THE ARRIVAL
TRILOGY

LUCY DANIELS

Illustrated by
Trevor Parkin

Hodder
Children's
Books

a division of Hodder Headline Limited

THE
ARRIVAL

This edition of *The Arrival*, *The Challenge* and *The Runaway*
first published in 2002.

ISBN 0 340 85238 0

10 9 8 7 6 5 4 3 2 1

The Arrival

Special thanks to Helen Magee

Text copyright © 1998 Ben M. Baglio
Created by Ben M. Baglio, London W6 OQT
Illustrations copyright © 1998 Trevor Parkin

First published as a single volume in Great Britain in 1998
by Hodder Children's Books

Typeset by Avon Dataset Ltd, Bidford-on-Avon, Warks

Printed and bound in Great Britain by
The Guernsey Press Co. Ltd, Vale, Guernsey, Channel Islands

Hodder Children's Books
a division of Hodder Headline Ltd
338 Euston Road
London NW1 3BH

1

'Come on, Nell,' Jenny whispered to the black-and-white sheepdog. 'You can do it.' She pushed her shoulder-length fair hair out of her eyes.

It was warm in the old stables though the weather outside in early January was still bitterly cold. It had been the coldest winter anybody around Graston could remember. The ground had been as hard as iron for weeks before the snow came. Now there was a deep covering of snow in the fields. Even the hardy Scottish Blackfaces that her father bred on his sheep farm were finding it impossible to graze. Fraser Miles, Jenny's father, had had to put out bales of hay for his flock of almost a thousand sheep in addition to their usual winter feed.

Jenny knew the extra expense of buying in the feed had been a drain on the farm's resources. But, right now, Jenny had other things to worry about. She and her father were keeping an anxious watch over the birth of Nell's puppies.

The Border collie looked up at Jenny with liquid brown eyes. Already three puppies lay snuggled into the sheepdog's side. Jenny looked at them and smiled. They looked so helpless with their eyes shut tight but they were already beginning to suckle.

'You're going to be great sheepdogs,' Jenny said softly to them. 'Just like your mum and dad.'

'I hope so,' Fraser Miles said, smiling at his daughter. 'I've got buyers lined up for them.'

'You never have any trouble selling Nell and Jake's puppies, Dad,' Jenny replied. 'They're the best working dogs in the Borders.'

Fraser Miles nodded. 'Good stock,' he answered. 'That's the secret. We've always had the best sheepdogs at Windy Hill.'

'And Windy Hill is the best sheep farm in the Borders too,' Jenny went on.

Mr Miles's eyes clouded and Jenny bit her lip and wished she hadn't said that. She knew her father was having trouble keeping the farm going. These puppies would bring in some welcome money. She didn't want to think about what would happen if he couldn't balance the books this year.

'Here comes the pup,' Mr Miles said suddenly.

Jenny watched, fascinated, as the next puppy was born. First the water bag containing the puppy appeared and started slowly to emerge.

As they watched, the puppy dropped on to the straw that lined Nell's whelping box. Nell immediately twisted round and began nuzzling at the birth sac, tearing the thin membranes away from the puppy's head.

Jenny waited anxiously as the newborn puppy raised its tiny head. Then the little animal snuffled as it took its very first breath.

'Well done, girl,' said Jenny, smiling.

Nell continued to lick at the membranes, uncovering the rest of the puppy's body.

'That stimulates the pup's blood flow,' her father told her. 'Let's just wait and make sure the pup is able to move. Then I think we can leave Nell alone. I reckon that's her last.'

The puppy wriggled slightly and lay still, a warm, wet little bundle with its eyes tightly shut. Then Nell lowered her head and began to nudge it towards her tummy. The puppy moved its head blindly and began to crawl. Jenny itched to help it but she knew better than that.

'Don't interfere so long as the pup is managing,' her father said, reading her thoughts.

Jenny grinned. 'It's so tempting to give them a hand,' she admitted.

Fraser shook his head. 'They have to learn to cope with life from an early age,' he explained seriously. 'Don't forget, these are working dogs, not pets.'

Jenny nodded and her hair fell over her face again. 'Oh, bother this hair,' she exclaimed, gathering it up and twisting it round her hand. She stuffed it down into the neck of her coat. 'I wish you'd let me get it cut.'

Her father shook his head. 'No, I think it suits you as it is,' he said shortly.

Jenny looked at her father and sighed. Mr Miles's eyes were on Nell and her puppies but Jenny could hear the pain in his voice. She knew that she reminded her father of her mother. People had always remarked on how like her mum Jenny was. Sheena Miles's hair had been shoulder-length too and exactly the same colour as her daughter's. Jenny thought that was why her father wouldn't let her get her hair cut, but she didn't dare ask him. He still missed her mother so much he got upset and even angry if he had to talk about her.

Sheena Miles had died in a riding accident the previous summer, when Jenny was ten. Jenny could remember the terrible pain on her father's face when Matt, her older brother, had haltingly told her about the accident. Fraser Miles hadn't been able to tell his daughter – he couldn't bring himself to say the words. He had looked the way Jenny had felt. It was as if the world had ended.

Jenny hadn't been able to cry – not at first. Not until her grandparents, her mother's mum and dad, had come home from Canada, and her grandmother had taken Jenny in her arms. She had cried then – she had cried as if she would never stop. Gran Elliot would talk to Jenny about her mother, and that had helped a lot. But then Gran and Grandad Elliot had gone back to Canada and Jenny had learned to cry quietly up in her own room. She had felt very lonely – and she still did.

She wished her father *would* talk about her mum. She sometimes thought of forcing him to talk about her. Her mother had often joked with Jenny about standing up to the men in the family. Jenny missed so much about her mother. She missed her affection and her understanding – but most of all she missed the sound of her laughter ringing through the house.

'I like it really,' she said in a small voice. 'My hair, I mean.'

Fraser Miles looked up. His hair was much darker than Jenny's. Both Fraser and Matt were tall and dark. Jenny was fair, like Sheena. 'I'd better get back to the sheep,' he said, changing the subject. 'I've still got a few more bales of feed to take up to the top field.'

Jenny nodded. 'The poor sheep,' she said. 'They aren't cosy and warm like Nell and her puppies.'

'Hill breeds like the Scottish Blackface have good thick coats,' Fraser reassured her. 'But even so, if this weather doesn't improve soon I think we might lose some of them. I had to haul seven of them out of snowdrifts last week.'

Jenny knew that in winter, sheep were always

in danger. They would turn their backs to the wind during a blizzard and could be quickly covered by the driving snow. She frowned. She knew Windy Hill couldn't afford to lose *any* sheep. 'Can't you bring any more of them into the shearing shed?' she asked.

'There's no more room,' said her father shortly. 'I've brought in the weakest of the pregnant ewes. The shearing shed doesn't give very much protection anyway. It isn't much more than a lean-to. What I really need is a new lambing barn.'

And lambing barns cost money, Jenny thought. The old lambing barn had been falling to bits for the last two years. It had finally had to be demolished after a particularly severe gale at the end of December.

'Will you be able to build one before the lambing?' Jenny asked.

Fraser shook his head. 'I'll need the money from the lambs to pay for the barn,' he said.

Jenny sighed. 'Lambing is such hard work – even in a barn,' she said sympathetically. 'If you've got to do it in the open fields it'll be even worse.'

'Don't you worry about that,' her father said, getting to his feet. 'The lambing isn't until spring and, besides, Borders farmers have been lambing in the open fields for generations. I can manage one season!'

'Of course you can,' Jenny said. 'Nell and Jake will help. Nell will be back to her old self in a few weeks' time.'

'You've been a good help with her, Jenny,' Fraser said. 'Thanks, love.'

'Nell did all the work,' Jenny replied. 'I didn't have to do a thing.'

'Oh, yes you did,' her father said. 'You kept talking to her, soothing her, keeping her calm.' He smiled. 'You've a way with animals, Jen.'

Jenny blushed with pleasure. Her father didn't hand out compliments easily. He was a man of few words – but he was a good sheep farmer.

Windy Hill had been in Gran Elliot's family for generations. Gran and Grandad Elliot had given the farm to their only child, Sheena, when she'd married Fraser Miles. Then Gran and Grandad Elliot had emigrated to Canada, which was Grandad Elliot's home.

Fraser had been determined to live up to the trust Sheena and her parents had shown in him to take good care of Windy Hill. That determination had been even greater since Sheena's death.

'Can I stay and watch the puppies for a little

while?' Jenny asked. 'I'd like to be sure they're feeding all right.'

Fraser nodded. 'That would be a good idea,' he agreed. 'Just don't go getting too attached to them. You know they've got to be sold when they're eight weeks old.'

Jenny dropped her head and gazed at the four puppies. 'I'll try not to,' she promised. 'It just seems such a shame for Nell, not being able to keep even one of her puppies.'

'Nell's a working dog,' said Fraser. 'She's used to it – and by the time the puppies are ready to leave their mother, she'll be busy with the pregnant ewes. There's a lot of work to be done, rounding them up for their vaccinations before lambing.' He ruffled Jenny's hair. 'You're the one who can't get used to it.'

'Dad's right,' Jenny said softly to Nell as her father walked towards the barn door. 'I'd like to keep all of your puppies at Windy Hill, Nell.'

'Call me if there are any problems, Jen,' Fraser Miles said over his shoulder.

Jenny nodded. She bent again and laid a finger on the last little puppy. 'I wish I could have a puppy like you as a pet,' she said. But her father had told her often enough there was no room for pets on a working farm. Jenny couldn't help herself, though. It was her constant dream to have a puppy of her own.

Nell whimpered and Jenny looked sharply at her. The Border collie's eyes rolled and she began to strain, her flanks heaving. Jenny gasped, then she jumped to her feet and ran towards the barn door. The pale winter sun cast a watery light over the cobbles of the yard, reflecting in the frozen puddles.

'Dad!' Jenny yelled across the farmyard.

Fraser turned and, at the sight of her worried expression, began to stride back across the yard towards her. 'What is it?' he asked urgently. 'Nell's all right, isn't she?'

'I don't know,' Jenny replied anxiously. 'She seems distressed.'

Fraser followed Jenny into the stables and crouched down beside Nell. She was panting now, her flanks damp and hot.

Jenny watched as her father put a hand on Nell's side.

'There's another puppy on the way,' he said. 'But I was *sure* that there were only four. This one must be very small.'

'Is Nell going to be all right?' Jenny asked,

anxiously. 'She wasn't like this with the others. What's wrong, Dad?'

Fraser Miles's face was serious. 'She must be exhausted by now,' he said. 'Perhaps that's all it is.' He moved his hand to Nell's hindquarters, gently probing. 'There it is. It's coming out the wrong way round.'

'You mean not head first, like the others?' Jenny asked.

Fraser nodded. 'This one is a breech birth. That's hard on Nell after all the work she's already done.'

'What can we do?' Jenny asked. 'Poor Nell. Look, she's pushed the other puppies away.'

Nell arched her back and the puppies fell away from her. The collie's eyes rolled towards Jenny as her body twisted in pain.

'Hold her head, Jenny,' Fraser said. 'I'm going to give her a hand with this one.'

'Oh, be careful, Dad,' Jenny urged him. 'If the puppy is back to front you might hurt it.'

Fraser looked up briefly. 'Nell is more important than any puppy, Jenny,' he said shortly. 'And I'll do what I have too.'

Jenny turned back to Nell and cradled the collie's head in her hands. She knew how vital Nell was to the farm – an experienced sheepdog *was* more important than a puppy. If her father had to decide between them, she knew he would save Nell.

Jenny closed her eyes. Please don't let it come to that, she prayed. Please let them both be all right.

She didn't dare to watch. Nell looked up at her with mournful eyes as she struggled to give birth to this last puppy. 'There, girl,' Jenny whispered. 'Just a little longer. Be brave!'

Suddenly Nell's head dropped heavily in Jenny's arms and Jenny's heart turned over. 'Nell!' she cried desperately.

The collie turned her head and licked Jenny's hand. Her body shuddered, tensing – then went still.

Jenny felt the breath stop in her throat.

'It's OK now,' Fraser reassured her, scooping something up in his hands. 'It's over, old girl. Just you concentrate on your other four pups.'

Jenny's breath came back in a rush as she watched the sheepdog open her eyes and move slightly. She cast a quick glance at what her father was holding and when she looked back Nell was already licking her other puppies again, encouraging them to feed. The tiny bodies scrabbled blindly towards her but Jenny hardly saw them. Her father's words rang in her ears.

'What do you mean, Dad? The last puppy isn't dead, is it?'

Fraser looked down at her and his usually stern expression softened. 'No,' he said gently. 'He isn't dead. But he might as well be. He'll never make a working dog.'

Jenny looked at the pathetic little bundle her father was holding. It was so tiny Fraser could easily hold it in one hand. He had torn away the birth sac from the puppy's head but there was no sign that the little animal was breathing. Jenny held out her hand and touched a finger to the puppy's body. It was warm and she could feel his heart beating under his skin.

Then, as her father removed the rest of the sac, the puppy breathed.

'It's going to live!' she cried.

'Look, Jenny,' her father said.

For the first time, Jenny noticed what her father had already seen. The puppy's right front leg was twisted at an impossible angle. 'His leg!' she gasped. 'What happened to it?'

'It must have been growing like that for some time inside the womb,' Fraser explained, cutting the umbilical cord and drying the puppy with a piece of old towel.

'Oh, the poor little thing,' said Jenny, gently taking the puppy in her own hands. She laid him down beside his brothers and sisters. 'There,' she encouraged him. 'You feed too.'

But the puppy was far too weak. The bigger pups scrambled over him, pushing him out of the way. Even Nell pushed him away from her.

'What's wrong?' Jenny asked. 'Why is Nell rejecting him?'

'Instinct,' Fraser explained. 'She knows he won't survive. Look at him. He's so weak he can hardly breathe.'

'But he *is* breathing,' Jenny insisted. 'That must mean he wants to live.'

Fraser leaned over and laid his hand on the puppy's bad leg, testing it gently.

'I'd never be able to sell him,' he said. 'And you can't expect Mrs Grace to look after a puppy as well as us.'

Jenny bit her lip. Ellen Grace was a widowed neighbour of theirs. Fraser had asked her to come and do the housekeeping at Windy Hill now that Matt was at college and away all week. She was taking a winter holiday at the moment but was due to start in a month's time.

'She wouldn't have to look after him,' protested Jenny. '*I'd* keep him. I'd look after him.'

'You know the rules, Jenny,' Fraser Miles answered. 'Every animal on this farm has to earn its keep. This crippled little pup could never do that.'

Jenny blinked back tears. 'What are you going to do then?' she whispered.

Fraser looked at her in real concern. 'I'll have to put him down,' he said gently. 'It's the kindest thing for him. The other puppies will crowd him out. He won't get fed. He won't even get near his mother to keep warm. He'll get chilled, and that alone would kill him in a few hours. He'll die anyway. At least this way he won't be in pain. He won't suffer.'

Jenny looked at the puppy's poor crippled leg. 'Is he in pain now, do you think?' she asked.

Fraser shook his head. 'It's hard to tell,' he replied. 'Now be sensible, Jenny. You know it has to be done.'

Jenny swallowed hard. She knew what her father said was true. She had lived on a farm all her life. There was no room for unproductive animals on a farm. The little puppy moved in her hands and yawned. The tip of a tiny pink tongue licked her finger.

Jenny just couldn't let him go – not just yet. 'Can I have a little while to say goodbye?' she asked.

Fraser Miles bent over Nell. 'All right,' he said. 'I'll just wait with Nell to see she's OK after that last birth.'

'Thanks, Dad,' Jenny said. 'I'll take him into the house. It's warmer there and Nell doesn't want him here.'

She was almost at the door when her father called her. 'Remember what I said, Jenny. Don't get too attached. That puppy has to go.'

Jenny nodded and looked down at the puppy. She knew what her father said made sense. But it was too late. It was *far* too late for common sense. She had already fallen in love with this puppy.

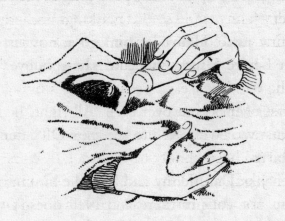

2

Jenny carried the little puppy into the big farm kitchen, kicking off her wellingtons in the porch on her way. She laid him gently down on the rag rug in front of the Aga, took off her coat, then set to work sponging the puppy clean with warm water and drying him.

When she had finished she went to the dresser and pulled out a soft blue blanket. 'There, that's better isn't it?' she said to the puppy as she wrapped him up.

She gazed down at him. Now that he was clean and dry Jenny could see his markings properly for the first time. He was mainly black with four white socks. His muzzle and chest were white and he had black ears, the marking running like patches over both eyes.

'You're so beautiful,' she whispered. The puppy turned his head blindly towards her, nuzzling her finger. Jenny found she had a lump in her throat.

'I'm not your mum,' she said softly to him. 'I can't feed you.'

The puppy continued to search blindly. Jenny couldn't bear it. 'Maybe I'm *not* your mum,' she told him. 'But I can at least give you some milk.'

Swiftly, cradling the puppy in one hand, Jenny looked amongst the baby bottles they used for feeding newborn lambs. There were some especially small bottles that they used for the very tiny lambs. Sometimes a ewe would have premature triplets and those lambs were nearly as tiny as this little puppy. A ewe could only feed two lambs so one of her babies had to be hand-reared.

Jenny took down one of the smallest bottles, not much bigger than a dropper. Then she heated a little milk in a pan on the Aga. Laying the puppy down on the rug once more, she poured the milk into the bottle. She tested the temperature on the back of her hand.

'Just right,' she said, picking up the puppy in his blanket. Holding the little animal gently, she guided the teat of the bottle into his mouth. It took several tries but at last the puppy got a taste of milk and began to suck enthusiastically. Jenny watched him feeding. He might not be very strong but he was certainly full of courage.

'At least the other puppies can't push you away from this,' she reassured him. 'You didn't stand a chance against them. But don't worry, I know how you feel. Fiona McLay is like that at school. Bigger than me and always pushing me out of the way.'

'Hi, Jenny! What's that about Fiona McLay?' said a voice from the door.

Jenny looked up and smiled. 'Matt!' she cried. 'Nell's had her puppies!'

Her brother strode into the kitchen. Matt was eighteen and, last September, he had gone away to agricultural college. But he came home most weekends to help out at Windy Hill.

He ruffled his little sister's hair and looked quizzically at the bundle in her arms.

Jenny explained: 'Nell had four healthy puppies.

24

But this one has a twisted leg, and the other puppies were pushing him out of the way so he couldn't feed. I was telling him they're just like Fiona McLay.'

'What's she been doing to you?' Matt asked, running a gentle finger along the puppy's nose.

'Oh, just the usual,' Jenny shrugged. 'She's telling everybody Dad will have to sell up Windy Hill and her dad is going to buy us out.'

Matt looked up sharply. 'Is she?' he said. 'Well, Calum McLay *has* had his eye on Windy Hill for years. But don't worry, Dad won't sell if he can help it. And even if he does, he'll *never* sell to McLay.'

'So you think he *might* have to sell?' Jenny asked.

Matt looked suddenly serious. 'Things are a bit tight just now,' he said. 'But we'll pull through. We always have in the past. What else has Fiona McLay been saying to you?'

'She teases me about not having the right sort of jeans and stuff,' said Jenny. 'But that doesn't matter to me. I'm not going to ask Dad to waste money on fancy clothes.'

'Good for you,' Matt said approvingly. He frowned. 'This puppy doesn't look too good.'

Jenny let Matt see the puppy's twisted leg. 'Dad

says he'll have to put him down,' she said.

Matt shook his head as he looked at the puppy's leg. 'That leg *does* look bad,' he said.

'I want to keep him,' Jenny confided.

'You know what Dad says about pets,' cautioned Matt. 'And you'll be at school all day. Who would look after it?'

'It's a *he*,' said Jenny. She thought for a moment. 'I don't suppose Mrs Grace would want him around. Anyway there's no point. Dad is going to get rid of him.'

'You're not still worried about Mrs Grace coming to look after us, are you?' Matt asked.

Jenny's mouth set in a stubborn line. 'We've managed all right until now,' she said. 'I don't see why we can't go on as we are.'

'No, we haven't, Jen,' her brother replied. 'It's been a struggle – especially since I started college and haven't been around to help out during the week.' Matt smiled encouragingly at his sister. 'Don't upset things now, Jen . . . It was hard enough to persuade Dad to have an outsider around Mum's kitchen. You'll like Mrs Grace. It's for the best, really it is.'

Jenny didn't say anything. She had enjoyed helping Dad and Matt with the housework. Now it was all going to be spoiled. Mrs Grace was sure to want to do everything her way.

'Hey,' said Matt. 'Come on. Come outside. I've got something to show you.'

'What is it?' asked Jenny. But Matt was already out of the door.

Jenny shrugged on her anorak, picked up the puppy in his blanket and pushed her feet back into her wellingtons before following Matt out into the farmyard.

'It's a horse!' she said. Then, as she looked, she began to take in the state of the animal. Its coat was dirty and dull and there were bare patches on its back where the skin had been rubbed almost raw. Its eyes were sunken and Jenny could clearly see the outline of the animal's ribs. 'Oh, the poor thing,' she exclaimed, her heart going out to it.

Matt's mouth set in a stern line. 'Poor thing, right enough,' he said. 'Somebody has been treating him very badly. It looks as if he's been beaten. I couldn't find out exactly what had happened to him. I got him for next to nothing at the livestock market in Greybridge. It was lucky I happened to be there today. If I hadn't bought him he would have been sent to the abattoir to be put down.'

Matt's comments stung Jenny. She was glad her brother had saved this poor horse from the abattoir, but what about the little animal curled up fast asleep in her arms? Didn't he deserve the same care?

Jenny gazed at the horse. He was coal black and, even with his coat patchy and unkempt, Jenny could see that he must once have been magnificent. Scars had formed unevenly over old injuries but they couldn't hide the quality of the animal.

Jenny frowned. There was something very familiar about this horse. She put out a hand to touch his neck. The horse rolled his eyes nervously at her gesture. She drew her hand back as the big animal stamped and pawed the ground.

'Careful,' said Matt. 'He's wary of people. Small wonder when you imagine the kind of treatment he must have had. Poor Mercury.'

Jenny stood frozen in shock. 'Mercury!' she exclaimed, her memory flooding back. 'This is Mercury? *Mum's* horse?'

'That's right,' Matt replied. 'Didn't you recognise him? I don't blame you. He looks entirely different. Mum always took such good care of him. She would be heartbroken if she

29

could see him now. I just *had* to rescue him, Jen.'

Jenny stood open-mouthed as Matt led the horse away across the farmyard towards the stables. Mercury! Her mother's horse. The horse that had thrown her! The horse that had killed her! How could Matt dare to bring that horse back here? What would her father say?

Jenny opened her mouth to warn Matt not to show this horse to her father. Her father would *never* keep him! He had sold Mercury immediately after the accident. But then Jenny recalled Matt's words. It was true, her mother had adored Mercury. What would *she* have done if Mercury had been in danger of being sent to the abattoir?

Fraser Miles came out of the barn as Matt passed with Mercury. Jenny watched as, at first, her father's reaction of frozen shock mirrored her own. He spoke briefly to Matt. But then, after a short hesitation, Fraser patted the horse, then set about assessing Mercury's damage, feeling his hocks, running his hands over the horse's flanks.

'Dad!' Jenny called, hurrying over to her father. 'You aren't going to keep him, are you? You sold him when . . . when . . .' she stopped at the sudden desolate look in her father's eyes.

'I sold him in a hurry,' her father replied gravely. 'I sent him to auction. I didn't even bother to find out who had bought him. Maybe it's partly my fault he's in this state now, poor beast. If I got hold of whoever did this to him I'd turn them over to the police.' Fraser Miles sighed deeply 'Once he's recovered, we'll make a decision about his future. Come on, Matt. Let's get some food into him. He looks half-starved.'

Jenny watched as her father and Matt slowly led the horse into the barn. She was torn between sympathy for the horse's mistreatment and shock that her father and Matt seemed willing to accept Mercury back at Windy Hill so easily. Why, after selling him, was her father taking him back?

But then, this wasn't just *any* animal, Jenny argued to herself. This was *Mercury*! And no matter how sorry she felt for him, she could *never* accept this horse at Windy Hill.

Suddenly Jenny felt very alone.

A small mewling sound caught her attention and she looked down. The puppy was curled in her arms, nestled in his blanket. Jenny gazed at him. A tear rolled down her cheek and landed on his nose. He stirred slightly but didn't wake up. Jenny cradled him closer. She wasn't alone. At least she had this puppy – if only for a little while. He was sleeping peacefully, his belly full. His life would be short but right now he was warm and happy.

'Dad says you have to die,' she whispered. A feeling of the unfairness of things swept over her once again. Then her head came up determinedly. 'Maybe you *do* have to die,' she said. 'But first I'm going to take you to my favourite place. I can't save you but I can give you a little more time.'

Jenny wrapped the blanket snugly round the sleeping puppy, unzipped her jacket and tucked the bundle securely into its fleecy folds. Then she set off for the place she always sought out when she felt unhappy – the keep.

'It's my very special place,' Jenny whispered to the sleeping puppy as she hurried out of the farmyard and up the frozen track to the hill beyond. 'And no matter what happens to you, I'll always have a memory of the two of us there.'

The wind lifted her hair as she crested the hill. Snow crunched under her boots. The wintry sun sparkled on the sea beyond the farm and gulls wheeled around the cliffs that marked the seaward boundary of Windy Hill. There was a rim of hard frost at the edge of the snow-covered fields and ice lay thick under overhanging hedges and fences. Blue shadows pooled at the foot of the drystone walls lining the farm track.

But Jenny didn't see any of this. Her eyes were fixed on a jagged stone structure perched on rising ground a mile away across the snowy landscape. That was where she was going – Darktarn Keep.

3

Jenny climbed the knoll to the ruined keep and sat in her favourite spot looking out towards the sea. From here she could see Windy Hill below her: the red roofs of the farm buildings bright against the snowy backdrop.

The farmhouse looked warm and snug, its grey stone weathered by years of sun and wind. The shearing shed stood at right angles to the house, its open side facing away from the prevailing winds; the small stable block made up the other side of the 'U' shape. The lambing barn had been tacked on to the end of the stables but it was gone now. Jenny sighed when she thought of the expense of replacing it.

In front of the farmhouse the fields stretched down to the cliffs and the sea. Down there, below the cliffs, was the fishing village of Cliffbay.

Jenny thought of Carrie Turner, a new girl at Graston School, who had moved to Cliffbay with her parents a month ago. At first Jenny had hoped they might be friends, but when Fiona McLay had overheard Jenny saying so, she'd laughed at her.

'Why would someone like Carrie Turner want to be friends with a boring little mouse like *you*?' she had said spitefully. 'Her mum is a famous artist – her parents are really well-off. My dad says their house must have cost a fortune. *And* they have a terrific boat.'

Fiona's jeering had upset Jenny, and discouraged her from attempting to make friends with Carrie. Maybe Fiona was right. Why would a bright and bubbly girl like Carrie want to be friends with Jenny? Carrie was outgoing and confident in a way that Jenny admired. She didn't think she could ever be like that. Not now that her mum wasn't there to support and encourage her.

Jenny often thought about her mum when she visited Darktarn Keep. Sheena Miles had always encouraged Jenny to speak her mind. 'Come on,' she would say when Matt teased Jenny. 'Are you going to let Matt get away with that? We girls have got to stand up for ourselves, Jenny!' Then Jenny would giggle and join in while her mother teased Matt in return.

Jenny smiled at the memory. It had been a long time since she had teased Matt. A lot of things had changed since her mother had died. Jenny knew Matt and her father loved her but they didn't seem to understand her the way her mum had. Jenny had grown even quieter since her mother's death early last summer, but Mr Miles hadn't noticed. For a long time he hadn't noticed anything very much.

Jenny couldn't help thinking that Carrie Turner would have handled her situation differently. Carrie would have had a good deal more to say about how unfair it was to get rid of Jess and to keep Mercury. When she was angry, Carrie's cheeks would flame as red as her hair and she never seemed to be at a loss for words. But Jenny hardly ever got worked up and when she did she always seemed to get tongue-tied.

The puppy moved in her arms, wriggling his small body into a more comfortable position. '*You're* my friend,' Jenny said to him. 'I wish I could keep you.' The puppy snuggled deeper into his blanket and Jenny lowered her face, feeling the warmth of him on her cheeks.

She looked down towards the farm. Her father was out in the top field now with Jake. The sheepdog moved like the wind along the edge of the flock, rounding them up, moving them into position at Fraser's command. The black faces of the sheep stood out against their white coats and the snowy surroundings.

Bales of hay hung from the winter feeding racks. She saw her father stoop at a drinking trough and raise his stick, bringing it down hard to break the ice that had formed on top. Jenny shivered. Even here, protected from the wind, the cold was beginning to bite her gloveless fingers. But the puppy, tucked in his blanket inside her anorak, was warm and snug.

'I bet you'd make the best sheepdog in the world if you didn't have a twisted leg,' Jenny said.

The puppy's nose twitched and his little pink tongue came out, licking her cold fingers, warming them. Settled in a corner of the old stone wall, Jenny watched the clouds that scudded across the sky. Out to sea the wind whipped the water into white horses.

Jenny loved this place. She spent hours here, remembering the stories her mother used to tell her about the keep in the olden days — stories about the Border reivers who had fought to protect their land and had run raiding parties across the border of Scotland and England to rustle sheep. Sheena had made the tales of the reivers come alive. Jenny's favourite character had been Jess of Beacon Brae, who had rustled more sheep than all the other reivers together.

According to legend, Jess had once sold an entire flock of stolen sheep back to his arch-enemy on the other side of the border. Another story told how he got his name. His leg had been broken in a skirmish with reivers from across the border. The rest of his party were killed, but Jess had escaped and climbed Beacon Brae, a hill near Graston, and lit a fire to alert the surrounding countryside to the danger to Graston's sheep. He walked with a limp for the rest of his life but he was a hero and ever afterwards he was known as Jess of Beacon Brae.

'Jess of Beacon Brae had a twisted leg too,' Jenny said to the sleeping puppy. She smiled. 'And he was brave like you.'

Jenny's gaze shifted towards the tarn, a small lake on the other side of a drystone wall below the keep. That was where Mercury had thrown her mother. She had died there, alone, because of that horse.

'I wish Mum was here now,' Jenny whispered to the puppy in her lap. 'Dad and Matt just don't understand.'

The puppy made a little mewling sound.

Maybe it was her imagination but she was sure he was looking better already. But when Jenny drew back the blanket and looked at his tiny twisted leg, she sighed. Her father was right. This little one would never make a working dog.

Jenny was lost in thought, her eyes closed, when she heard a voice and looked up. It was Matt, standing silhouetted against the sun.

'I thought I'd find you here,' he said. 'How's the pup?'

Jenny dropped her head. 'He's lovely,' she said. 'And he's feeding. But I know it's no good. Did Dad send you to get me?'

Her brother sat down beside her and reached out a hand, turning back the blanket. 'Dad was worried about you,' he said. 'He doesn't want you to get too attached.'

Jenny swallowed and a tear rolled down her cheek. 'I can't help it,' she whispered. 'He's so brave – and he's strong. You should have seen him drinking his milk.'

Matt ran a hand through his hair. 'You really love this little scrap, don't you?'

Jenny nodded, unable to speak.

'Dad can't afford to be sentimental about animals,' Matt said, looking unhappy.

Jenny didn't answer. She couldn't help thinking that Mercury had been saved but Jess wouldn't be. It was so unfair. She looked up at her brother. 'Do you want me to come now?'

Matt nodded. His dark blue eyes were full of sympathy. 'It's getting really cold now,' he told her. 'You'll freeze here.'

Jenny turned away, shivering suddenly. There was nothing Matt could do even if he wanted to. There was nothing anyone could do. She got up slowly. 'We're ready,' she said.

'We?' said Matt.

'Jess and me,' Jenny replied.

Matt's eyes opened wide. 'You've given him a name then?'

Jenny nodded. 'I called him after Jess of Beacon Brae. He had a bad leg too.'

Matt smiled. 'I remember Mum telling me that story when I was little.' He looked towards the tarn. 'You miss Mum a lot, don't you?'

Jenny wiped a hand across her eyes. 'She would understand how I feel about Jess,' she said.

Matt looked at her helplessly. 'Come on, Jen,' he said kindly. 'If it's got to be done, we'd better get it over with.'

Jenny got up slowly and followed Matt back down towards the farm. For all his sympathy, even Matt didn't understand.

Fraser Miles was just coming into the farmyard with Jake at his heels when Matt and Jenny arrived. Jenny reached down to stroke the sheepdog, running her cold fingers through his thick coat.

'You and Nell have a beautiful litter,' she whispered to him. 'And the littlest one is the most beautiful of all.'

Jake wagged his plumy tail and reared up, putting his front paws on her chest, nuzzling at Jess tucked inside Jenny's jacket. Jess stirred sleepily as Jake licked his tiny head.

'Down, Jake,' Fraser commanded and, at once, the sheepdog dropped to the ground.

'I've given Mercury a bran mash, and he seems to have settled OK in the barn,' Matt said to his father.

Mr Miles nodded gravely. 'I'll get the vet out to him as soon as possible.' He shook his head. 'I'll never understand how people can mistreat an animal like that.'

Jenny stared at her father, unable to speak. She couldn't ask him to get rid of the horse. But she still thought it was unfair to put Jess down and keep Mercury.

Fraser turned to Jenny. 'Did you have enough time to say goodbye?' he asked her.

Jenny nodded, holding back the words that filled her mind. She wanted to shout at her father – how could he keep the horse that killed Mum and not an innocent little puppy? But she didn't dare. She couldn't bear the thought of mentioning her mother's accident to him. She had *never* mentioned it to him. She didn't want to cause her father any more pain.

Matt glanced at her and pursed his lips. 'Wait a minute, Jen,' he said softly. He turned to his father.

'Jenny has really got attached to this puppy.'

Fraser Miles looked impatient. 'That's what I was afraid of,' he said shortly. 'If I'd just disposed of the pup straight away this wouldn't have happened.'

'No!' Jenny burst out. 'I'd rather have had a little time with Jess than no time at all.'

'Jess?' said her father.

'That's what she's called him,' Matt explained.

Fraser Miles closed his eyes in exasperation. 'So now it's got a name, has it?' he said. 'When will you ever understand, Jenny? I can't afford animals that can't earn their keep.'

'I know,' Jenny replied, resentment building up in her. 'But even a crippled puppy is entitled to have a name. You can't begrudge him that, Dad. It was only for a little while. Here – take him!'

She kissed Jess on the top of his head, hugging him gently, then with a whispered goodbye, held him out in his blanket to her father.

Fraser Miles didn't move.

'Aren't you going to take him?' Jenny asked brokenly. Her throat was clogged with tears and she was having difficulty holding them back.

Her father looked at her for a long moment.

'You know, Dad, Mercury won't exactly earn his keep,' Matt said quietly.

Jenny saw her father go pale. A spasm of pain crossed his face. He drew a hand across his brow and closed his eyes. Fraser Miles was silent for a long time. At last, he looked over at Jenny and gave her a strained smile. 'Matt's right,' he said at last. 'If we can keep and feed Mercury we can surely afford to keep a puppy.'

For a moment Jenny couldn't believe her ears. 'Keep him?' she whispered. 'You mean you aren't going to put him down? He can be my puppy?'

Mr Miles grunted and turned away. 'That's what I said,' he told her. He turned back for a moment. 'But remember, Jenny, he's your responsibility. You'll have to look after him – and it won't be easy with him crippled the way he is.'

Jenny swallowed back her tears. Suddenly she was ablaze with happiness. 'Oh, yes, I know,' she said holding the puppy in the blue blanket close to her chest just in case her father changed his mind. 'I'll do everything for him,' she promised.

'See that you do,' said her father. He looked at his son. 'Come on, Matt, there's work to be done. I want to house some of the ewes from the bottom field in the far end of the stables.'

As Matt passed his sister he laid a hand on her shoulder. 'Happy now, Jen?' he asked.

Jenny beamed up at him, overjoyed. 'Thanks, Matt,' she said. 'Thanks for sticking up for us.'

Matt laughed. 'Us!' he repeated. 'I've a feeling it's always going to be "us" from now on.'

'Matt!' called his father. Jenny's brother hurried off.

Jenny looked down at her puppy. He slept on, oblivious to the fact that his life had just been spared.

'Us,' Jenny said. 'You and me, Jess – for ever!'

4

Jenny was sitting in the kitchen, still holding Jess in his blue blanket, when Matt returned from helping their father.

She looked down at her puppy. 'I hope I can look after him properly,' she said. 'It's all right for the other puppies: they have Nell. But poor Jess only has me.'

'I think you'll make a wonderful substitute mum,' Matt assured her, smiling. 'Come on, I'll give you a hand to get his bed sorted out.'

Jenny looked around the kitchen. 'A bed!' she said. 'I hadn't even thought about that yet. We don't have a dog basket.'

'A dog basket would be too big for him,' Matt told her. 'We'll find a nice cosy box and line it with newspaper for insulation. We can put that blanket in too for him to cuddle into. Jess looks as though he's really taken to that.' The puppy was snuggled deep in his blanket, eyes tightly shut, fast asleep.

Matt rummaged in the big pantry in the corner of the kitchen. He brought out a cardboard box. 'This will do,' he decided, setting it down near the Aga. 'You'll have to keep him in a warm place at first. Newborn puppies can get chilled very easily.'

Matt took a sheaf of newspaper and expertly lined the box. 'That should do,' he said.

Jenny laid Jess down in the box, tucking his blanket round him. 'It's perfect,' she said, standing up. 'But do you think he'll be warm enough? Won't he miss his mother?'

'You could put a hot-water bottle in beside him,' Matt advised her. 'Wrap an old jumper round it so that it's soft and furry – as much like his mother's body as possible. A ticking clock is a good

THE ARRIVAL

idea too. Jess will think it's his mother's heartbeat and it'll stop him feeling lonely.'

Jenny sorted out an old jumper and prepared a hot-water bottle, as Matt had suggested. 'What about feeding him?' she asked.

'Ah, well,' said Matt. 'That's going to be a little more difficult. If he was still with Nell he would feed whenever he was hungry. You're going to have your work cut out feeding him often enough.'

'I don't mind,' said Jenny firmly. 'I'll feed him as often as he wants. I could even sleep in the kitchen with him.'

Matt laughed. 'I don't think Dad would be too keen on that,' he said. 'But you're going to have to make sure your alarm clock is working. This little one will need feeding every four hours – and that means getting up in the middle of the night to do it. How do you feel about that?'

'No problem!' she declared. 'Jess is worth weeks of getting up in the middle of the night.'

'Let's see if you still think that when you have to get out of your warm bed when it's freezing!' Matt teased.

But Jenny *didn't* mind. She set her alarm clock

for four-hourly intervals and, when it went off, she slipped out of bed as quietly as she could, padding downstairs in slippers and a warm dressing-gown. She cradled Jess in her arms as she gave him his bottle, watching in delight as he sucked.

For the first two weeks the puppy went straight off to sleep after he'd fed, but gradually he was able to stay awake for a little while. The first time Jenny saw his eyes open was during one of the night-time feeds. He had nearly finished his milk when, quite gently, he opened his eyes, looked at her for a moment and then closed them again as he drifted into sleep. Jenny sat there holding him for a long time afterwards, too thrilled to want to leave him.

As the weeks went on, Jenny made time to play with Jess for a little while after his feed – until he grew tired and fell asleep in her arms. Her father came down one night and found both of them fast asleep, curled up in the armchair at the side of the Aga. He woke Jenny gently and sent her off to bed with instructions to turn her alarm clock off – he would do the next feed. Jenny agreed – after all, the sooner her father and Jess got to know each other, the better. But next day Fraser Miles was just as firm about the puppy as he pointed out that Jess had dirtied the floor, not the newspaper Jenny had laid out. Jenny went to clear it up. Maybe it would take Jess a *little* longer to win her father over completely.

'Mrs Grace is coming this morning,' Fraser Miles told Jenny when Jess was four weeks old. 'I hope you're going to make her welcome. She's looking forward to getting to know you properly.'

Jenny looked up from tidying Jess's box and yawned. She had been able to cut down on the middle of the night feeds as Jess grew bigger and stronger, but she was still tired. Right at this moment Jess was lapping up an egg whisked in milk.

'I *do* know her,' she replied. 'She always says hello when I see her in Graston.'

'This is a bit different,' her father said. 'After all, she's going to be round the house a lot.'

Jenny reached out a hand and stroked Jess's coat. The puppy's eyes had been open for two weeks now and he was even beginning to cut his first teeth. Soon he would be chewing everything in sight. What would Mrs Grace say about that?

Jess lifted his head from his bowl and sneezed,

looking surprised at the sound. He was learning to lap but sometimes he blew out into his milk and the bubbles tickled his nose.

'Whoops!' said Jenny. 'Lap, don't blow, Jess.'

'If you can get him on to solids you'll be able to cut down even more on the feeds,' Mr Miles said.

Jenny yawned again and nodded. 'Matt says I can try him with baby cereal or porridge, or a tiny bit of minced meat.'

Her father nodded. 'The more protein he gets the stronger his bones and muscles will grow,' he told her, coming over to have a look at Jess. 'You've done well, Jenny. Looking after such a young puppy is a lot of work.'

Jenny flushed with pleasure. 'I don't mind the work so long as Jess is well.'

Jess polished off the last of his egg and milk, and turned his head, looking for Jenny. He wobbled uncertainly on his three good legs. His right front leg was twisted to the side and the paw didn't reach the floor. He took a few steps towards Jenny before tumbling sideways. Jenny watched as Jess tried to struggle to his feet again but his twisted leg gave way under him.

'He can find his balance on just three legs if I

put him down on the floor,' Jenny explained. 'It's just that he finds it difficult to get up again if he falls over. He's trying his best though.'

Jenny picked Jess up gently and gave him a cuddle before laying him back in his box. Jess promptly closed his eyes and fell fast asleep.

'Learning to walk isn't easy for him,' Fraser said. 'You can't expect him to walk as soon as a normal puppy.'

Jenny nodded. She visited Nell and her litter every day but she was careful not to make pets of the other puppies. Jess's brothers and sisters were much bigger than he was and already starting to explore their surroundings.

'He'll catch up,' she said.

Fraser Miles ruffled her hair. 'If his determination is anything like yours, he certainly will. You've thought of nothing but that puppy for the last month.'

Jenny had spent all the time she could with the little dog, feeding him and looking after him. She even managed to dash home from school at lunchtime to feed him. But Jess would soon be getting out of his box by himself when Jenny wasn't there, and scrambling about the kitchen. He was sure to get in the housekeeper's way.

'Do you think Mrs Grace will mind Jess?' Jenny asked anxiously. 'Puppies can be a lot of trouble round the house. Maybe she won't like him.'

'I've told her about Jess,' her father said. 'She says she doesn't mind him in the kitchen.'

Jenny looked up, alarmed. 'Do you mean she won't let him run round the rest of the house — even when he's house-trained?' she asked.

Her father shrugged. 'You'll just have to wait and see,' he said. 'After all, Mrs Grace will be in charge of the house from now on.'

The sound of a car engine came from outside and Fraser looked round. 'That'll be her now,' he said. 'Be nice to her, Jenny. I'm not going to be around much to welcome her; I'm so busy on the farm. Some of the sheep need their feet trimmed, and I'm trying to get records up to date, ready for the lambing.'

Her father looked tired and strained. Foot-trimming was a hard job. It had to be done by hand, with clippers. If the horny outer surface of the sheep's foot wasn't trimmed it could make the animal lame.

Jenny also knew that until her death last year, her mother had done most of the record-keeping for the farm. This was the first year that her father was having to tackle it on his own.

'Oh, and I'm expecting Calum McLay some time today,' Fraser added, running a hand through his hair. 'If you see him before you go to school, tell him I'll be up in the top field.'

Jenny nodded, feeling rather alarmed. Calum McLay and her father had fallen out with each other years ago, before she was born. Mr McLay really seemed to hate her father and Fraser Miles avoided him whenever he could. Why had her father agreed to see Mr McLay today? Not about selling Windy Hill to him, surely! Matt had told her that their father would never sell to McLay!

'Anybody home?' called a voice at the open kitchen door.

Jenny took a deep breath. It was Mrs Grace. She cast a quick look round the kitchen, wondering what the housekeeper would think of it. She frowned as her eyes took in the dusty surface of the dresser and the dullness of the row of brass jelly moulds hanging from one of the wooden beams. Even the blue-checked curtains at the window looked as if they could do with a wash. A pile of newspapers, weeks old, was stacked by the back door.

Jenny bit her lip. The kitchen hadn't always been

untidy. When her mother had been alive the brass shone, the wooden surfaces gleamed and there were potted plants in the windows. She sighed. Everything at Windy Hill had been different since her mother died. And now here was Mrs Grace – and everything was going to change again.

5

Fraser Miles invited Mrs Grace into the kitchen. Jenny picked Jess up. The puppy yawned and nuzzled her finger. 'You've got to be good, Jess,' Jenny whispered. 'Best behaviour.'

'Hello, Jenny,' Mrs Grace said as she came into the kitchen. She smiled. 'This must be Jess.'

Jenny nodded. 'I've started to toilet-train him,' she blurted out. 'He won't be any trouble.'

Ellen Grace laughed and her eyes lit up. She wasn't very tall and her brown hair was soft and curly. Her blue eyes were the warm blue of a summer sky, not dark blue like Matt's and Fraser's.

Mrs Grace was a widow. Jenny couldn't remember her husband. He had died a long time ago, her dad had told her.

'I expect Jess'll have the odd accident for a while yet,' Mrs Grace said, her eyes twinkling. 'But I'm sure we can cope with that. I'll keep lots of newspaper handy just in case.' She looked at the pile of newspapers by the door. 'Those will be perfect. Do you put him on the newspaper just after his feeds?'

Jenny relaxed a little. Maybe things wouldn't be so bad after all. 'If you watch him you'll see that he whimpers a little and tries to turn in a circle. That usually means he's ready. Sometimes he sniffs the floor. But sometimes he forgets.'

'He's very young,' said Mrs Grace kindly. 'You can't expect him to get it right all the time. What about feeding him?'

'Oh, you don't have to feed him or anything,' Jenny assured the new housekeeper. 'I've started him on solids now. I feed him before I go to school and I come home at lunchtime to do his midday feed. The next one isn't due until four o'clock so I'll be home for that one too.'

'That's excellent,' Mrs Grace replied. 'After all, you know how he likes his food prepared. But I could watch how you do it and, any day you don't have time to come home at lunchtime, I can feed him. I'll need to talk to you about what you and your dad like to eat as well. There's no point in me giving you meals you won't enjoy.'

Jenny smiled. 'I'll make a list of all our favourite meals.'

'Wonderful,' said Mrs Grace. 'Now, why don't you and Jess take me on a tour of the house and show me where everything is?'

Jenny set Jess down on the floor. Immediately the puppy wobbled over to Mrs Grace, holding his twisted leg up. He began to sniff at her shoes.

'Oh, the poor thing,' said Mrs Grace. 'I didn't know he was injured. What happened?'

Jenny looked warily at the woman. Maybe she wouldn't have time for Jess now she knew he was crippled. 'He was born like that,' she said. 'But he's learning to manage on just three legs.'

Mrs Grace bent down and held out her hand. Jess put his little pink nose into it and licked her fingers. 'The poor little scrap!' she said. She looked up at Fraser Miles. 'What does Tom Palmer say?' she asked.

Fraser looked surprised. 'The vet?' he said. 'I haven't asked Tom to look at Jess.'

Ellen Grace didn't say anything. She just looked calmly at Jenny's father.

'I was going to ring Tom tomorrow to come and check up on Mercury,' Mr Miles said quickly. 'Maybe I can get him to have a look at the pup then.'

'I think that would be a very good idea,' Mrs Grace said firmly. She looked at Jenny. 'Maybe it would be best if you asked him to call on Saturday when Jenny is here.'

Jenny gazed at Mrs Grace. She hadn't felt able to ask her father to go to the expense of sending for the vet. But the new housekeeper had suggested it just like that!

'Well, I'll be getting on up to the top field then,' Fraser Miles said, looking slightly embarrassed. 'You can show Mrs Grace where everything is, Jenny.'

Jenny watched her father stride out of the kitchen. Through the window she could see Nell and Jake lying in the sun. The frost had all gone now and already there was warmth in the sun. Her father had taken the ewes out of the shearing shed and the stables and put them back in the fields to graze. Spring wasn't far away.

Mr Miles crossed the yard, gave a low whistle and got into the jeep. The sheepdogs sprang to their feet and leaped up into the back of the vehicle as it started up. Her father didn't even look round. He knew they'd be there. The two working dogs obeyed every command.

'You're not that obedient, are you, Jess?' Jenny giggled as Jess lolloped over to her and began trying to undo her shoelaces. 'One word from me and you do as you like.'

'Puppies are like that,' said Mrs Grace. 'But with training they learn.'

'Thank you for asking Dad to let the vet see Jess,' Jenny said shyly.

'I'm surprised it's taken so long,' said Mrs Grace, her face puzzled.

'Dad's been busy lately,' Jenny explained. 'I didn't like to bother him. And anyway . . .' she stopped.

'What?' asked Mrs Grace.

'Vets cost money,' Jenny finished.

Mrs Grace smiled comfortably. 'I'm sure it wasn't the money,' she said. 'You're probably right. Your father has just been too busy to think about it.'

'Do you think the vet could help Jess?' Jenny asked.

Mrs Grace shook her head. 'I don't know, Jenny,'

she replied. 'We'll just have to wait and see. But we can hope, can't we?'

Jenny looked at Jess, hobbling around on three legs, his twisted leg held up.

'Yes,' she said. 'We can hope.' It sounded nice, that 'we'. Maybe having Mrs Grace here wasn't such a bad idea after all.

Jenny was leaving for school when Calum McLay arrived. Mr McLay farmed the land adjoining Windy Hill. His farm was the biggest in the area and he never let anyone forget it. He drove up to the gate just as Jenny was closing it behind her. 'Where's your father?' he asked gruffly.

Jenny looked at him, sitting behind the wheel of his shiny new Land Rover. Mr McLay's dark hair was cut very short and right now he was looking even more bad-tempered than usual. 'He's gone up to the top field,' Jenny answered.

'What's he doing there?' McLay barked. 'I told him I was coming to see him.'

'He's foot-trimming,' said Jenny, trying to be polite.

'Well, I don't have time to go running all over the countryside trying to find him,' Mr McLay said. 'Tell him I'll up my offer if he's prepared to see sense. He'd be a fool not to take it with Windy Hill in its present state.'

'What offer?' said Jenny, alarmed.

'My offer to buy Windy Hill,' snapped Calum McLay. He looked narrowly at her. 'So he hasn't told you about it, has he? Well, you know now. I want Windy Hill, and what I want, I get.'

With that, Calum McLay revved the engine and turned his Land Rover in the muddy track. Mud spurted from its wheels, splashing Jenny's skirt, but she barely noticed. An offer! She hadn't realised things had gone as far as that. She turned as Mrs Grace came across the farmyard and stood on the other side of the gate.

'I see my landlord has come calling,' she said easily. 'What did he want?'

'Your landlord?' asked Jenny.

Mrs Grace nodded. 'Calum McLay owns the cottage I rent,' she explained. 'I've been trying to get him to repair the roof for months but he just ignores me. I'm afraid Calum and I don't get on very well.'

'He and Dad don't get on either,' said Jenny absently. Mrs Grace put a hand on her shoulder. 'What is it, Jenny?' she asked.

Jenny looked at the housekeeper. 'Mr McLay

THE ARRIVAL

says he's made an offer to buy our farm,' she said. 'You don't think Dad's going to sell Windy Hill, do you?' she asked, anxiously.

Mrs Grace pursed her lips. 'No, I don't, Jenny,' she said firmly. 'But if you're worried about it you should speak to your father.'

Jenny nodded. 'I'll do that,' she said. 'Thanks, Mrs Grace.'

Jenny couldn't get Mr McLay's visit out of her mind. It worried her all morning.

Carrie Turner noticed. 'What's wrong, Jenny?' she asked at mid-morning break. Jenny had hardly spoken to Carrie before but Carrie looked so sympathetic she couldn't help telling her what was worrying her.

Carrie pushed her bright red hair back from her face, her blue eyes sparkling fierily. 'Well, of all the cheek,' she said. 'Mr McLay must think he can do whatever he likes just because he's got plenty of money. I reckon Mrs Grace is right. You ask your dad about it, Jenny. Don't take Mr McLay's word for it.'

'It's true that Windy Hill is short of money,' Jenny confided. 'Maybe Dad *can't* afford to keep it going.'

'Don't you think he would have told you if he was going to sell it?' asked Carrie.

'Maybe,' answered Jenny. 'But maybe he didn't want to worry me.'

Carrie put her hands on her hips. 'My mum says there's no point in meeting trouble halfway,' she announced. 'Worrying doesn't solve anything. If he *is* thinking of selling, *then* you can worry, but not before you find out the truth.'

Jenny smiled. Carrie was so positive. 'How can I stop worrying?' she asked.

'Oh, that's easy,' said Carrie breezily. 'It's geography next. You can help me with my project. It's a complete mess. It needs somebody to tidy it up and sort it out.'

Jenny burst out laughing. 'You think that'll take my mind off things?' she said.

Carrie shook her head. 'Just you wait till you see my project,' she said darkly. 'It's *monumentally* awful.'

The bell went for end of break and Carrie took Jenny by the arm, leading her towards their classroom. 'Where is Paraguay anyway?'

'Calum McLay had no right to speak to you about it,' Fraser Miles said at lunchtime.

Jenny had cycled home from school in double-quick time. Now she was sitting on the floor with Jess on her lap. The puppy had eaten every scrap of the porridge Jenny had prepared for him.

'But is it true, Dad?' she asked.

Fraser Miles looked at her sternly. 'It's true he's made me an offer for the farm,' he replied. 'A very good offer.' Jenny's heart sank.

Then her father started to speak again. 'But there's no way I'll ever sell Windy Hill and certainly not to him. You can stop worrying, Jenny. Windy Hill belongs to this family – and it always will.'

Jenny buried her face in Jess's soft fur and the little puppy wagged his stumpy tail and licked her face.

'There now,' said Mrs Grace comfortably. 'You've had a morning's worry for nothing, Jenny.'

Jenny looked up and smiled. 'Half a morning,' she said. 'I spent the other half sorting out Carrie Turner's geography project.'

'That was kind of you,' Mrs Grace complimented her.

Jenny put her head on one side. 'Actually, it was kind of Carrie. She was really nice to me.'

'Why don't you ask her to tea?' Mrs Grace suggested.

Jenny looked up, surprised. She hadn't had anybody to tea since her mother had died. That was one of the things that had changed at Windy Hill. Her mother had liked her to have friends for tea. Mr Miles never seemed to think about it.

'Maybe I will,' Jenny said. She kissed Jess on the nose. 'You'd like to meet Carrie, wouldn't you, Jess?' she asked.

Jess snuffled and sneezed. 'I'll take that as a "yes",' Jenny told him, laughing. 'Now, don't you go catching cold or Mr Palmer will have to give you medicine. He's coming to see you on Saturday.'

Jenny could hardly wait for Mr Palmer's visit. The vet first examined Mercury out in the yard, and seemed pleased with his progress.

'He's a lot better,' the big, red-faced man pronounced.

Jenny stood well back, in the kitchen doorway, while Tom Palmer completed his examination. Jenny's mum had taught both her and Matt to ride when they were young, and Jenny was usually perfectly at ease around horses. Indeed, she remembered being perfectly at ease around Mercury – until last summer, when he'd caused her mother's death. Now things were different, and Jenny was very nervous of him.

Mercury was recovering well. He was putting on weight; his ribs didn't show through his skin any longer, and his coat was growing back thick and glossy.

'He'll always have a few scars,' Tom Palmer said. 'He must have had some rough treatment. But good feeding and grooming should take care of the rest of his troubles.' The vet looked round, his face serious. 'Have you found out who did this to him yet, Fraser?'

Fraser Miles nodded. 'I made inquiries,' he said. 'I've handed the name of his previous owner over to the police and I've informed the RSPCA. It seems Mercury was a bit too much for him to handle so he resorted to ill-treatment to try and tame him. I don't think it'll be easy for him to talk his way out of a prosecution.'

'Good for you,' Tom Palmer boomed approvingly. 'Animals are just like people. They respond to kindness, not cruelty.'

Jenny really liked Mr Palmer. He was always cheerful but she wondered if he was a bit noisy for Jess. Maybe he would frighten the puppy. But Mercury didn't seem to mind Tom's booming voice and the horse was usually very skittish.

'How would you like to ride Mercury one day?' Tom Palmer called to Jenny. She shrank back instinctively, shaking her head. She still couldn't bring herself to go near Mercury. She didn't like to see any animal in pain but she couldn't *like* him. Not after what he'd done to her mother.

'He's a bit frisky for Jenny,' Matt said. 'Maybe once he's been here a while and calms down she'll change her mind.'

'No,' said Fraser Miles shortly. 'You can exercise Mercury if you're careful, Matt, but I don't want to see Jenny up on him.'

Jenny looked gratefully at her father. He might have taken Mercury in, but it was clear that he didn't think the big horse was safe for her.

'I guess you're right, Dad,' Matt said. 'I've got a lot more experience as a rider than Jenny.'

Jenny frowned. Her mother had been an excellent rider and look what Mercury had done to her. 'You *will* be careful, Matt, won't you?' she said.

Matt ruffled her hair. 'Don't you worry, Jen,' he reassured her. 'I won't take him out until I'm sure he's recovered.'

Jenny frowned again. That wasn't what she had meant. It was *Matt* she was worried about, not

Mercury. But, looking at the way Matt was stroking Mercury, Jenny could see that her brother wouldn't listen to any criticism of the horse. He had rescued the animal and all he could think about was Mercury's wellbeing.

Tom gave Mercury a slap on the rump and the big horse danced, hooves clattering on the cobbled yard. Jess wriggled in Jenny's arms but she kept a firm hold on him. She didn't want Jess going anywhere near those big, dangerous hoofs.

'Let's have a look at this little fellow then,' Tom Palmer boomed, striding across the yard.

Jenny held Jess out to him and he took the puppy in surprisingly gentle hands.

'Now, Jess,' he said softly. 'What's happened to you?'

Jenny looked at the vet with surprise. Maybe he wasn't always noisy after all.

'That's a pity,' Tom said, as he looked at Jess's leg. 'I hate to see something like that.'

'Does that mean you can't do anything for him?' Jenny asked, her heart in her mouth.

'It depends,' the vet replied.

6

'First we'll take Jess inside where I can examine him properly,' Tom Palmer said.

Jenny followed the big vet inside, along with Matt and her father. Mr Palmer laid the puppy carefully on the kitchen table and began to examine him. 'How old is he? About four weeks?'

'Nearly five weeks,' Jenny replied. 'He's a bit small for his age because he had to be hand-reared.'

'Did you rear him yourself?' Tom asked. 'You've

done very well, lass. I'll have to try extra-hard with this little one.'

Jenny looked on anxiously, watching the vet run his hands over Jess's leg and shoulder.

At last, he looked up. 'I'll have to do some x-rays,' he said. 'But I'm pretty sure what the problem is: the shoulder joint on this front leg is out of line,' he explained. 'That's why the leg has grown at an awkward angle.'

'But can you do something for him?' Jenny asked hesitantly.

'Well, we might not be able to get his leg completely straight,' the vet told her. 'But I'm sure we can do *something*. The only thing is, he's not going to like it very much,' Tom warned her. 'I'll have to dislocate the joint and reset it. That way we can try and get the leg back into its normal position.'

Jenny swallowed. It *did* sound terrible. 'Will it hurt?' she asked.

Tom pursed his lips. 'I'll put Jess to sleep for the operation,' he said. 'He'll have to wear a cast for a while until the joint recovers. He won't like it, but he won't be in too much pain.'

Jenny swallowed. 'And it would be best for him in the end?'

Tom held Jess's twisted leg in his gentle fingers. 'I think so,' he said. 'But I can't make promises.'

'What do you think, Dad?' Jenny asked. 'Should we try? I mean, if it's going to be hard on Jess and then not work after all . . .' Her voice trailed off.

Fraser Miles looked serious. 'It's really up to you, Jenny,' he said. 'Jess is your dog. I only feel bad that I didn't send for Tom right away.'

Jenny put her arm through his. 'You let me keep him,' she said.

Fraser patted her hand. 'And as I said, he's your responsibility. What do you want to do – try Tom's treatment or leave Jess as he is?'

Jenny frowned. Mr Palmer had said that the treatment would be hard for Jess – maybe even painful. But the alternative was that Jess would never get any better than he was now. She found herself thinking of Jess of Beacon Brae. He would have taken the risk. If there was a chance of Jess having a more normal life, surely they should take the opportunity.

'Let's try it then,' Jenny decided. 'How long will it take before we know if he's all right?'

'A few weeks,' Tom Palmer replied. 'Of course,

when the cast comes off, his leg will be very weak. He'll need to exercise it. It'll be a lot of work for you.'

'I don't mind,' Jenny declared. 'I'll do anything if it makes him better.'

'Just remember,' said Tom, 'this may not work. And, even if it does, there's no guarantee that Jess's leg will be completely normal. It might always be weak. But I think it's worth a try.'

Jenny nodded. 'I understand,' she said, stroking Jess. The puppy looked up at her and licked her hand. 'Mr Palmer is going to do his best for you, Jess,' she whispered. 'His very best.'

'Oh, I'll do that all right,' said Tom Palmer, smiling down at Jenny. 'And I'll tell you another thing. I don't think Jess could have a better nurse than you, Jenny.'

Jenny looked up at him. 'Thank you,' she said. 'When will you do it?'

Tom frowned. 'I'd like to leave it until he's a little bit older – let's say three weeks from now. By that time he'll be stronger but his bones will still be soft enough to grow into a more normal position with the help of the cast. You go on doing what you're doing and he should be more than fit for the operation.'

'I will,' Jenny promised. 'I'll take *extra* special care of him.'

Matt laughed. 'You couldn't take more care of him than you are doing, Jen,' he said.

But Jenny had made up her mind. From now until Jess's operation the little puppy was going to come first every time. *Nothing* would be too much trouble.

Over the next three weeks Jenny read everything she could get her hands on about the rearing of puppies. Carrie Turner got interested too and together they made up a diet sheet for Jess. Carrie had started coming to tea once a week at Windy Hill. The first time she had seen Jess she had been completely hooked.

'Oh, he's gorgeous!' she said, stooping to pet the little puppy.'

'Come and see Nell's other puppies,' Jenny said, lifting Jess up. 'They're gorgeous too.'

'Aren't they allowed in the house?' asked Carrie as she followed Jenny into the stables.

Jenny shook her head. 'They're going to be working dogs,' she explained. 'They have to get used to it.'

'Poor little things,' said Carrie, bending down

to stroke the puppies. 'But at least they've got their mum.'

Nell looked up at them and Jenny gave her a pat. The puppies scrambled over each other, tumbling and playing. Jenny couldn't resist it. She put Jess in the box with them and watched as he began to make friends.

'He isn't really supposed to play with the other puppies,' she told Carrie. 'But he's managed to find his way into the stable several times. He can't see why they shouldn't all be friends.'

'They're much bigger than he is,' Carrie commented. 'But I still like Jess best.'

'Nell's puppies will be going to their new homes this afternoon,' Jenny said. 'Maybe it's just as well Jess wasn't allowed to play with them. He'd miss them when they went.'

'Oh, I don't know about that,' said Carrie, grinning. 'I can't see what harm being friends *ever* does. I mean you can't always be worrying about what's round the corner.'

Jenny grinned back. Carrie was so good to be with. She was showing Jenny a different way of looking at things. Jenny decided to stop worrying about Jess's operation and just enjoy him. After all, she was lucky to have the puppy at all!

★ ★ ★

'That's the last one,' Fraser Miles said later that afternoon. He tucked the fourth puppy into the big basket in the back of the jeep. 'Say goodbye now, Jenny.'

Jenny leaned over the basket with Jess in her arms. She stroked the puppies. Jess squirmed, eager to join the others but Jenny held him firmly. 'You're all going to lovely homes,' she said softly to his brothers and sisters.

'They are that,' said Mr Miles. 'There's been quite a bit of competition for Nell's pups. I got good prices for them. I reckon we'll see one or two of these at the sheepdog trials in Graston in a few years' time.'

'I'll take Jess to watch them,' Jenny announced, cuddling her pet.

Mr Miles smiled. 'I reckon Jess might sire a sheepdog or two in his time,' he said.

Jenny stared at him. 'Oh, Dad, do you really think so?'

Jenny's father looked at Jess. 'I don't see why not,' he said. 'After all he comes from good stock. Just because he can't be a working dog doesn't mean he can't sire good working animals.'

'Wow!' said Carrie as Mr Miles drove off with

the pups. 'Just imagine, Jen – a whole dynasty of champion sheepdogs all sired by Jess!'

'Protein and vitamins to help him grow strong and healthy,' Jenny announced to Mrs Grace on the morning of Jess's operation. 'And carbohydrates for energy – but not too many or he'll get fat.'

Ellen Grace laughed as she watched Jess scamper under the kitchen table. Jenny looked round the kitchen. Already it looked more like it had done when her mother had been alive. The jelly moulds were shining and Mrs Grace had run up new curtains from some material she had at home – red checks this time. She had also sorted out some different curtains and a pretty bedspread for Jenny's room. The flowered pattern looked much more grown-up than the old cartoon characters Jenny had had since she was tiny.

'Oh, Jess has got plenty of energy,' Mrs Grace said.

Jenny made a dive for Jess and scooped him up in her arms. The puppy was managing very well with only three good legs and he had grown amazingly. 'I hope you won't mind the cast too much, Jess,' she said, rubbing her cheek against his head. 'You won't be able to run about as easily with that on.'

'I'm sure he'll manage,' Mrs Grace put in. 'He's very brave. You'd better get off to school. You'll be late otherwise.'

Jenny gave Jess a final cuddle. 'Next time I see you your operation will be over, Jess. Oh, I hope it goes well.'

Jess looked up and licked her chin.

'Now, don't worry, Jenny,' Mrs Grace advised. 'Your dad will collect you from school and take you to the surgery to visit Jess.'

School, thought Jenny. How on earth was she to keep her mind on her schoolwork while Jess was having his operation? She wondered if Carrie would have any bright ideas about taking her mind off that!

'Why don't you get a decent schoolbag instead of that old thing?' Fiona McLay sneered at Jenny, as she arrived at the school gates.

'Jenny's schoolbag is OK,' said Paul, Fiona's seven-year-old brother. 'It's a *sports* bag.'

Jenny looked at Matt's battered old sports bag and smiled at Paul. Paul was deaf but he was a marvellous lip reader. Often people didn't even realise he was deaf – until Fiona told them.

'What do you know about anything?' Fiona snapped at him. She turned to Jenny. 'Well?'

Jenny was hardly listening. Jess would be on his way to the vet's about now and she couldn't think of anything else.

'Oh, I forgot,' Fiona said, looking down her nose at Jenny. Fiona was a lot taller than Jenny with short dark hair and ice-blue eyes. 'Your father can't afford to buy you decent things. When is he going to sell that old farm of yours? My dad says he can't last much longer – not with his money worries.'

Jenny looked at the other girl in frustration. Fiona always made her feel tongue-tied. 'I don't care what kind of schoolbag I have,' she said. 'And Windy Hill isn't for s-s-sale.'

'Oh, now you've got a stutter,' Fiona mocked. 'Windy Hill isn't for s-s-sale. We'll s-s-see about that.'

'Leave her alone,' said a voice behind Jenny.

Jenny whirled round. Carrie had just arrived. Her bright red hair was escaping from its ponytail and her green eyes were flashing. 'I'm fed up with you always getting at Jenny,' Carrie went on. 'You're just a bully. Why can't you pick on someone your own size? Can't you *see* she's worried?'

Fiona went bright red. 'She's worried about losing her tatty little farm,' she retorted nastily and she flounced off.

Little Paul looked embarrassed at his sister's behaviour and gave Jenny an apologetic smile. Jenny smiled back and looked at Carrie in admiration. Even the freckles across Carrie's nose seemed to glow with indignation as she watched Fiona storm off into the playground.

'I wish I could stand up to Fiona like that,' Jenny said. 'Thanks.'

'Don't mention it,' Carrie replied. 'I've been itching to give her a taste of her own medicine for ages. Anyway, how was Jess this morning? When will you know how the op went?'

'Dad's picking me up from school this afternoon to go straight to the vet's surgery,' Jenny replied. She saw Paul's face looking puzzled. 'It's my puppy,' she explained to him. 'He's having an operation today and I'm worried about him.'

'You're so lucky to have a puppy,' the little boy said. 'I wish I had a pet.'

'I haven't got a pet either, Paul,' said Carrie comfortingly.

'At least you can go to Puffin Island and watch the birds any time you want,' replied Paul. 'I love bird watching.'

'Do you?' asked Carrie. 'Then you should come for a trip to the bird reserve one day.'

'You mean in your dad's boat?' asked Paul excitedly.

Carrie nodded. Jenny knew that Mr Turner had a boat which he used to take people on trips to Puffin Island, just off the coast. The little island was a bird reserve and was home to nesting seabirds.

'You could come too, Jenny,' Carrie said. 'Mum wants to go out there anyway. She's got a commission to illustrate a book on birds and Puffin Island is perfect for it. We could *all* go.'

'Oh, I'd love to,' Jenny said. 'But shouldn't you ask your mum and dad, first? I wouldn't want to be in the way.'

Carrie put her head on one side. 'Typical Jenny!' she said. 'You're always putting yourself down.'

'Sorry,' said Jenny.

'See what I mean?' said Carrie, her hands on her hips.

They both laughed.

'You need someone to stand up for you,' Carrie decided.

'I'll stand up for you, Jenny,' Paul said. 'Fiona bullies me too.'

Jenny was shocked. How could Fiona bully her deaf little brother? That was really mean. Paul and Fiona were so different they didn't seem like brother and sister at all. Jenny could see Fiona crossing the playground towards them again. She suddenly felt sorry for Paul – not because he was deaf but because he had to put up with a sister like Fiona.

'How would you like to come and see Jess some day?' Jenny asked him.

Paul's face lit up. 'Can I really?' he said. 'I'd love that.'

Fiona came to stand beside Paul. 'No, you can't,' she said. 'You know Dad would never let you set foot on Windy Hill – at least not until we own it.'

Paul's face fell and Jenny felt a rush of sympathy for him.

'Well, I intend to visit Windy Hill as often as I like,' said Carrie.

'You!' said Fiona. 'What do you want to go visiting Jenny for?'

Carrie stuck her chin out. 'Because she's my friend,' she declared.

'Hmmph,' said Fiona. 'Your mum's a famous

artist. She wouldn't want you to waste your time on a nobody like Jenny Miles.'

'My mother would love Jenny,' Carrie retorted. 'In fact, she's invited Jenny to tea!' Carrie gave Jenny a look and Jenny blushed. She had been putting off going for tea at Carrie's, preferring to rush straight home to feed Jess. Maybe she should make time to visit Cliff House, the Turners' home in Cliffbay.

For the first time Fiona looked put out. Her face flushed an angry red and she grabbed Paul's hand. 'Come on, Paul. Dad wouldn't want us to waste our time talking to Jenny Miles.'

Jenny felt a hot surge of anger. Why should she always let Fiona get away with it? 'By the way, Fiona,' she said sharply, 'Windy Hill is *not* for sale – to your father or anybody else.'

Fiona looked as if she couldn't believe her ears, then she turned on her heel, dragging Paul after her. The little boy looked back as he went and gave her a weak smile. Jenny waved and smiled back.

'Wow!' said Carrie admiringly. 'Maybe you *can* stick up for yourself after all. Well done, Jenny!'

Jenny flushed. She felt elated, triumphant. She had stood up to Fiona McLay.

'I hope you didn't mind me saying that about coming to Windy Hill whenever I liked,' Carrie went on. 'I just got so *mad* at Fiona. She's always trying to wangle an invitation to Cliff House. She thinks Mum will want to paint a portrait of her. Some chance!'

'I didn't mind,' said Jenny. 'And, Carrie, I *will* come to tea. I promise – as soon as Jess gets home.'

'How about Saturday?' Carrie asked.

Jenny nodded. 'Saturday!' she agreed. 'And I'll bring Jess too, if I may.'

'I knew I'd talk you round,' said Carrie. 'Now, can you have a look at this maths homework of mine? I just don't know what algebra is *for*!'

Jenny shook her head. 'Sure,' she said. 'It'll take my mind off Jess.'

Talking to Carrie was a bit like dealing with a whirlwind but Jenny liked it. For the first time ever she had felt more important than Fiona McLay. Carrie had made her feel like that, by standing up for her and showing her how to stand up for herself. And, better than anything else, at last she had a friend!

7

Tom Palmer was smiling when he opened the door of the surgery to Jenny and her father.

'It went very well,' he said reassuringly. 'Jess is still a bit sleepy but come and see him. He's doing fine.'

Jenny's heart hammered as she followed Tom Palmer through reception and into the recovery room. Jess looked very small, lying in his cage. The cast on his leg seemed too big for the little puppy. Jenny touched it through the bars of the cage.

'It's lighter than it looks,' said Tom Palmer, guessing what she was thinking. 'It's a special plastic bandage called a vetcast. It isn't nearly as heavy as a plaster cast.'

Jenny moved closer to the cage and gazed down at Jess. The puppy's eyes were closed but when she said his name they opened slowly and his tail thumped against the bottom of the cage.

'Oh, Jess,' whispered Jenny. 'I was so worried about you.' She turned to Tom Palmer. 'Can I hold him?'

The vet nodded and opened the door of the cage, lifting Jess out carefully. He laid the puppy in Jenny's arms and Jenny bent her head and gave Jess a cuddle. Jess licked her cheek and his tail wagged harder.

Jenny touched the cast again. Mr Palmer was right. It wasn't so heavy after all.

'Will he have to lie still while he has the cast on?' Jenny asked anxiously.

'Not at all,' Tom Palmer assured her. 'He's so young he'll adapt to it very quickly.'

'It looks like you've done a good job there, Tom,' Fraser Miles said. 'What happens now?'

'I'll keep him in overnight just to make sure he's completely recovered from the anaesthetic,' the vet replied. 'You can come and collect him tomorrow.'

Jenny bent her head to Jess. 'Tomorrow, Jess,' she promised. 'You're coming home tomorrow and I'm going to take *such* good care of you.'

Tom Palmer was right. Jess soon got used to having the cast on his leg. Too used to it, Jenny thought, as she and Carrie watched the little puppy chase after Jake and Nell three weeks later.

The working dogs trotted across the yard, heads low and plumy tails waving. Jess limped behind the sheepdogs, yapping furiously but the older dogs took no notice.

'Keep Jess in the yard,' Fraser Miles warned Jenny as he opened the gate and the two sheepdogs followed him through. 'I don't want him anywhere near the sheep. He's a house dog and he has to learn to behave like one.'

Jenny hid a smile. Jess just couldn't help trying to follow Jake and Nell.

'It isn't Jess's fault,' Carrie whispered to her as Mr Miles whistled for the working dogs and set off up the track. 'Jess was bred from a long line of sheepdogs. It's in his blood.'

Jenny nodded. 'I know,' she said. 'But Dad is

right. He can't afford to risk Jess frightening the sheep or trying to play with Jake and Nell. It won't be long till lambing now and the ewes are easily upset when they're pregnant. Dad needs a good lambing. Everything depends on it.'

Carrie looked serious as she and Jenny walked back towards the house. 'Are things really that bad then?' she asked.

Jenny nodded her head. 'I think so. Dad doesn't talk about it. But Matt says if we don't get a good yield of lambs Dad will have to think about putting Windy Hill on the market.'

'And you know who'll be ready to buy it,' Carrie said.

'Fiona McLay's father,' Jenny replied, frowning. 'It would break Dad's heart to sell Windy Hill – and it would be even worse if he had to sell to Mr McLay. The trouble is, Fiona's dad seems determined to get our farm.'

'Why?' Carrie asked.

Jenny shook her head. 'Mrs Grace says he wants to buy up all the land round his farm. But I think it's to do with an argument they had years ago. I reckon Mr McLay still holds a grudge against Dad.'

'Well, I think you should concentrate on Jess

and forget about Mr McLay,' said Carrie. 'Come on, it's time for Jess's exercise.'

Jenny grinned as she followed Carrie into the kitchen porch. Carrie was always so full of enthusiasm. She had been a real help these last weeks.

'Just another week, Jess,' Jenny whispered to the puppy. 'Then we'll see what you can do without your cast.'

Jess looked up at her and gave a short bark. He was growing fast now. Jenny scooped her pet up into her arms. 'Now, where's your stick?'

Jenny found the stick behind the porch door and they took Jess out into the yard.

'It isn't very sophisticated, is it?' asked Carrie, looking at the stick.

'It works,' said Jenny. 'That's all that matters.'

Carrie looked at Jess as Jenny threw the stick. The puppy ran after it, sometimes forgetting to hold his bad leg out of the way in his excitement to fetch the stick. 'You're right,' Carrie said. 'Anything that makes him use that leg must be good for him.'

Matt came out of the house and stood watching for a while as the girls threw the stick for Jess. 'Why don't you try taking him down to the beach for a swim once his cast is off?' he suggested.

'Swimming?' said Jenny. 'Would that be good for him?'

'I've started taking Mercury down to the beach at Cliffbay,' Matt said. 'I gallop him along the edge of the water. That's really good for his legs. Maybe you should try it with Jess.'

'That sounds like a good idea,' Carrie said.

'Check it out with Tom Palmer,' Matt advised. 'But I don't see why it shouldn't work.'

Jenny watched as Matt went into the stable. A moment later he led Mercury out. The big horse looked sleek and well fed and he stood quietly while Matt saddled him. Jenny stared at Mercury. She was beginning to remember why her mother had loved the horse so much. He was *beautiful*.

He turned his head and looked at her, blowing softly through his nostrils. For a second, Jenny was tempted to move closer and touch the gleaming creature. But she couldn't. No matter how beautiful he was she still couldn't forgive him.

'The seawater certainly seems to have worked for Mercury,' Carrie said. 'What do you think, Jenny? Do you want to give it a go?'

Jenny didn't answer. She was still looking at

Mercury. Matt led the big black horse through the farm gate, mounted and rode off down the track. Jenny turned to Carrie and saw concern in her friend's eyes.

'You don't like Mercury, do you?' asked Carrie.

'No,' Jenny said quietly.

'But why?' Carrie asked.

'Because he killed my mother,' Jenny replied.

Carrie gasped in shock. 'What do you mean? How?'

'He threw her and she died,' Jenny explained. 'I just can't understand why Dad wants to keep him.'

'So why don't you ask him?' Carrie asked.

Jenny shook her head. 'I can't,' she said. 'Dad won't talk about Mum's accident.'

Carrie looked thoughtful. 'Your dad must have his reasons for keeping the horse,' she said.

'I suppose it's because he feels guilty that Mercury was so badly treated after he sold him,' said Jenny. 'It's the only reason I can think of.'

'Then why don't you tell Matt you're not happy about Mercury being here?' Carrie suggested.

'Because Matt loves Mercury,' Jenny said. 'Anybody can see that. I think he loves Mercury as much as I love Jess. Though I can't understand it.'

Carrie sighed. 'So what are you going to do then?' she asked.

Jenny shook her head. 'There isn't anything I *can* do,' she said. 'I've just got to accept it.'

Carrie was silent for a moment. 'What about Matt's idea of taking Jess swimming?' she said at last.

Jenny looked down at Jess. He was scampering round the farmyard, chasing a tuft of sheep's wool. Every time he caught up with it the breeze blew it away from him. Jenny felt better just watching him. She nodded. 'It's worth a try,' she said. Anything was worth a try if it helped Jess. But she would check with the vet first.

Mrs Grace came out of the kitchen into the yard. 'Tea's ready,' she announced. 'It's your favourite, Jenny – sausage casserole. Now leave some for your dad and be sure to put the dish back in the oven to keep warm after you've finished. I've got to dash into Greybridge to do some shopping.'

Jenny nodded. Mrs Grace had fitted in really well at Windy Hill and she was a terrific cook.

'Yummy!' said Carrie. 'I *love* sausage casserole. Come on, Jess, race you to the kitchen. That'll count as exercise.'

★ ★ ★

Carrie's mum drove up in her battered old Mini just as Jenny and Carrie were finishing tea. The two girls dashed outside to meet her. Jenny loved Mrs Turner's Mini. It was bright orange and she had painted big yellow sunflowers on the roof. Mrs Turner had had the Mini since she was an art student and refused to part with it, even though she could afford something smarter. Mrs Turner's hair was red like her daughter's but cut short. She looked as bright and cheerful as a sunflower herself. She and the Mini were a good match.

'How's the patient?' she asked as she got out of the car and caught sight of Jess.

'The cast is coming off next week,' Jenny replied.

Mrs Turner was studying Jess closely and looking very thoughtful. 'Next week,' she murmured. 'Mmm. Do you mind if I do a few sketches of Jess while he still has his cast on, Jenny?'

Jenny's mouth dropped open in surprise. 'Sketches! Oh, that would be great. But I don't know if he'll sit still.'

Carrie laughed. 'Don't worry about that,' she said. 'I've seen Mum chase animals all over her studio while she's been sketching them.'

'Cats are worse than dogs,' Mrs Turner said, reaching into the back seat of the Mini. She brought out a sketch–pad and a box of pencils. 'Just put him down and I'll get on with it, Jenny. He's perfect.'

Jenny put Jess on the ground and the puppy began to chase his tail, falling over several times when he lost his balance. Carrie's mum perched herself on the bonnet of the Mini and began to sketch furiously. Her eyes flicked from Jess to the sketching block in front of her. It was clear to Jenny that she wasn't doing just one sketch. She was doing one after another.

As Jenny watched, Mrs Turner tore off the sheet she had been working on and tossed it on top of the bonnet behind her. Carrie made a dive and caught it as it slid off the car. Mrs Turner didn't even seem to notice.

'When Mum's hard at work the *sky* could fall in and she wouldn't notice,' Carrie explained, as another page slithered down the bonnet.

Jenny giggled. Jess was rolling round the yard now, trying to eat his cast. Mrs Turner's pencil was flying across the paper and Carrie was diving for pages as quickly as her mum tore them off and threw them behind her.

THE ARRIVAL

At last Mrs Turner stopped her frantic sketching and looked up. 'That should do to be going on with,' she announced. 'Thanks, Jenny.'

'Do you mean you might want to do more?' Jenny asked.

Mrs Turner grinned. 'I'll work some of these up and then I'll see if I need any more,' she replied.

'What for?' asked Carrie.

Mrs Turner's eyes twinkled. 'Just wait and see.'

She handed Jenny one of the pages. It had five or six thumbnail sketches of Jess on it. Jenny gasped with pleasure as she looked at the drawings. Though they were composed of only a few quick lines, Jenny thought they captured Jess's playfulness perfectly.

'Can I keep these?' she asked.

'Sure,' said Mrs Turner. 'Now, Carrie, let's get going.'

Carrie leaped into the car as her mother revved the engine.

Jenny grinned. Mrs Turner was amazing. Carrie has said her mother could sit for hours just looking at something she was painting, but when she moved, she moved *fast*!

Jenny looked again at the sketches as the Mini disappeared round the bend of the track in a cloud of dust. There was Jess sitting up, wide-eyed and innocent looking; Jess rolling on the cobbles, looking like an animated ball of black and white fluff; Jess chasing his tail, tumbling over his feet; Jess in all his moods – naughty, soulful, mischievous, adorable! The cast on his front leg made him even more appealing. Jenny turned to show the pictures to Jess but the puppy was nowhere to be seen.

'Jess!' she called in a panic. 'Where are you?'

There was a short bark from the kitchen and Jenny dashed inside. She stopped at the kitchen door, horrified. 'Oh, Jess!' she said. 'What have you done?'

But it was all too obvious what Jess had done. The casserole dish was still on the kitchen table. Jenny had forgotten to put it in the oven when she and Carrie had rushed outside to meet Mrs Turner. Jess stood over it, his tail wagging furiously. Somehow he must have managed to jump up on a chair and on to the table. He was licking his lips and the dish was wiped clean.

'You've eaten Dad's dinner,' said Jenny. 'What *is* he going to say?'

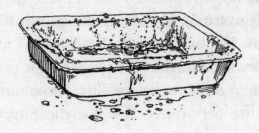

8

Jenny picked Jess up off the table and put him down firmly on the kitchen floor. 'Jess, that was really naughty,' she scolded, trying her hardest to sound severe.

Jess put his head on one side and looked up at her appealingly. Jenny couldn't help smiling as she took the empty casserole dish away from the table. 'At least there's nothing wrong with your appetite,' she joked. And, secretly, part of her was thrilled that Jess had ignored his weak leg in order to jump up to get the food. This must be a good sign! 'I suppose I'd better do something about Dad's dinner,' she said.

Jenny opened the larder door and scanned the contents. The larder was much better stocked since Mrs Grace had come to Windy Hill.

'Pasta,' Jenny decided, reaching down a packet of spaghetti. She frowned, then opened the fridge and considered the options. 'With cheese and tomato sauce,' she announced.

Jess wagged his tail and Jenny looked at him severely. 'Not for *you*, Jess. You've already had two dinners!'

Jenny unhooked an apron from the back of the kitchen door, put it on and set to work. By the time she heard her father arriving home the smell of the sauce was wafting through the kitchen and the pasta was ready.

Swiftly, Jenny drained the spaghetti and piled it into a serving dish. She poured the sauce over it, whipped off the apron and sat down in the corner armchair beside the Aga, cuddling Jess on her lap. 'Not a word!' she warned the little puppy.

Jess barked and licked a spot of sauce off her hand.

'Oops! Thanks, Jess,' she giggled.

Mr Miles came through the kitchen door, sniffing appreciatively. 'Hello, lass. Something smells good,' he said approvingly as he went to wash his hands.

Jenny set the serving dish in front of him at the table and watched anxiously as he helped himself.

'You know,' he said, taking a bite of his pasta. 'Mrs Grace really is a wonderful cook.'

Fraser Miles repeated his compliments next morning after breakfast.

'That pasta you left for me last night was delicious, Mrs Grace,' he said warmly.

Mrs Grace looked puzzled and she opened her mouth to say something. Jenny felt her heart sink. She looked quickly at Jess and away again. Then she saw Mrs Grace's eyes on her and felt herself blushing.

'I'm glad you enjoyed it, Fraser,' the housekeeper said solemnly. 'And don't you think it's time you called me Ellen?' she added, as Mr Miles made for the door.

'You've made quite a difference to Windy Hill since you've been here, Ellen,' he called back as he went out into the yard.

Jenny looked at the pots of spring bulbs on the

window ledge, the blue and white crockery gleaming on the dresser, the vase of bright yellow daffodils on the table. Mrs Grace certainly had made a difference – but would she be angry with Jess?

The housekeeper raised her eyebrows. 'Is there something I should know?' she asked, smiling.

Jenny couldn't help smiling back, and blurted out the whole story.

'I wondered if it might be something like that,' Mrs Grace said when she had finished.

'I thought you might be angry,' Jenny confessed.

Ellen Grace gathered up the plates from the kitchen table and dumped them in the sink. 'Angry?' she repeated. 'Not at all. It's nice to know that Jess likes my cooking too. But you might regret this episode, young lady.'

'Why?' asked Jenny, alarmed.

'Because now that I know you're such a good cook you won't be able to get out of helping me now and again.'

Jenny grinned. 'Oh, I'd love that,' she said. 'Thanks for not giving Jess away.'

Mrs Grace turned from the sink to look at her. 'That'll be our secret.'

Jenny smiled with relief. Mrs Grace was turning

out to be a very good addition to Windy Hill. 'You don't mind Jess being around, do you?' she asked. 'I mean he doesn't get in your way, does he?'

Mrs Grace laughed. 'He does,' she admitted. 'But I'm learning to put anything I don't want chewed out of *his* way! I didn't realise he could get up on to the table. I'll remember that in future. He'll be worse when he gets that cast off. Next week, isn't it?'

Jenny nodded. 'Mr Palmer is coming over after school on Wednesday to take it off. I hope everything will be OK. Carrie said she'd come over too if that's all right.'

'Of course it is,' replied Mrs Grace. 'It's good to see you've got a friend.'

Jenny opened the dresser drawer and started searching for something to tie her hair back with.

'Oh, I nearly forgot,' said Mrs Grace, wiping her hands on a towel. She went to her bag and brought out an elasticated hair-tie. It was yellow with blue splodgy flowers on it. 'This is for you.'

Jenny took the hair-tie and examined it. 'Thank you. I usually just tie it back with anything I can find,' she said.

Mrs Grace put her hands on her hips and gave

Jenny a look. 'I know,' she said. 'That's what comes of living in a house with no other women in it. This is much prettier. Now turn round and I'll fix it for you.'

Jenny did as she was told and Mrs Grace gathered her hair up and pulled it into a loose pony-tail. Then she twisted it up and fixed the hair-tie round it.

'There, what do you think of that?' she asked.

Jenny looked at herself in the dresser mirror, twisting round so that she could see the back of her head. 'Oh, that looks great, Mrs Grace,' she said. 'Carrie has a hair-tie just like this. What do you think, Jess?'

The puppy barked and wagged his tail.

'That looks like the seal of approval,' Mrs Grace said, laughing.

Jenny looked at her shyly. 'It was really good of you,' she said.

'Nonsense,' replied Mrs Grace briskly. 'I don't have any girls of my own to buy pretty things for. I've got a nephew but I can't buy hair-ties for him.'

Jenny giggled. 'I suppose not,' she said. 'What's he like?'

'You'll see soon enough,' Mrs Grace replied. 'He's coming for a long visit. His parents are going to Canada through his father's work and they need time to get settled down before they can send for him. They have to find somewhere to live and look at schools. It could take a while so he's coming to me for the time being. He'll be going to Graston School while he's here.'

'My grandparents live in Canada,' Jenny informed Mrs Grace. 'Grandad is Canadian. He came over here with the Canadian airforce. He was based at the old airfield on the other side of Greybridge. Then he met Gran and they got married. But he always said he would go back to Canada when he retired.'

'I remember your grandparents,' Ellen Grace said. 'I hope they're enjoying their retirement.'

'They love it,' Jenny enthused. 'They go camping and skiing and all kinds of things. Your nephew will have a great time in Canada. I'll show him some photos if you like.'

Jenny was about to ask more questions about Mrs Grace's nephew but she caught sight of the clock and jumped. 'Cripes! I'll be late for school if I don't hurry.' She gave Jess a quick cuddle and dashed out of the door. 'Try to be good, Jess,' she called over her shoulder.

'That'll be the day!' Mrs Grace called after her.

★ ★ ★

'There,' said Mr Palmer the following Wednesday. He stood back from the kitchen table. 'Let's see how he manages.'

Jenny and Carrie stood silently by as Jess looked up at the vet. The cast was lying on the table beside him and, for the first time in weeks, Jenny could see his leg. She drew in her breath.

'It looks straight,' she said.

Mr Palmer ran a hand over Jess's bad leg and the puppy wriggled. 'Not quite,' he said. 'I think he'll always have a bit of a limp, but what we're more concerned with is getting some strength into it.'

Jess licked furiously at his leg.

'That'll be good for it,' Tom Palmer assured Jenny. 'Licking will stimulate the blood flow to the muscles. His leg muscles need building up.'

'Yes, it looks thinner than the other leg,' said Carrie sympathetically.

'That's only to be expected,' said Tom Palmer. 'You'll have to try and get him to exercise the leg.'

'We were going to ask you about swimming,' Jenny said. 'Do you think it would be good for him?'

110

'I think that's a brilliant idea,' the vet replied. 'Swimming would strengthen the muscles in his leg and, because he'll be suspended in the water, it won't put too much strain on him.'

Jenny picked Jess up gently. 'Do you hear that, Jess? You're going swimming. Won't that be fun?'

9

'Go get it, Jess!' Carrie shouted the following Sunday afternoon as she threw a stick into the sea.

Jenny laughed as Jess hurtled after the stick, splashing in the waves and throwing up sprays of seawater that sparkled in the sun. Jess was three months old now and well on his way to catching up on his growth. He was still a little small for his age but Tom Palmer had told Jenny not to worry about that. He would grow faster now that he was able to take regular exercise.

'He's certainly coming on,' said Mrs Turner, coming to stand beside Jenny.

Jenny nodded happily. 'The swimming is a great success,' she said. 'And he loves chasing sticks.'

Mrs Turner laughed as Jess raced up the beach and began to shake himself.

'Oh! I've had a shower already today,' Jenny cried, bending down to take the stick and fuss over Jess's cleverness. The puppy wagged his tail so hard he overbalanced and sat down suddenly on the sand.

'Still not entirely steady,' commented Mrs Turner, laughing.

'His right front leg is still pretty weak,' said Jenny.

'But you'd hardly notice he had a limp,' Carrie put in, running up to them. 'Oh, *look!*' She pointed to a sketch Mrs Turner was working on. 'He's still got his cast on.'

Jenny looked at the drawing. Mrs Turner was working up one of the sketches she had done of Jess. It looked very strange now that Jenny was getting used to Jess without his cast.

Mrs Turner held up the sketch and looked at it critically. 'I think I like this one best of all,' she said, examining her handiwork. The drawing showed Jess sitting, head on one side, looking up plaintively. The cast made him look very sweet and vulnerable.

Mrs Turner was lost in thought. 'Yes, I think this is the one I'll use,' she said softly.

'What for?' asked Carrie, plonking herself down on the sand beside Jess and rolling around with him.

Mrs Turner smiled. 'I don't want to say anything yet. If my idea works out I might have a very nice surprise for Jenny and Jess.'

Jenny longed to find out more but Mrs Turner shook her head. 'Time for tea,' she announced. 'Would you like to have tea with us, Jenny?'

Jenny had kept her promise to Carrie. Now she had tea at Cliff House as often as Carrie did at Windy Hill. This time Jenny shook her head. 'No, thank you. I'd love to, but I can't. Mrs Grace's nephew has arrived to stay with her for a while, and she's asked him to tea at Windy Hill today. I promised I'd be there.'

'What's he like?' asked Carrie, getting up and dusting sand from her clothes, as her mother walked on ahead.

Jenny shrugged. 'I haven't met him yet,' she replied. 'He only arrived last night.'

'Tea, Carrie,' Mrs Turner called from further along the beach. 'I've got a meeting of the Wildlife Association in an hour's time so we'll need to get a move on.'

Carrie grinned. 'Got to go. See you tomorrow,' she said, darting off.

'Come on, Jess,' Jenny called, picking up the stick. 'Let's go home.'

As they made their way along the beach towards the path at the far end of the cliffs, Jenny threw the stick as far as she could along the edge of the water. Jess scampered after it. Jenny watched him in delight. A wave caught the stick and drew it out to sea. Jess paddled after it, his legs working furiously as he swam. Matt was right. Swimming *was* good for Jess's leg.

Jenny watched as the puppy retrieved the stick and made his way back to shore, shaking himself and racing up the beach towards her. She took the stick and made to throw it again. Jess backed off, eyes alert.

'Oops! Sorry, Jess,' Jenny apologised as her aim went wide and the stick landed behind a rock at the base of the cliff.

Jess lolloped after it and disappeared behind the rock. Jenny waited but Jess did not reappear.

She frowned. 'Jess!' she called.

There was a muffled barking and Jess's head appeared round the side of the rock. He stood there, ignoring the stick, barking at her.

'What is it?' she called, walking over to him. 'Have you found a crab? Careful it doesn't nip you!'

Jess continued to stand there, legs stiff, barking urgently. Then he disappeared once more behind the rock.

Jenny began to run. 'What *is* it, Jess?' she cried. Then, as she reached the rock the breath caught in her throat. It wasn't a crab Jess had found. It was a sheep, lying motionless on the sand.

Jess stood over the sheep, barking furiously. But even without touching it, Jenny could see it was too late. The poor animal was dead.

Jenny looked up. The cliffs tumbled towards the beach in a mass of rock and scrubby grass. Shading her eyes from the sun, Jenny searched the top of the cliff. There was movement up there. More sheep.

Jenny's heart beat faster as she bent towards the dead sheep and examined it. It was a Blackface. The body was still warm and the blue marking on the sheep's fleece was visible. It looked like the

THE ARRIVAL

Windy Hill mark. Quickly she checked the tattoo on the inside of the animal's ear. It was one of her father's flock.

Jenny tried to picture the lie of the land above her. One of her father's fields was up there but it was fenced off from the cliff. Had some of the flock somehow broken through? Had somebody left a gate open?

As she looked up Jenny could see more movement. She listened and could hear the agitated bleating of frightened sheep. Jenny knew that if she didn't do something, more of her father's flock might panic and topple over the cliff. And it wasn't just the ewes that were in danger. Most of the flock was pregnant. If the ewes were lost, then their lambs would be lost too. Her father's whole livelihood was at risk.

Jenny looked at the cliff face. Was there any way she could climb it? Could she turn the sheep back? The cliff wasn't as sheer at this point as it was further along towards Cliffbay, but it was still steep. And there were loose rocks and stones that would make getting a foothold difficult. Jenny looked down at her trainers. They weren't the best footgear for climbing a cliff like that. But she knew she had no choice. It was either climb the cliff to try and turn the sheep, or watch as her father lost everything he had worked so hard for.

Jenny placed one foot on the side of the cliff. Jess looked up at her. 'I've got to do something, Jess,' she whispered, her throat dry. 'At least I've got to try.'

10

Jenny was a third of the way up the rocky slope before she realised that Jess was behind her. She turned, clutching at a spur of rock. 'Go back, Jess! It's too dangerous.'

But the little dog ignored her command and carried on up the cliff behind her, finding crevices and tufts of vegetation to give him footholds.

Jenny didn't know what she could do to stop him. What if he tumbled off and fell like that poor sheep down there? She opened her mouth to call to him but her handgrip slipped and she had to cling on to a tuft of grass to save herself from falling. One foot scrabbled at the surface beneath her as sand and gravel rolled away under her trainers.

At once there was a flurry of black and white and Jess was beside her, negotiating his own way up the cliff, testing, finding footholds. Jenny let out a sigh of relief as her foot found a grip, then she glanced at Jess. The little dog turned his head and looked at her, then began to scramble up the cliff in front of her.

Jenny let out a shaky breath of laughter. Jess was doing a lot better than she was. 'OK, Jess,' she admitted. 'You win. I'll follow you.'

Jenny was so intent on following where Jess led that at first she didn't hear the voice yelling from the top of the cliff. Then she became aware that somebody was shouting at her.

'Get back! What do you think you're doing? That cliff isn't safe.'

Jenny looked up, annoyed and ready to give as good as she got, but looking up made her dizzy. She gritted her teeth and kept on climbing. The voice above continued to shout.

'Nearly at the top, Jess,' she muttered as the cliff

face sloped inwards. Jenny leaned gratefully against the warm rock, clinging to it. Her nails were broken from scraping handholds. Her knees were scratched where the rock had grazed through her jeans.

'How stupid can you get?' came the voice.

Jenny looked up again, the sun dazzling her eyes. She could make out the shape of a boy, leaning over the cliff.

'Grab my hand,' he yelled.

Jenny reached up and grabbed the outstretched hand with her right one. Just as she did so the rock her foot was resting on rolled away from under her and crashed down to the beach below. 'Jess!' she cried.

The boy's other hand grabbed at Jess's collar and he hoisted the dog up on to the clifftop. 'Now grab that ledge,' he yelled, pointing at a narrow ledge near Jenny's left shoulder.

Jenny grasped the ledge, hauled on the boy's hand and heaved herself over the top of the cliff. She lay there for a moment, the breath rasping in her throat while the boy stood up.

'What on earth do you think you were doing?' he yelled. 'You could have killed yourself!'

Jess bared his teeth and growled at the boy. Jenny

had never seen him growl at anyone before. He was defending her.

Jenny looked at the boy. He looked about her own age. He stood up, towering over her, hands on hips. He had short brown hair and his green eyes were stormy with anger. 'The sheep,' she gasped, trying to get her breath back. 'I've got to turn them back.'

'And kill yourself while you're at it?' mocked the boy. 'People are more important than sheep.'

Jenny looked just beyond him to where the flock was huddled together, bleating pitifully. She took in the open field gate in the distance just as another of the sheep made towards the edge of the cliff.

The boy whirled and flapped his arms at the sheep. 'Get back!' he yelled.

Jenny scrambled to her feet. 'Don't!' she cried. 'You'll frighten them even more and then they'll all be over the cliff. Don't you know anything?'

The boy turned on her, furious. 'So what are *you* going to do about it?' he yelled.

But Jenny wasn't listening. Quick as a flash, Jess sped towards the straying sheep as it lumbered its way towards the cliff edge. The little dog crouched in front of the sheep, head low, eyes on the animal.

Then he darted forward, chivvying the ewe back out of harm's way.

'Jess,' Jenny breathed. She lifted her head and gave a low whistle. Jess's ears flattened and he sidled alongside the sheep, forcing it ever farther back.

Another animal broke from the flock. Jess scampered towards her, cutting off the sheep's progress and herding it back towards the rest.

Every time a sheep tried to break loose Jess crouched, eyes alert, head low, cutting off its route.

'Get round the other side of the flock,' Jenny ordered the boy. 'Make sure they don't break away. And *don't* raise your voice – *or* flap your arms! Can't you see they're nervous?'

Something in Jenny's voice must have told him she knew what she was talking about. He marched off, following her instructions to the letter.

Together girl, dog and boy edged the sheep away from danger towards the field gate. Now came the tricky bit – getting them safely back into the field. But Jenny needn't have worried. Sheep herding was bred into Jess's bones. The little collie was everywhere, nipping at the sheep's heels, weaving his way in and out of them, rounding them up, peeling off from the flock when one went astray to bring it back.

'Wow!' said the boy admiringly as the last of the sheep trotted through the gate. 'That dog is amazing. We've done it!'

Jenny closed the gate safely on the flock. 'That'll do, Jess,' she called, just as she had heard her father call many times to Jake and Nell after a job well done.

Jess came flying towards her and Jenny fussed over him, patting him and rubbing his ears. Jess licked Jenny's face, wagging his tail hard. 'If it hadn't been for you, Jess, those ewes would have been lost,' she said. Jess wagged his tail ecstatically. 'You'd make the best sheepdog ever, if it wasn't for your poor weak leg,' Jenny said, a little wistfully.

'I don't suppose *I* helped at all, did I?' the boy asked sarcastically. 'I mean *I* only saved you from falling down the cliff. But I suppose saving the sheep was more important!'

Jenny turned on him, all her pent-up anger breaking free. 'If they *are* safe it's no thanks to you, leaving the gate open. Don't you know how dangerous that is?'

The boy looked at her in astonishment. 'I *didn't* leave the gate open,' he protested. 'I was taking a walk along the clifftop when I came across these sheep all over the place. I was trying to *stop* them stampeding over the cliff.'

'By flapping your arms like a madman?' she snapped. 'That's the best way of frightening them.'

'How was *I* supposed to know that?' the boy retorted. 'I don't know anything about sheep. I was just doing my best.'

Jenny bit her lip. Maybe she had been a bit harsh on the boy, but she was so angry that someone had left that gate open. She frowned. Had someone left the gate open by accident – or had someone left it open on purpose?

She marched over to the track that bordered the field and looked at the ground. There were tyre marks. They looked quite fresh. 'Did you see anybody?' she asked the boy.

'No, I didn't,' he answered. 'And I'm getting fed up with you treating me like some kind of criminal. Anyway, how could anyone be stupid enough to risk their life for a flock of sheep?' the boy asked.

'You don't know the first thing about it,' Jenny snapped. 'Those are my father's sheep. They're ewes and they're pregnant. It wasn't just the flock that was in danger. It was all the unborn lambs as well.'

'And I suppose your father wouldn't mind you falling off the cliff so long as his sheep were saved,' the boy threw back at her. He looked at her stonily. 'You're off your head,' he said and turned and stomped off.

Jenny sighed. The boy had only been trying to help.

A wet tongue licked her hand and Jenny reached out and cuddled Jess to her. '*You* understand, Jess,' she said into the puppy's soft fur. '*You* know how important the sheep are.'

She looked up. The boy was fast disappearing along the clifftop.

Jess looked up at her, head cocked to one side. 'Come on, boy,' Jenny said, standing up. 'Let's get home and tell Dad about this. I've a feeling the gate being left open wasn't an accident at all.'

11

'You did well, lass,' Fraser Miles said, as Jenny finished her story.

'Jess did well too,' Jenny replied. She had washed and changed into fresh clothes. 'If it hadn't been for him we'd have lost some of the flock – maybe all of them. Perhaps he could help with the sheep now.'

Mr Miles ran a hand through his hair and smiled, his worried expression relaxing for a moment. 'Of course he did well,' he assured her.

'But you can't have a house dog working the sheep.'

Jenny bent and rubbed Jess's ears. 'I know that, really,' she agreed. 'But you *are* glad we kept him, aren't you?'

'Of course I am,' Fraser Miles said. 'But right now I want to find out what's going on. Where exactly did you see those tyre marks?'

Jenny told him and her father rose to his feet. 'We'd better go up there now, Matt,' he said to Jenny's brother. 'I'll get the jeep.'

Matt nodded and looked out of the window. 'We'll have to hurry. It's started to rain,' he said. 'Those tyre marks won't last long if we get a downpour. And we need to have a look at the ewes as well.'

'But the ewes are safe,' said Jenny.

'Look, Jen,' Matt said. ''Jess saved the ewes and that's wonderful, but they'll be upset and that could mean premature births. You know how much we're depending on them giving us a good yield this year. A bad lambing is the last thing we need.'

'Now, now, there's no need to worry about things before they happen,' Mrs Grace put in as the jeep's horn tooted from the farmyard. 'You

130

get on up there with your dad, Matt. I'll have a cup of tea waiting for you when you get back.'

Matt grinned. 'That's your answer to everything, Ellen,' he said.

Mrs Grace laughed. 'I suppose it is,' she replied as Matt strode out into the farmyard.

Jenny watched as the jeep drove away.

'This boy you saw up on the cliff – what was he like?' Ellen Grace asked.

'Mmm?' Jenny murmured, gazing after the jeep. 'Oh, him. He was really rude and bad-tempered! Horrible!'

Just as Jenny finished speaking there was a sound at the door. 'Aunt Ellen,' said a voice. 'You'll never guess what happened.'

Jenny looked up and gasped as the boy from the cliff walked into the kitchen.

Jess growled, and the boy looked at him warily.

Jenny's mouth had dropped open. 'Oh, no! I don't believe it!' she burst out before she could stop herself.

The boy looked at her in dismay, his green eyes wide with surprise. 'You!' he exclaimed.

'This is Ian Amery, my nephew,' Mrs Grace said gently.

'But it can't be,' Jenny protested. 'He's the one I

was telling you about. He's the boy I had the argument with.'

'I thought it might be,' Mrs Grace replied. 'That's why I asked you what he was like.'

'And he's come for a *long* stay with you,' Jenny said mournfully.

'Don't worry. I'll be sure to stay well out of *your* way,' Ian retorted.

'You can start by going to get cleaned up,' Mrs Grace told him. 'You're nearly as dirty as Jenny was.'

Ian looked at his dirty hands. There were grass stains and streaks of mud on his jeans and sweatshirt. 'I was only trying to help,' he said, looking accusingly at Jenny.

'I'm sure Jenny understands that,' his aunt replied. 'And I'm sure she'll be very grateful when she thinks about it. The bathroom is that way.'

Ian trudged off and Jenny looked apologetically at Mrs Grace. 'Sorry,' she said. 'He's right. He *did* try to help.'

Ellen Grace smiled. 'I'm sure you two will be firm friends in no time,' she said confidently.

Jenny tried to feel as confident about that as Mrs Grace sounded, but, remembering the look Ian had given her when he came into the kitchen, she didn't think it was very likely.

By the time Ian had washed most of the mud off himself and his clothes Jenny had other things to think about. 'That's Dad and Matt,' she cried, hearing a car door slam.

Mrs Grace placed two mugs on the table as the two men came in. Jenny waited impatiently while the housekeeper introduced her nephew.

'I hear you saved Jenny from falling off the cliff,' Mr Miles said, looking intently at Ian. 'Thank you doesn't seem enough somehow.'

Ian blushed. 'I don't think she really would have fallen,' he protested. 'I just gave her a hand, that's all.'

Jenny danced with impatience. 'What about the *sheep*?' she asked. 'Are they all right? Did you find the tyre marks?'

Fraser Miles sat down at the table. 'The sheep seem OK but the rain had washed the tyre marks away. I'm pretty sure that it was Calum McLay but we'll never prove anything.'

'Calum McLay?' Jenny echoed. 'What makes you think that, Dad?'

'The tyre marks you described sounded like they were made by a Land Rover,' Matt said to her. 'Who else has a Land Rover round here?'

Mrs Grace sighed. 'And who else has a reason to do something like this?' she asked.

Jenny looked at them in dismay. 'Surely even *he* wouldn't do a terrible thing like that?'

'He might well be ruthless enough,' Fraser Miles replied. 'Calum McLay has wanted to take Windy Hill from me ever since I came here,' he explained. 'And now he is all the more determined. He wants to turn his own land over to forestry, but it won't be worth his while unless he buys up the rest of the land around here too – including Windy Hill.'

'Forestry!' Jenny burst out. 'But this is *sheep* country. He can't do that!'

Fraser smiled grimly. 'I suspect McLay might have more dirty tricks up his sleeve to get Windy Hill,' he concluded.

'What did you do to him all those years ago?' Matt asked his father. 'Beat him in a sheep-shearing competition? Walk off with the prize?' he joked.

Surprisingly, Fraser Miles smiled. 'A prize,' he mused. 'Something like that.'

Jenny wanted to ask more questions but Matt tipped his chair back and looked out of the window. 'We've got visitors,' he announced. A bright orange Mini drove through the gate.

'It's Carrie and her mum,' Jenny called, dashing outside.

Mrs Turner brought the Mini to a halt halfway across the farmyard and leaped out. Today she was wearing a bright pink shirt and purple leggings. 'I've got a surprise for you, Jenny,' she called.

Jess ran to meet her. The little dog's tail was wagging furiously. 'You'll wag that tail right off one day,' Mrs Turner laughed, bending down to pet him. Jess's tail wagged even harder. He loved Mrs Turner.

Carrie climbed out from the other side of the car as her mother dived into the boot and started to rummage about.

'Mum doesn't ever park the car,' she said to Jenny as they looked at the Mini skewed across the yard. 'It's more like she abandons it.'

'Come in out of the rain,' Mrs Grace called from the kitchen door.

'What's the surprise?' Jenny asked Carrie.

Carrie's face lit up. 'I can't tell you. Mum would *kill* me if I told you first,' she replied. 'But you'll love it.'

Mrs Grace was pouring water into the teapot. She set it down on the table and opened the oven door, drawing out a tray of hot, fluffy scones.

'Oh, Mrs Grace, I could *die* for your scones,' Carrie moaned.

'There's no need to go that far, Carrie,' Mrs Grace told her, laughing.

'Here comes your mum,' said Jenny as Mrs Turner lurched across the farmyard, lugging an enormous folder tied with strings at one edge. Jess danced around her feet, threatening to trip her up as they both tried to get through the door together.

'Oops!' said Jenny, making a dive for the folder as Mrs Turner staggered into the kitchen. She caught it just in time and laid it down on the table.

'Thanks,' breathed Mrs Turner. 'Oh, Ellen, a cup of tea. Lovely!'

The folder was Mrs Turner's portfolio. Jenny knew that she used it to carry sketches and paintings to save them getting crushed.

'Have a look inside, Jenny,' Mrs Turner said.

Jenny undid the strings and opened the portfolio. She gasped at what she saw. There was Jess staring out at her. Not just quick sketches but a proper painting. Jess was looking straight at her, his head on one side. His leg was still in the cast and the look in his eyes was both pleading and friendly.

'Oh, Mrs Turner, it's beautiful,' Jenny breathed. Everyone else in the kitchen agreed.

Mrs Turner looked pleased. 'It's one of the best things I've done,' she said happily. 'But then, I had a very good model, didn't I, Jess?'

Jenny picked Jess up and showed him the painting. 'That's you, Jess,' she said softly. 'Aren't you just the most beautiful puppy in the world?'

'You aren't the only person to think so,' Mrs Turner said.

Jenny looked at her in surprise. 'What do you mean?'

Mrs Grace was leaning over the picture, admiring it. 'Something tells me this isn't the only surprise,' she said to Mrs Turner.

Pam Turner's eyes twinkled.

'Go *on*, Mum,' urged Carrie. 'Don't keep Jenny in suspense.'

'Jess is going to be famous – if you agree, of course,' Mrs Turner said.

'Famous?' asked Jenny, her eyes still on the painting. 'But how?'

'I was asked to do an illustration for an animal welfare fund-raising campaign,' Mrs Turner explained. 'I thought Jess was perfect for it – and so did the organisers.'

'You mean *Jess*'s picture will be used?' Jenny said, unable to believe her ears.

'Yes, on billboards, advertisements, leaflets – the lot,' Mrs Turner replied. 'The campaign organisers are really excited about it. They think Jess is just the image they're looking for. But I wouldn't be happy about letting them use my illustration unless you agreed, Jenny.'

'You said it was for animal welfare,' Jenny said. 'That means Jess will be helping other animals. Of *course* I agree. I'd be so proud of Jess.'

Mrs Turner smiled. 'I'm so glad,' she said. 'This campaign could really help animals that have been maltreated.'

Jenny thought of Mercury and the state he had been in when he first came to Windy Hill. Although she was still uncomfortable having the horse at the farm, she didn't like to think of other animals going through what he had gone through with his last owners.

'Jess and I would be proud to help,' she said. 'You're going to be famous, Jess!' she said, leaning down to hug her pet. Jess put his two front paws on her knees. Jenny stroked his bad leg. It seemed to be getting stronger every day. Soon, she hoped, it would be almost as strong as his others.

'The campaign organisers will pay a fee to use my illustration,' Mrs Turner went on. 'It won't be much, of course, because they're a charity, but I insist on sharing it with you, Jenny.'

Matt threw his head back and laughed. 'There you are, Dad,' he said. 'Jess is earning his keep after all.'

Fraser Miles smiled. 'After what he and Jenny did today they deserve a treat,' he said. 'What are you going to spend the money on, Jenny?'

Jenny put her head on one side thoughtfully. 'A proper dog basket for Jess to sleep in,' she announced. 'Instead of his old cardboard box!'

'Good idea,' said Fraser Miles.

Jenny was suddenly filled with happiness. She was surrounded by people she loved. For the first time since her mother had died the old kitchen was alive with voices and laughter. She thought how happy her mother would be to hear that laughter ringing round the kitchen again. The farmhouse looked much more like its old self.

There was only one difference – her mother wasn't there. Her mother would never be with them again. Some day Jenny would talk to her father seriously about her feelings. But right now she was happy to let herself bask in the warmth of the friendship that flooded the kitchen.

A small, wet tongue licked Jenny's hand. She looked down. Tears blurred her eyes for just a moment as she scooped Jess up and cuddled him to her. 'Oh, you would love Jess, Mum,' she whispered into his soft fur. 'You would just *love* him.'

THE
CHALLENGE

The Challenge

Special thanks to Helen Magee

Text copyright © 1998 Working Partners Ltd
Series created by Ben M. Baglio, London W6 0QT
Illustrations copyright © 1998 Trevor Parkin

First published as a single volume in Great Britain in 1998
by Hodder Children's Books

1

'Fetch, Jess!' Jenny Miles called, throwing a stick into the sea. She shaded her eyes with her hand. The early spring sunshine glittered on the waves as they curled towards the shore. Jess, Jenny's sheepdog puppy, scampered into the sparkling water and swam strongly towards the floating stick.

'His leg's really much better now, isn't it?' commented Carrie, Jenny's best friend.

Jenny nodded happily as Jess retrieved the stick and swam towards her. Jess had been born with a badly twisted leg. At first, Jenny's father had wanted to put the little puppy down but Jenny had persuaded him to let her look after the runt of the litter – and now Jess was a happy, healthy puppy, even though his leg had had to be in a cast for a while.

'He only limps a little now,' Jenny replied. 'Nobody notices – well, almost nobody.'

Carrie looked sympathetically at her friend. 'Nobody except Fiona McLay, you mean,' she said. 'Don't take any notice of what she says. She's only jealous.'

Fiona McLay was in Jenny's class at Graston School. She was always taunting Jenny about not having the right kind of trainers or wearing fashionable clothes. Jenny didn't care about clothes, but Fiona's spitefulness still hurt.

Fiona had started calling Jess 'Jenny's lame dog'.

'*Jealous?*' echoed Jenny, turning to Carrie in surprise. The wind whipped her shoulder-length honey-brown hair into her eyes and she shoved it back from her face. 'Why on earth would Fiona McLay be jealous of *me*? Her parents are really well off. She has everything she wants.'

'Because you've got the best dog in the world and he's *famous*, after his picture was used for the animal welfare campaign,' Carrie replied.

Carrie's mum was an artist. They lived in Cliffbay, a fishing village not far from Windy Hill, the farm where Jenny lived. Mrs Turner had painted Jess for an advertising campaign to help maltreated animals. Jenny still couldn't get used to seeing Jess's picture on posters and in newspapers. He looked so small and vulnerable with his leg still in its cast. She bent down as Jess came hurtling out of the water towards her, sending up glittering sprays of seawater. He was a lot bigger now.

'Ow!' she yelled as Jess dropped the stick on her feet and then shook himself. 'I'm so wet now, I might as well have gone for the stick myself!'

Jess looked up at her and wagged his tail. Jenny laughed. 'Home now,' she said firmly. 'Mrs Grace will have tea ready.'

'You like Mrs Grace, don't you?' Carrie

asked, as they walked along the beach.

Jenny nodded. 'At first I didn't want a housekeeper at Windy Hill,' she explained. 'I thought we could manage all right the way we were but I'm really glad we've got Mrs Grace now.'

'What about Ian?' Carrie went on.

Jenny pulled a face. Ian Amery was Mrs Grace's nephew. He was staying with his aunt until his parents got themselves settled in Canada, and it looked like being quite a long visit.

'We didn't get off to a very good start,' Jenny said, remembering how she had accused Ian of letting her father's sheep out of the cliff field. 'He still hasn't forgiven me for calling him an idiot.'

Carrie giggled and tossed her bright red hair out of her eyes. She had a dusting of freckles over her nose and bright blue eyes. 'I can't imagine you getting angry,' she said. 'You're usually so calm.'

Jenny blushed. 'It was the sheep,' she said. 'I thought he had put them in danger.'

'And sheep are important,' Carrie stated.

'Of course,' replied Jenny. 'This is Border country. Sheep are *everything*.'

'Especially at lambing time,' Carrie agreed. 'How is your dad getting on?'

Jenny frowned. 'Poor Dad,' she sighed. 'He's exhausted. There's so much work to do, and Calum McLay has offered higher wages to the casual workers Dad usually employs for the lambing. Dad just can't afford to compete with that, so the workers have gone to the McLays' farm instead of Windy Hill. Dad is going to be really overworked this lambing.'

'Can't Matt help?' asked Carrie.

'Matt only comes home from college at weekends,' Jenny explained. 'Dad won't let him interrupt his studies to help on the farm.'

Matt was Jenny's eighteen-year-old brother. He was away at agricultural college.

'Your dad won't have to sell Windy Hill, will he?' asked Carrie, concerned.

Jenny sighed. 'I hope not,' she said fervently. 'If the lambing is good then things should be all right. Dad doesn't talk about it much but I know it's touch and go.' She lifted her head to look far down the beach to where the cliffs rose to the fields above – and Windy Hill. 'I think I'd *die* if I had to leave Windy Hill,' she said.

Carrie whirled round and put a hand on each of Jenny's shoulders. 'You won't have to,' she said firmly, her blue eyes unusually serious. 'You're Jenny of Windy Hill. It's where you belong.'

Jenny gave a shaky smile and her chin came up. 'Of course I won't,' she said.

'And don't let Fiona McLay get you down either,' Carrie continued. 'Remember what I said. She's just jealous!'

'Oh, Carrie,' Jenny laughed. 'You always make me feel better!'

Carrie grinned. 'Mum says there's an up side to everything,' she declared. 'It just takes a bit of finding sometimes – that's all.'

'I'll remember that,' said Jenny, whistling to Jess as they reached the path to Cliffbay. 'See you at school tomorrow.'

Jenny made her way up the winding track that led from the beach to the clifftop. At the top she stood for a moment, shading her eyes against the sun. The wind teased at her hair and ruffled Jess's black and white coat. The sea gleamed silver in the spring sunshine and Puffin Island lay like a green jewel in its silver setting. Carrie's dad ran trips to Puffin Island in his boat. The island was a bird sanctuary. Jenny had never been there but she hoped to go some time soon.

She turned and looked inland. From here she could see the ruins of Darktarn Keep standing high on its hill. The keep was Jenny's favourite place – especially when she was upset. She let her eyes move down to the farm fields stretching below the keep to the clifftop. They were dotted with sheep.

Fraser Miles, Jenny's father, bred Scottish Blackfaces, which were a hardy hill breed. The climate could often be harsh here on the border of England and Scotland – even in the spring at lambing time. Border sheep needed to be tough enough to withstand everything the weather could throw at them.

Jenny was looking forward to the lambing, despite the problems. She loved the tiny newborn lambs with their sweet little black faces. Last year at this time her mother had still been here to help with the lambing. But that was last year and now her mother was dead, killed in a riding accident shortly after last year's lambing had finished. The lambing was going to bring back memories for all of them, especially her father.

Jenny brushed a tear away as she shifted her gaze to the farm buildings in the distance, remembering how things used to be. The farmhouse stood four-square in the middle of the fields, its red-tiled roof gleaming in the sunlight. Windy Hill – her home. She raised her head and let the wind blow through her hair.

'Carrie's right,' she said to Jess. 'I'm Jenny of Windy Hill – and you're Jess of Windy Hill. Come on, let's go home.'

'Just in time. Tea's ready,' said Mrs Grace comfortably, as Jenny came into the big farmhouse kitchen with Jess at her heels. The little dog scampered up to Ellen Grace and rubbed himself against her legs.

'Don't worry, you'll get fed too,' said Mrs Grace to him, patting his head affectionately.

Jenny smiled. Mrs Grace and Jess got along really well.

'Is Dad in from the fields yet?' she asked, going to the dresser that ran along one wall of the kitchen and taking down a stack of blue-patterned plates.

'He's just gone up to check on the fences in the top field,' Mrs Grace replied. 'He should be back soon.'

Jenny frowned. 'Those fences belong to Calum McLay,' she said, setting out the plates.

Mrs Grace nodded. 'Your father is worried about them. They're in need of some repair and you know what ewes are like when it comes to lambing time. They've got a tendency to bolt.'

Jenny knew that ewes in labour sometimes took fright and ran off. 'If they got out of the field they'd be on McLay land,' she said.

'And then there would be trouble,' agreed Mrs Grace.

Jenny frowned. Calum McLay was Fiona's father. He wanted to acquire more land to plant trees – trees in sheep country! Jenny thought it was outrageous. But that wasn't the worst of the problem. Calum McLay was determined to take over Windy Hill – by hook or by crook.

'Now, now, don't you go worrying over the lambing,' Mrs Grace advised Jenny. 'Lambing might be a hard time on a farm like this but there's the common riding at the end of it to look forward to.' The common riding was when all the towns and villages in the Borders turned out to ride round the boundaries or marches of their towns.

Jenny smiled suddenly and her whole face lit up. Mrs Grace looked at her heart-shaped face framed by her honey-coloured hair. 'You know, you look just like your mother, when you smile like that,' she said.

'I was thinking about her up on the cliffs,' Jenny replied. 'I was trying to remember all the good times we had – like the stories she used to tell me about the Border reivers. I'm glad I look like her.'

'You're a lot quieter than your mum was, though,' Mrs Grace went on. 'I remember her as a girl. She was always a bit of a daredevil but she enjoyed life. She could always make me laugh.'

Jenny's cheeks flushed pink with pleasure at the memory of how her mother had been able to make *all* of them laugh. It was good to talk to Mrs Grace about her mother. Jenny's father never talked about her. He still found the whole subject too painful.

'I like talking to you about Mum, Mrs Grace,' Jenny confided. 'The more I talk about her, the more I remember.' She hesitated a moment, looking down at Jess. The puppy licked her hand, sensing her sudden sadness. 'Sometimes I'm afraid I'll forget her,' Jenny finished.

Ellen Grace put her arm round Jenny's shoulders. 'You'll never do that,' she comforted her. 'All you have to do is look in a mirror. I think it's your hair. It's the exact shade your mum's was.'

'I'd really like to get it cut,' Jenny said. 'It's a pest. It blows into my eyes all the time.'

'Where's that hair-tie I got for you?' Mrs Grace asked.

Jenny dug in her jeans pocket and pulled out a blue and yellow hair-tie. She twisted her hair into a knot and fastened it with the tie.

'One day I'm going to fix your hair properly,' said Mrs Grace.

Jenny pulled a face and Ellen Grace laughed. 'We'll get it properly done for the common riding,' she said. 'Everybody gets dressed up for that.'

The Graston common riding was in May and Jenny was really looking forward to it. It was the biggest day of the year. The lambing would be over, all the really hard work done, and there would be time to celebrate – if the lambing went well.

'Are you on the common riding committee?' she asked Mrs Grace.

Ellen Grace bent down to open the oven door of the Aga and took out a big shepherd's pie. The potato topping was browned to a turn and it smelled delicious. 'I certainly am,' she said, laying the pie dish on top of the Aga to keep warm. 'And I hope I'll get some help from you. I've got a mound of baking to do as well as making bunting and helping to decorate the floats for the procession.'

Jenny looked into Ellen Grace's warm blue eyes. 'I'd love to help,' she said, smiling.

The kitchen door opened just then, and Fraser Miles entered. 'Something smells good,' he said.

Ellen Grace put her hands on her hips and tried to look severe. 'And about time too,' she said. 'That pie is nearly ruined.'

Fraser Miles just laughed. 'That'll be the day, when anything you cook is ruined, Ellen,' he said, as he passed Jenny and ruffled her hair. 'How's my lass?'

Jenny looked up at him and saw the weariness and worry behind his smile. 'Fine,' she said. 'What about the fences?'

Her father ran a hand through his hair and shook his head. 'They need attention, that's for sure,' he said. 'I've contacted McLay about it, but the fences were just as bad when I went up there just now.'

'Can't *you* fix them?' asked Jenny, concerned. 'If our sheep get out we could lose them.'

'I don't think Calum would take too kindly to my interfering with his fences,' Mr Miles answered her. 'But it might come to that.'

Jenny studied her father more closely. He looked exhausted. Jess lolloped up and wagged his tail. Fraser Miles gave the puppy a brief pat. Jess scampered off to the corner of the kitchen and picked up a slipper in his mouth. He trotted back and laid the slipper in front of Mr Miles.

Fraser laughed. 'If you go on like this I might be glad we kept you after all,' he said.

Jess barked and Jenny felt a warm glow. Her father had been dead against keeping Jess. His own dogs, Jake and Nell, were working sheepdogs and never came into the house. Fraser Miles always said animals had to earn their keep on a farm. But Jenny had great hopes that he would love Jess as much as she did – in time.

There was a sound from the farmyard and Mrs Grace looked out of the window. 'Uh-oh!' she said. 'It's Calum McLay.'

Fraser turned at once. 'What on earth does *he* want?' he said in exasperation. 'As if he isn't causing me enough problems with his fencing!'

Jenny watched her father stride out of the kitchen into the farmyard and went to stand by the open window with Mrs Grace.

A big, burly man was getting out of a Land Rover. He slammed the door and stomped

across the yard to meet Fraser. Hands on hips, Mr McLay stopped and stood with his feet planted firmly on the cobbles of the yard.

'He acts as if he owns the place,' Jenny muttered.

'What can I do for you, Calum?' Fraser Miles said politely.

Calum McLay thrust his chin forward, his heavy face red with anger. 'You can stay off my land, that's what you can do,' he said.

Fraser Miles looked down for a moment. Jenny could see him holding on to his temper. Then he looked up and said, his voice calm, 'I haven't been on your land, Calum.'

'You've been messing around with my fences!' the other man yelled, taking a step forward.

'Your fences need fixing,' Fraser replied quietly.

Jenny saw that Calum McLay's face was getting redder by the minute. Even his short black hair seemed to bristle with anger. It was as if Mr Miles's calmness made him all the madder.

The big man stuck out a finger, stabbing the

air in front of Fraser Miles's face. 'If you mess around with my fences, I'll have you up for trespass!'

'Your fences are putting my sheep at risk,' Fraser said reasonably.

Calum McLay drew himself up. '*Your* sheep are *your* business,' he sneered. 'And a poor sort of business you're making of them as far as I can make out. You can't afford the wages I'm paying so you can't get help. You can't handle the lambing on your own and you know it. You're finished, Miles. Why don't you give in and sell out now – to me?'

Fraser Miles looked down again. He was being very patient with Calum McLay. Jenny held her breath as the silence went on.

Even Calum McLay grew uncomfortable, shifting from foot to foot. 'Well?' he said at last, his voice cracking slightly.

'You won't get Windy Hill, Calum,' Mr Miles replied very quietly – so quietly that Jenny could hardly hear him through the open window. 'Not while I'm alive.'

Calum McLay swallowed hard and looked away. 'Just keep off my land,' he blustered, making for his Land Rover. 'You touch my fences and I'll prosecute – I mean it. Then where will your precious Windy Hill be?' Then he got into the Land Rover and drove off, racing the engine.

Fraser Miles stood quite still in the middle of the farmyard, his head down. Jenny felt a touch on her arm.

'Come on, love,' Mrs Grace said. 'Let's just pop this pie back in the oven for a moment. Your father will be wanting a bit of time to himself.'

Jenny watched as her father moved slowly towards the farm gate and stood looking out over the land belonging to his beloved Windy Hill.

'OK,' she said, her throat tight. 'It won't matter if it's a bit burnt, will it?'

'It won't matter at all,' said Mrs Grace. 'And don't you worry about Windy Hill. Your father will keep it safe.'

Jenny nodded, trying to hold back tears. Her father wasn't a magician. He couldn't do the impossible. She was old enough to know how hard things were for him. If he went bankrupt

the farm would be sold to the highest bidder –
and that was sure to be Calum McLay. Why
was Calum McLay so intent on ruining her
father? Why did he want Windy Hill so much?
She stole a brief look out of the window at
Fraser Miles's uncompromising back. One
thing was sure. She couldn't ask her father.

2

Jenny was riding her bike down the farm track on her way to school the next day when she noticed her father in the bottom field. He was standing quite still, looking at a ewe. Jake and Nell lay beside him, also perfectly still. Jenny braked and drew into the side of the track. At that moment her father turned and saw her. He beckoned to her and Jenny dismounted, scrambling over the drystone wall that separated the field from the track. Her father held his finger to his lips and, as he did so, Jenny looked beyond him.

The ewe was pawing the ground and bleating softly. The breath caught in Jenny's throat. She had seen enough pregnant ewes to know the signs. This one was about to give birth.

'The first Windy Hill lamb of the season,' her father whispered softly to Jenny as she reached him. 'It shouldn't be long now.'

Almost as he spoke, the ewe lay down with her legs stretched out to one side and began to strain. Jenny and her father were about twenty metres away but Jenny knew Fraser wouldn't go any closer, not unless the ewe looked as if she were in trouble. Ewes frequently gave up the attempt to lamb if they had an audience.

'Is she coping all right?' asked Jenny.

Fraser nodded. 'I don't often get to see the very first lamb,' he said. 'Usually I come out one morning and find that a dozen or more have been born during the night. I just couldn't resist watching this one.'

Jenny looked at her father, standing quietly beside her. There was real excitement on his face.

Even after all these years of lambing, the thought of the first lamb still meant so much to him.

'Look, Jenny!' he said softly. 'Here it comes.'

Jenny shifted her gaze to the ewe. As she watched, the animal began to strain harder, raising her head and curling her top lip. The waterbag, a transparent membrane enclosing the lamb, began to appear. It slid gently from the ewe's body and on to the ground behind the mother. As it did so, the waterbag burst, and Jenny gasped as the lamb's nose and front feet appeared. She heard her father sigh.

'That's OK,' he said. 'If the waterbag hadn't burst we'd have needed to do something about it, otherwise the lamb could suffocate.'

Jenny was barely listening. She was gazing in wonder as the tiny lamb began to kick and cough. The ewe turned and started to lick her baby.

'Oh, Dad, isn't it wonderful?' she breathed.

Her father looked at her, smiling. 'It's the best sight in the world,' he said. 'A good birth and a healthy lamb. That licking will dry the little fellow and establish a bond between lamb and ewe,' her father told her.

Jenny knew that sometimes a ewe failed to bond with her lamb and then a substitute mother had to be found. But these two looked as if they were going to be all right. The ewe was nuzzling her baby, licking furiously to stimulate its circulation. Early lambs often died of hypothermia.

Jenny shivered in the chill breeze off the sea. 'Will the lamb be warm enough?' she asked her father.

Fraser Miles looked out to sea. The wind was whipping spray off the tops of the waves. 'I'd rather get them both to a more sheltered spot,' he confessed. 'It's a bit exposed just here. Have you got time to give me a hand, lass?'

Jenny looked at her watch. 'Just about,' she replied, delighted. 'What do you want me to do?'

Her father pointed towards the drystone wall. 'If we can get them under the lee of the wall, that'll keep the wind off them,' he said. 'But we have to make sure the ewe doesn't lose contact with the lamb. If she loses sight of it she'll return to the spot she chose for the birth and abandon the lamb.'

169

'So how do we manage that?' asked Jenny.

'If you can take the lamb by the front legs and draw it along the ground in the direction we want the ewe to go then the ewe will follow,' Fraser Miles told her.

'But won't that hurt the lamb?' Jenny asked.

Mr Miles shook his head. 'Not if you're careful. The lamb must stay on the ground so that the ewe can continue to lick it as we move.'

Jenny and her father moved quietly towards the ewe. 'Just take the legs,' Fraser instructed as Jenny hesitated. 'I'll clear the afterbirth away.'

Jenny did as she was told, grasping the little animal's front legs firmly but gently between her hands. Then she began to draw the lamb along the grass towards the spot her father had chosen. The ewe followed, head down, licking her lamb.

'That's it, Jenny. You're doing fine,' her father encouraged her.

Jenny laid the tiny lamb down in the shelter of the wall and watched as the ewe settled down to take care of her baby.

'Just one more job to do,' Fraser Miles said.

Jenny watched as her father drew his thumb

and forefinger gently down the ewe's teats.

'That breaks the seal at the end,' he said. 'Now the lamb can suck much more easily and get that all-important colostrum — the first milk the ewe produces. The colostrum has antibodies in it that protect the lamb in the early stages of its life,' Jenny's father explained. 'If a lamb can't get it naturally it has to be fed colostrum by bottle.'

Jenny nodded as she watched the lamb wobble precariously to its feet and start searching for its mother's teat. The ewe nudged her baby into place and the lamb began to suck, its tiny stub of a tail wagging furiously.

'I like feeding the orphaned lambs,' Jenny said, watching mother and baby.

'Let's hope we don't have too many of those this year,' Fraser Miles replied. 'I don't know how I'll manage if we do. There's more than enough work out here in the fields as it is.'

'I'll help,' said Jenny, looking up at her father.

Fraser Miles smiled down at her. 'It might come to that,' he said. 'But lambing is hard work, you know that.'

'I don't mind the hard work,' Jenny said.

'It's for Windy Hill, isn't it?'

Fraser Miles looked out over his land. 'It is, lass,' he agreed. 'It's all for Windy Hill – and worth it!'

Jenny was full of her news about Windy Hill's first lamb when she arrived at school. She met Carrie just as both girls turned into the playground on their bikes.

'That's marvellous,' Carrie enthused. 'I wish I'd seen it.'

'It *was* marvellous,' Jenny agreed, as they propped their bikes up in the bike shed, then walked across the yard as the bell rang for them to line up with their class, ready to go into school.

Ian Amery, Mrs Grace's nephew, was standing just in front of them, with his back to Jenny. He turned as they approached. Jenny was describing the tiny Blackface lamb to Carrie.

'Don't you ever think about anything else?' he asked Jenny.

'Sheep are important,' Jenny retorted.

'So you told me – yelled at me, I should say,' Ian said.

Ian was the same age as Jenny, and in the same class. He barely spoke to her which made Jenny feel alternately guilty and exasperated. Right now she felt exasperated. She had *tried* to apologise about the sheep incident. If he didn't want to be friends that was all right by her. He was a real bossyboots anyway.

'Mum wants to sketch Jess again,' Carrie put in hurriedly. 'The animal campaign people have asked for another illustration of him.'

'Wow!' breathed Jenny. 'They must really like Jess.'

'I don't see how anybody could like a lame dog,' said a voice behind Jenny.

Jenny turned round. Fiona McLay towered over her, looking down her nose. She was a lot taller than Jenny, though they were the same age. Jenny looked up at her, too angry to speak.

'He isn't lame,' Carrie retorted. 'He hardly limps at all.'

'He still *limps*,' declared Fiona, spitefully.

Fiona's little brother, Paul, stood beside her. '*I* like Jess,' he said stoutly. 'I think he's really brave.'

Jenny smiled at the little boy. Paul was seven.

He looked a little like his sister, but he was never bad-tempered like Fiona.

'Maybe you could come and visit Jess sometime,' Jenny offered. She spoke clearly, looking straight at Paul.

Paul had become deaf after a bad viral infection. But he was now a marvellous lip-reader, and Jenny always made sure she spoke directly to him.

'No, he can't,' Fiona snapped. 'Dad would never let Paul set foot on Miles land.'

Jenny's heart sank when she saw the disappointment on Paul's face as he lip-read his sister's words.

Ian flicked a cold look at Fiona. 'You like bird-watching don't you, Paul?' he asked, turning to Paul. 'I saw the report on the ringed plovers you did for the school noticeboard. It was really interesting.'

Paul flushed with pleasure and nodded eagerly. 'I got a gold star for it,' he said proudly.

'Hmmph!' said Fiona. 'I don't know why Paul is so keen on bird-watching. He can't even hear them.'

Jenny drew in her breath sharply. How could

Fiona say such a horrible thing? Luckily, Paul was still looking at Ian and didn't read the cruel words coming from Fiona's lips.

Ian turned round and looked full at Fiona, his green eyes full of anger, then he shifted his gaze back to Paul. 'I'll go bird-watching with you, Paul,' he said. 'I like it too, and I can describe all the bird calls to you.'

'Wow!' exclaimed the younger boy. 'Would you?'

Jenny looked at Ian in surprise. He was usually so brusque and unfriendly – at least to her. 'That's really nice of you, Ian,' she said.

Ian shrugged. 'It's no problem,' he said shortly. 'I'd enjoy it. And at least it's not sheep.'

Jenny rolled her eyes at Carrie. You just couldn't please some people no matter how hard you tried.

The bell rang and Fiona charged past Jenny and Carrie, pushing Paul towards his own line of classmates.

Carrie's face flushed. 'Of all the horrors!' she exclaimed. 'What has she got against Paul?'

Jenny thought for a moment. 'It's almost as if she's ashamed of having a deaf brother,' she said.

'Ugh! That's terrible!' Carrie declared.

'Is that you on your high horse again, Carrie?' Mrs Barker, their teacher, said as Jenny and Carrie walked past her into the classroom. 'You're always getting worked up about something.'

'Mum says I'm an activist,' Carrie told her, smiling.

Mrs Barker raised her eyebrows. 'Don't think I haven't noticed,' she said as the class settled down. 'Come to think of it, we're going to need some activists for the Graston common riding – or at least some active people.'

'When is the common riding committee going to choose the Graston Lass, Miss?' Fiona demanded from the back of the class.

Several of the boys groaned. Every year a girl from the senior class at Graston School was chosen as a sort of queen for the day. She had to ride at the head of the procession as it marked out the boundaries of the village. There was always a lot of excitement about who was going to be the Graston Lass – at least among the girls in the class. Fiona had been boasting for weeks that she was going to be chosen. After all, her father owned a good portion of the land around Graston.

'All you girls will get the opportunity to enter the competition when the time comes,' Mrs Barker said firmly, as Fiona flicked her hair into place, shaking her head back. The teacher continued: 'What I want you to think about in the meantime is the Graston Hero Prize. That's much more important.' She pointed to a box on the window ledge, saying, 'As most of you will know, the Graston Hero Prize is a prize that the common riding committee awards each year for things like bravery or community spirit. If you know of any examples of outstanding effort that should be rewarded you can submit your nomination to the committee. The box on the window ledge is there for your ideas.'

'I'd like to nominate little Paul for putting up with Fiona and for being so cheerful even though he's deaf,' Carrie whispered in Jenny's ear.

Jenny thought for a moment. 'I don't know if that would be a good idea,' she said at last.

'Why not?' asked Carrie indignantly.

'Because it might make Paul feel even more different,' said Jenny. 'I know it can't be easy for him being deaf but it doesn't seem right to give him a prize for it.'

Carrie's mouth dropped open and she shook her head. 'I never thought of that,' she said in wonder. 'You know, Jenny, you're really good at putting yourself in other people's shoes. I just go charging in like a bull in a china shop.'

Jenny grinned. 'You're an activist, remember?'

'And you're a – thoughtfulist,' Carrie added, giggling.

3

Jenny and Carrie stayed on for a while after school, discussing with Mrs Barker what they would do for the celebrations, so Jenny was a bit later than usual getting home. The first thing she saw as she cycled up the track was Matt's old motorbike parked in the farmyard. Jenny's face split into a smile. Matt was home! She hadn't been expecting him and that made it all the better.

Then Jenny saw Mercury. The big black horse was tethered to a ring on the stable wall. He whinnied as Jenny came through the gate and stamped his feet restlessly. Matt must have taken him out earlier. It was the first thing he did whenever he came home.

Jenny's smile disappeared and she gave the horse a wide berth. Mercury had been her mother's horse, the horse that had thrown and killed her. Fraser Miles had sold the animal immediately afterwards. But Matt had found Mercury at the Greybridge livestock market months later. The horse had been maltreated and Matt had bought him for next to nothing and brought him back to Windy Hill, much to Jenny's dismay. She couldn't understand how her father and Matt could stand having Mercury around after what the horse had done to her mother.

But Jenny's mood was instantly lifted when Jess came flying out of the farmhouse and launched himself at her in delight. Jenny scooped him up in her arms and gave him a cuddle. 'And what have you been up to today?' she asked him, burying her face in his fur.

The little dog licked her cheek, leaped out of her arms and ran round her feet, barking and wagging his tail furiously. Jenny laughed. 'Come on, let's go and see what Matt is doing home.'

Jenny dumped her bike against the wall and, together, they raced into the kitchen.

'Matt!' Jenny exclaimed, throwing herself at her brother. 'How come you're home?'

The tall, dark-haired young man caught her and swung her round. 'Hi, Jen,' he said, setting her back down on her feet. 'How are things?'

Jenny smiled up at him. 'Great now that you're here,' she enthused. 'I didn't know you were coming. How long are you staying?'

Matt ran a hand through his hair. It was a habit Fraser Miles had too and it made Matt look very like his father. 'I'm here for the lambing,' he said, grinning at his sister.

'*What!*' said Jenny. 'How? Why? That's great! *All* of the lambing?'

'Hey, slow down,' Matt said, laughing. 'Yes, I'm here until the lambing is done.'

'But how did you get away?' Jenny asked.

Matt grinned at her amazed face. 'It was easy,

really,' he said. 'I'm doing agriculture after all, and everybody on the course has to do a placement on a farm at some point in the year. As I've always intended to go into sheep farming, I put it to them at college that for my practical experience this year, I would come to Windy Hill to help with lambing. Of course, I'll have to study the books about lambing as well.'

'But that's brilliant, Matt,' Jenny enthused. 'And guess what! We had our first lamb today!'

'Really?' said Matt. 'In that case it looks as if I've arrived home just in time. Even *Dad* can't handle the lambing entirely on his own.'

Mrs Grace was standing by the Aga, stirring a pot on the stove. 'Your father *is* tired,' she agreed. 'And this is just the beginning of it. It's going to get much worse over the next few weeks. He doesn't have any of the extra workers this year, thanks to Calum McLay's dirty tricks.'

Matt gave her a reassuring smile. 'Don't worry, we'll pull through,' he said.

Jenny looked up at her brother's confident face. She only hoped he was right. She had been so worried about her father. But now

Matt was here, everything seemed better. She smiled in spite of her worries.

'Mercury isn't getting much exercise,' Mrs Grace informed Matt. 'Your dad doesn't have time for him.'

'I don't know where *I'll* find the time either,' Matt sighed. 'It's the lambing that's important at the moment.'

'Why don't you sell him?' Jenny asked.

Matt looked surprised. 'I couldn't do that,' he said. 'Anyway, he's still recovering. His physical injuries are better but it'll take him a while to get over his nervousness.'

Jenny clamped her mouth shut. Matt thought the world of Mercury and nothing she could say would change his mind about that.

'Ian rides,' Mrs Grace put in. 'He's a good horseman. He could exercise Mercury. I'm sure he'd love that.'

Matt looked thoughtful. 'I don't know about that, Ellen,' he said. 'Mercury can still be a little unpredictable.'

Jenny snorted. 'You mean dangerous, Matt,' she said.

Matt looked at her sympathetically.

'Look, Jen, I know you're a bit nervous of Mercury but that makes him even *more* nervous when you're around. You don't see him at his best.'

Jenny shook her head. 'How can you trust him?' she asked.

'That's the point,' said Matt. 'You've got to give trust to get it. You don't trust Mercury so you don't have his trust.'

Jenny shook her head. 'I'll never trust that horse – *never*!' she said.

Matt spread his hands out. 'So he'll never trust you,' he said.

'Why don't you try Ian out on Mercury?' Mrs Grace suggested. 'He's coming for tea. He should be here soon.'

'Good idea,' agreed Matt, making for the door. 'I'll just go and work off some of his energy before Ian arrives. I wouldn't want him to be too fresh for a new rider.'

Mrs Grace looked sympathetically at Jenny when Matt had gone. 'Your mother loved horses, you know,' she said. 'When we were girls she was always horse-mad. She used to jump the highest fences and walls.'

'I like horses too,' said Jenny. 'It's just Mercury I don't like – and I never will.'

Mrs Grace's face grew even more sympathetic. 'That's understandable,' she said. 'After what happened to your mother.'

'So why does Dad keep him?' Jenny asked.

Mrs Grace shrugged. 'Grief is a strange thing,' she said. 'Maybe Mercury reminds him of when your mother was alive.'

Jenny swallowed back the tears. 'He reminds me of how Mum died,' she said.

Mrs Grace was silent for a moment. 'Maybe you should tell your father that,' she said.

Jenny looked up at her, tears spilling over. 'I can't,' she said. 'He doesn't talk about her. You're the only one that ever talks about her to me.'

Mrs Grace didn't say anything else. She just held out her arms to Jenny and let her cry.

Ian arrived shortly afterwards but Jenny was in no mood to be friendly. Not that Ian made much of an effort.

'Why are your eyes so red?' he asked her.

Jenny glared at him. 'I've got an allergy,' she snapped, then blew her nose.

'So have I,' Ian replied. 'To rude people like you!'

'I wish you two could be friends,' Mrs Grace said, as Ian and Matt went out into the yard.

Jenny shrugged. 'Don't worry about it, Mrs Grace,' she replied. 'I don't care.'

'He'll come round,' Ellen Grace went on. 'He's always been stubborn.'

'Bossy!' corrected Jenny, as she and Mrs Grace followed them.

Matt handed Ian a riding-hat. 'That should fit,' he said. 'Now just take it easy to begin with. Walk him round the yard.'

Ian put one foot into the stirrup and hoisted himself into the saddle. He settled himself and ran a hand over Mercury's neck. The big horse whickered and Ian leaned forward, whispering in the horse's ear. Mercury's ears pricked but he still moved restlessly under Ian's weight.

Ian clicked his tongue. 'Walk on,' he said steadily to the horse. Mercury began to move forward, then stepped sideways, tossing his head. Ian gathered in the reins and brought the horse's head round. 'It's OK, boy,' he said. 'Walk on now.'

Jenny watched as Mercury moved forward again. Mrs Grace was right. Ian *was* good with horses.

'You're doing really well,' Matt congratulated the boy. 'Just keep him steady.'

But Mercury had other ideas. He didn't seem to like having a strange rider on his back. His big hoofs danced on the cobbles of the yard. Ian at once shortened the reins then let them out again almost immediately, deliberately confusing the horse to give himself time to get Mercury under control.

Jenny watched with interest. Ian was in no danger. Mercury was just testing him. Jenny had seen horses do this before. It was a battle of wills but she wasn't at all sure that Ian would win.

Jess suddenly ran forward and began to trot at Mercury's heels. Jenny was horrified – Jess might get trampled! She *had* to save him, but she just couldn't bring herself to go near the big horse. 'Jess!' she cried.

But Matt was already striding towards the puppy. However, he suddenly stopped and stood quite still, watching the two animals. 'Look at that,' he said.

Jenny *was* looking. Mercury had stopped dancing. He bent his head and Jess raised his. The two animals nuzzled each other, then Jess trotted calmly to the big horse's side and began to walk beside him. Mercury began to walk forward steadily with no sidestepping, and no skittishness.

'Jess is often in the stable with Mercury while you're at school, Jenny,' Mrs Grace said, coming to stand beside her. 'They're good friends.'

'But Mercury is *dangerous*,' said Jenny, appalled.

'Just a little nervous,' Matt corrected her. 'But just look at Jess. He's calmed Mercury right down.' Matt turned to face his sister. 'Jen, would you let Jess help with Mercury's training? Look how well they get on. Jess is herding Mercury.'

Jenny looked at Jess in amazement. Matt was right. Jess's sheepdog instincts were plain to see. He worked round Mercury's feet, keeping the horse steady. Jenny couldn't help but admire what Jess was doing but she was horrified at Matt's suggestion.

She couldn't possibly agree. This was the horse that had killed her mother. Then she saw

Matt's face. He didn't have time to train Mercury properly. He had to help their father and he was right. Jess *did* seem to calm Mercury down. If it could take some of the worry off Matt's shoulders how could she refuse?

'I'd certainly be happier with Jess along until Mercury gets used to me,' Ian said. 'The difference in Mercury with Jess at his heels is amazing.'

'I'd be happier too,' Mrs Grace told her nephew. 'I think you'd be a lot safer exercising Mercury with Jess on the job.'

Jenny looked at the others. They were all looking at her expectantly. She looked again at Jess. It was true. Mercury was as gentle as a lamb with Jess at her heels. The lambing, Jenny thought. That was what was important. Her father needed *all* the time Matt could spare. She swallowed.

'All right,' she said reluctantly. 'I don't have any choice, do I? But that doesn't mean I have to like it.'

4

Over the next few weeks, Ian was often at Windy Hill, exercising Mercury. Jenny still didn't like the idea but she found herself becoming interested in Mercury's progress. With Jess's influence. Mercury soon learned to tolerate Ian. Jenny was glad, however, when Ian was able to take Mercury out for rides on his own.

'You don't need Jess any longer, do you?' she

asked Ian on the first day of the Easter holidays. She was crossing the farmyard with a crate of babies' feeding-bottles filled with milk for the orphaned lambs.

Ian was in the yard, saddling Mercury, and Jess was sitting, watching the proceedings. Ian shook his head. 'Not really, but Jess enjoys being with us.'

'If you don't need him then you and Mercury can go out on your own,' Jenny said. 'I only agreed to let Jess help for a little while.'

Ian shrugged. 'Please yourself,' he said. 'Jess is your dog.'

'Yes he is,' agreed Jenny, as Ian mounted Mercury.

Jess rose at once to follow them but Jenny called him back. Jess looked round at her, puzzled.

'Here, Jess,' Jenny said firmly.

Jess trotted over to her and they both watched as Ian rode Mercury out of the yard. Jess whined a little and Mercury tried to turn his head but Ian kept the horse's head straight and didn't even turn round to wave goodbye.

'Come on, Jess,' Jenny said to the puppy.

'There's work to do. Let's go and see how the lambs are doing.'

Jenny and Jess made their way to the shearing shed where Fraser Miles had rigged up a lamb warmer for the newborn lambs whose mothers had died or rejected them. Sometimes a ewe had twins or triplets and couldn't care for all her lambs. Sometimes a ewe simply rejected her lamb and, if Mr Miles couldn't get another ewe to foster the lamb, then it had to be hand-reared for a few weeks.

The lamb warmer was a closed box with holes in the bottom and fan heaters underneath to blow warm air in. It was divided into two parts so that the lambs could be separated as Jenny fed each one. Every year there were a lot of lambs that had to be cared for in this way and Jenny loved looking after them.

She lifted the top of the box gently and, at once, the lambs scrambled towards her, lifting their little black faces and bleating piteously. There were almost thirty lambs in there. Jenny tickled the nearest lamb's nose and reached for a bottle. The lamb immediately opened his mouth and Jenny put the teat of the bottle between his lips, reaching at the same time for another bottle.

'I wish I had more than one pair of hands,' she said as the lucky lambs sucked greedily at their milk while the rest crowded round, eager for their turn.

'We all wish that at lambing time,' said a voice from the door.

Jenny turned her head. 'Hi, Dad,' she said. 'How are things going?'

Fraser Miles came over to stand beside her, looking down at the lamb warmer. 'I've had to bring six more lambs down,' he said. 'But none of these are ready to go out in the fields yet and there isn't room for any more in there.' He picked up a couple of bottles and began to help Jenny feed the lambs.

'What will you do with them?' Jenny asked.

'I guess I'll have to bring them into the kitchen,' Fraser said. 'I hope Ellen won't mind.'

'I'm sure she won't,' said Jenny, setting down the now empty bottles and picking up two more. 'And I can look after them just as well in the kitchen as here.'

Fraser smiled. 'You're doing a grand job with these, lass,' he said.

'I love doing it,' Jenny said, smiling. 'But I wish you'd let me help out in the fields as well. I've got time now that the Easter holidays have started. I could help you and still look after the lambs.'

The number of lambs had increased dramatically in the last week and Fraser was finding it difficult to cope. Jenny knew that the births would reach a peak soon and begin to tail off but, until then, the work would increase.

'It's hard work,' Fraser replied. 'It's hard enough for Matt and me, never mind a young girl. But I'll keep your offer in mind. I might just take you up on it if things get out of hand.'

Jenny looked at her father as he replaced his own empty bottles. 'That's good enough for me,' she told him. She allowed herself a small smile. She wouldn't push it. She knew her father too well to do that but she would remind him of what he had said, if things got really tough.

Jenny helped her father deposit the extra lambs in the kitchen before he headed back to the fields.

'Boxes,' said Mrs Grace. 'I'm sure I've got some that would do.'

'You don't mind them being in here, do you, Mrs Grace?' Jenny asked anxiously.

Ellen Grace smiled. 'Mind?' she said. 'I was brought up on a farm. When I was a girl we used to put the really small orphaned lambs in the Aga to warm them.'

'In the oven?' squeaked Jenny. 'You mean like cooking them?'

'Of course not.' Mrs Grace laughed. 'The oven was warm, not hot, and we left the door open. It was the quickest way to get very weak and tiny lambs warm,' Mrs Grace explained. 'Undersized lambs can get cold very quickly, and die. We didn't have lamb warmers in those days. Of course, most of the lambs were perfectly fine just laid around the oven in boxes. We can put these lambs around the Aga. That will be perfect for them.'

Jenny looked at Jess. 'How are you going to feel about that, Jess?' she asked. 'Your favourite spot is right in front of the Aga.'

But Jess took to the lambs very well. He even started herding them gently as Jenny put them down on the kitchen floor before transferring them to the prepared boxes.

'That should do it,' said Jenny as she popped the last lamb into its cosy cardboard box. She had lined the boxes with newspaper, just as she had done for Jess when he was an abandoned puppy.

Jess padded over to the nearest box and nuzzled it. At once a soft bleating came from inside and a small black nose peeked over the rim of the box. Jess sniffed and his tail began to wag. Then he went from box to box, sniffing each lamb in turn.

'He's saying hello,' said Jenny delightedly. 'He doesn't mind in the least losing his place in front of the Aga.'

'Just as well,' said Mrs Grace. 'Something tells me he won't get it back for a while!'

Mrs Grace was right. A week later, Jenny looked round the kitchen. There seemed to be orphaned lambs everywhere. Jess was curled up between two boxes, keeping a wary eye on the lambs. If any of them tried to climb out, Jess herded it back into its box.

'Poor little things,' Jenny said, as one lamb poked its head over the rim of a basket and bleated. 'But we haven't lost any of them.'

Mrs Grace smiled. 'That's because you've been looking after them so well, lass,' she said.

'I'm going to move another batch out of the lamb warmer later today,' Fraser Miles said from his seat at the kitchen table. He was snatching a quick bite to eat while Matt was working the top field. He and Matt tried to make sure that one of them was always with the ewes during daylight. 'We should be able to get some of these out of the kitchen.'

Jenny had taken the job of looking after the orphaned lambs very seriously and she knew her father was pleased with her work. It gave her such a thrill to see the little animals growing stronger by the day.

Just then Matt thrust his head round the kitchen door. His hair was standing on end and his face was flushed. 'Can you come, Dad?' he said to his father urgently.

'What's the matter?' his father asked sharply, standing up at once.

'It looks like a case of hypocalcaemia to me,'

Matt replied. 'But I'd rather you had a look.'

'What's that?' Jenny asked, worried.

'It's a deficiency in calcium,' Matt replied. 'It sometimes happens with pregnant ewes.'

Fraser Miles was already at the door, picking up his lambing bag from the dresser.

'Things have got really busy up in the top field,' Matt went on. 'I wish we had a bit more help.'

Jenny jumped down from the table. '*I* can help,' she said. Fraser hesitated a moment. 'You promised, Dad,' Jenny reminded him. 'You said you'd let me help if things got out of hand.'

'*Are* things getting out of hand up there, Matt?' Fraser Miles asked.

Matt grinned. 'I reckon we've reached peak lambing,' he said.

Fraser nodded. 'I'd call that out of hand,' he said. 'Come on, lass. Get your wellingtons and let's go.'

Though excited, Jenny cast a worried glance at the lambs.

'Don't worry about them,' Mrs Grace said. 'I'll make up their bottles and feed them if you aren't back in time.'

'Thanks, Mrs Grace,' Jenny said. She grabbed her wellingtons from the back porch and turned to Jess. 'Come on, boy.'

'No, Jenny,' said her father firmly. 'Jess can't come. He's a house dog.'

'But he's so good with the lambs,' Jenny protested. 'Look at him.'

Jess was gently nudging a tiny black lamb back into its basket. The little animal bleated but didn't try to climb out again.

'No arguments, Jenny,' her father said.

Jenny bit her lip as she followed Matt and her father out into the yard. The jeep's engine was running. Jess scampered out of the house. The puppy raised his head and howled as Jenny got in and the jeep drove off.

Jenny turned to look back. Mrs Grace had Jess by the collar to stop him running after the jeep. The housekeeper raised a hand and waved. Jenny waved back as the jeep turned up the track towards the top field. Poor Jess. He'd think she'd abandoned him, just as some of the ewes had abandoned their lambs.

She changed from trainers into her wellingtons as the jeep rattled along the rough farm track. Her father was looking worried. Jess would just have to put up with being left behind. The lambing was the important thing.

Matt drew the jeep to a halt beside the field gate. Jenny could see Jake and Nell amongst the flock, weaving their way in and out, keeping the ewes together.

Her father had already jumped out of the jeep, and now he was striding towards a ewe lying on the ground. The poor animal lay on her side, her body arched and her legs stiff. He kneeled down beside the ewe and opened his lambing bag.

'You were right, Matt, it is hypocalcaemia,' he said grimly. 'I'll need to give her an injection. Can you hold her head for me?'

Jenny watched as her father took a syringe and a bottle of clear liquid out of his bag. She had seen the lambing bag many times before. It was a sort of first-aid kit for sheep farmers. In it was fluid for marking the lambs with the Windy Hill symbol and penicillin in case the mother needed a quick injection to prevent infection. There was also lambing oil for the farmer to rub on his hands if he had to help ease the lamb out of the mother's body, and protein drinks for exhausted ewes. The bag itself was lined with soft sheep's wool so that if her dad had to transport a lamb into the house it wouldn't get cold.

Matt kneeled beside his father and made to take the ewe's head in his hands. Fraser Miles primed the syringe and examined it for air bubbles. There was a loud bleating and a flash of black and white as a sheepdog sped past them in pursuit of a ewe. Matt looked up.

'A bolter,' he said.

Jenny watched as Nell chased after the lumbering sheep.

'The ewe is making for the fence at the top,' she said.

Fraser Miles clicked his tongue. 'Get up there, Matt,' he said. 'That's Calum McLay's fence. It's in a bad state of repair and that ewe must be just about to give birth. Don't let her injure herself – or the lamb.'

Matt nodded and jumped to his feet, running across the short grass, whistling to Jake.

The other sheepdog sped to his side and

moved beside him like a shadow.

'I guess *you'd* better hold the ewe's head, Jenny,' Fraser Miles said.

Jenny crouched down, drawing the ewe's head on to her lap and stroking it. The animal's eyes had been closed but suddenly they opened and the sheep bleated weakly. Fraser Miles stretched a patch of skin on the sheep's flank and plunged the syringe home.

'Will she be OK?' Jenny asked, concerned.

Fraser Miles nodded. 'She should be,' he reassured her. 'We'll have to wait and see. The injection should take effect pretty quickly.'

The ewe's eyes were closed again, her body motionless. Jenny held her breath, willing the ewe to open her eyes, to get up. It wasn't just the ewe that was in danger. It was her unborn lamb as well.

The minutes seemed to drag by, then Jenny felt a shudder run through the ewe's body. The animal opened her eyes and began to struggle to her feet.

'Let her go,' Fraser told his daughter. 'But be ready to catch her if she bolts too.'

Jenny watched as the ewe scrambled to her

feet and began to crop the grass, pawing at the ground.

'It's amazing,' she breathed. 'A minute ago she seemed nearly dead.'

'I don't think it'll be long before her lamb is born,' Fraser said. 'Now, let's go and give Matt a hand.'

Jenny trudged up the field after him. As they approached Matt, her father turned to her and smiled. 'That was well done, Jenny,' he said. 'I was glad of your help.'

Jenny flushed with pride but one look at Matt's face told her something was wrong. Her brother was crouched beside the ewe, running his hands over her distended stomach.

'No wonder she bolted,' he said. 'I think it's a breech birth — and twins, too!'

Fraser dug into his lambing bag, drew out the bottle of lambing oil and rolled up his sleeves. 'Do you remember, lass?' he said to Jenny. 'Jess was a breech birth. That's when the baby animal is facing the wrong way in the womb,' he explained, as he rubbed the oil on his hands and forearms. 'Usually they're born head first, and, with twins, that's hard enough for a ewe. But with a breech birth the baby begins to come out backwards, and it can get stuck. So the ewe is going to need my help to ease the lamb out.'

Matt stationed himself at the ewe's head as Fraser got down on his knees and began to examine the ewe. Suddenly the animal began to bleat pitifully and strain against Matt. Matt had his work cut out holding on to her. The poor thing wanted to get away from the pain of imminent birth and the only way she knew how was to bolt.

'Here it comes,' said Fraser Miles. 'Get ready to take it, Jenny.'

Jenny watched, fascinated, as her father eased the little creature into the world. Tiny back legs appeared first, encased in the birth sac. Fraser moved his hands, supporting the little body as it emerged from its mother's womb.

'Push again, old girl,' Matt whispered to the ewe.

As if she had heard him, the ewe gave an almighty push and Fraser Miles was suddenly holding a slippery newborn lamb. He looked at it for a moment and Jenny watched his face.

All the usual worry and seriousness had gone. Her father must have delivered a thousand lambs, but he looked as if this was the very first one he had seen. Jenny understood more than ever before how important sheep farming was to him.

The ewe bleated and began to strain again.

'And here comes the other one,' Fraser said, handing the warm, wet lamb to Jenny. 'Put this one down beside his mother,' he said. 'The sooner she starts licking him clean the better.'

Jenny took the little lamb in her arms and laid him gently beside the ewe. Almost at once the lamb tried to get to his feet, bumping blindly into his mother's side. Jenny guided him towards the ewe's head but the ewe was already giving birth to the other twin.

'This one is the right way round,' Fraser said triumphantly. 'That's it girl – steady now.'

The second lamb slid easily on to the grass and the ewe shook her head and stopped bleating. Jenny's lamb nuzzled at his mother's neck and the ewe turned to him. As Jenny watched, the mother began to lick her lamb, cleaning him and stimulating his circulation.

Then she nudged him towards her flank. Jenny smiled as the tiny lamb searched for what instinct told him he needed.

'Can I give him a hand? He doesn't know how to feed,' she said.

'Better not,' said Matt. 'Sheep often reject lambs if you interfere too much.'

As Jenny watched, the little lamb at last found what he was looking for and fastened on his mother's teat, sucking furiously.

'I think he's going to be all right,' said Jenny.

'Here's the other one,' Fraser said, laying the second lamb in front of its mother.

'The ewe has got the hang of it too,' said Matt as the ewe began to lick her second lamb. 'I think we can leave them to it.'

'Isn't it wonderful?' breathed Jenny.

Fraser Miles took a rough towel out of his bag and wiped his arms.

'I feel that, every time I see a lamb born,' he said. 'But it's hard work.'

'Oh, I wouldn't mind that,' said Jenny seriously. 'I mean, what could be better than helping lambs to be born?'

Fraser looked at his daughter seriously for a

moment. 'You really believe that, don't you, Jenny?'

Jenny nodded, equally serious. 'I love the farm and I love the sheep,' she said. 'Windy Hill is just the best place in the world.'

Fraser turned away and looked out over the fields to the sea beyond. 'You're right, lass,' he said. 'And we'll hang on to it, I promise you that.'

Jenny looked at the twin lambs snuggled close to their mother. Everything she loved was here on this farm.

'What's next?' she asked stoutly.

Matt grinned. 'Talk about a glutton for punishment. Come on, Jenny. There's *plenty* to be done.'

5

From then on, Jenny divided her time between looking after the orphaned lambs and helping her father and Matt in the fields. She was up at first light every morning to give the lambs their feeds, then handed them over to Mrs Grace when she arrived. Matt usually popped back into the farmhouse to collect her and take her back with him.

Every so often, he arrived with new

abandoned or orphaned lambs. He would then collect some of the stronger lambs from the lamb warmer, leaving Jenny to divide the new arrivals between the lamb warmer and the kitchen. Jenny selected the lambs she thought needed the extra attention they could get in the farmhouse and separated them from those that could safely be put in the lamb warmer.

'I'm off back up to the top field, Jenny,' Matt told her, one morning. 'I'll come back for you in a couple of hours, all being well.'

Jenny waved goodbye to her brother. The back of the jeep was full of lambs that were ready to go back into the fields. They bleated piteously, tumbling over one another but Jenny knew they were fit to be outdoors now. There were always new lambs to replace them.

'Come on, Jess,' she said. 'Let's get these lambs settled.' But Jess was already hard at work, herding the tiny lambs into a corner of the kitchen.

Jenny was carrying a boxful of lambs out to the lamb warmer when Ian came out of the stables. He must have been exercising Mercury.

Jenny hadn't known he was around. She'd been far too busy with the lambs.

'Want a hand?' Ian asked as she passed him.

Jenny hesitated. She and Ian didn't get on but right now she reckoned Windy Hill needed all the help it could get.

'Sure,' she said. 'There's another box of lambs to come out to the lamb warmer. Can you fetch it?'

Ian nodded and strode off towards the house. Moments later, he joined her in the shearing shed and handed the box of lambs to her.

'Aren't they great?' he said, peering into the lamb warmer.

'I thought you didn't like sheep,' Jenny said.

'I never said that,' Ian replied. 'You accused me of not knowing anything about sheep – which I don't. But I could always learn.'

Jenny looked at him. 'Are you serious?' she asked. 'Because, if you are, there's a mountain of work you could help with.'

Ian grinned, suddenly looking much more friendly. 'Try me,' he said.

Jenny smiled back. 'Oh, don't worry, I will,' she told him.

★ ★ ★

Mrs Grace was looking round the kitchen in mock despair as Jenny and Ian came back into the house. 'This lot is going to keep you busy,' she said, shaking her head. 'I'll get the bottles ready.'

'Ian's going to help,' Jenny said.

'So he told me when he came for those lambs,' Mrs Grace replied. 'Well, you know what they say – many hands make light work.'

Jenny and Ian began filling boxes with fresh straw and tucking up the tiny lambs warmly. By the time they had finished Mrs Grace had lined up a row of bottles for them. The kitchen was filled with the sound of bleating.

'Where do I start?' asked Ian.

'Just pick a couple of lambs and do as I do,' Jenny told him. 'Look, I'll show you.'

'I'd help but I've got to get on with cleaning the house,' Ellen Grace apologised. 'After all, the humans need looking after too.'

'You've been great, making up the bottles, Mrs Grace,' Jenny called, as the housekeeper went upstairs. 'We'll manage.'

Jenny scooped up two bottles. She

approached a box with two lambs in it, inserting the rubber teats into the little animals' hungry mouths. She smiled as she felt the tug on the bottles. The lambs were so tiny but they would soon be strong enough to go back to the fields.

'That's all you do, Ian,' she said.

There was a scampering sound and Jenny turned round. Ian was chasing after a lamb that was skittering across the kitchen floor

'It got away,' Ian said, flushing, as the lamb staggered under the kitchen table on its wobbly little legs. 'I didn't want to grab it too hard and it slid out of my hands.'

'They're stronger than you think,' Jenny reassured him. 'You won't hurt it if you pick it up firmly.' She turned and whistled to Jess. The puppy leaped up and shot under the table after the lamb. A moment later the tiny creature teetered out, Jess behind it.

'That'll do, Jess,' Jenny said as Ian bent to pick up the lamb. Jess immediately moved back and lay down but he didn't take his eyes off the lamb.

'That's what shepherds say to their dogs,' Ian

said, tucking the lamb under his arm and picking up a bottle.

Jenny nodded. 'Jess knows all the commands,' she told him. 'I taught him right from the start.'

'It's a pity he couldn't be a working dog,' Ian said. 'But if he had been you wouldn't have had him as a pet.'

'I'd much rather have Jess as a pet,' she agreed. 'But Dad says maybe some day he'll sire pups that will be working dogs.'

Ian smiled. 'That would be great,' he said.

Jenny looked up, surprised. Maybe Ian wasn't so bad after all.

Ian looked round the kitchen. 'Are there usually this many orphaned lambs?'

Jenny shook her head. 'Not usually,' she said. 'But there have been a lot of premature births and a few other complications. We've lost more ewes than we normally do. Dad thinks it's because of the fright the ewes had when they got out of the cliff field.'

'Look,' said Ian. 'Can we just forget that? I mean, you know it wasn't my fault.'

Jenny frowned. At first she had blamed Ian for letting the ewes out, but on further investigation it had looked as if Calum McLay had been the culprit except there was no way of proving it. 'You mean start again?' she said.

Ian nodded. 'If you like.'

'We could try,' said Jenny doubtfully. 'But don't go bossing me around.'

'Fair enough,' Ian replied. They both smiled.

A tiny lamb scrabbled at the side of his box, overturning it. The little creature tottered towards Jenny on thin, spindly legs.

'Oh, do you want milk too?' Jenny said. She transferred both bottles to one hand and reached for another, holding it out to the escaped lamb. The lamb fastened on it eagerly, then collapsed on the floor in a heap.

Jenny giggled and positioned the bottle so that the lamb could continue sucking. Her other two lambs were protesting at the awkward position of *their* bottles. Jenny turned back to them. 'Hurry now,' she whispered. 'There are lots more to feed.'

There was a bleating behind her and Jenny turned her head. The bottle of milk had rolled away from the other lamb's reach and the poor thing was trying to stand. He kept collapsing again on his weak little legs.

Suddenly Jess darted forward and gently rolled the bottle back towards the tiny lamb. The animal fastened on to it again, closing his eyes with pleasure as he sucked on the teat.

'Good boy, Jess!' Jenny congratulated him.

'Look at that!' said Ian. 'Now there are three of us feeding the lambs. It's a pity Jess can't help out like that in the fields. Matt was telling me that some of the lambs aren't getting enough nourishment and they might die.'

Jenny nodded. 'Even lambs in the fields sometimes need extra feeding,' she said. 'But, without more help, we just can't get round them all.'

'I could help out there too,' Ian offered.

But Jenny was watching Jess. 'Ian,' she said. 'Do you think we could rig up a harness for Jess and attach a couple of baby bottles to it?'

'What for?' Ian asked.

'I've just had the most marvellous idea,' Jenny said, excitedly. 'We could make some kind of harness so that Jess could carry milk to the weaker lambs. If Dad could see Jess doing that

I'm sure he'd let him help in the fields,' she explained.

Jenny and Ian finished feeding the lambs in the kitchen while Jenny outlined her idea, trying to think of the simplest way of making a harness.

'We could try straps,' said Ian.

Jenny frowned. 'They might get caught on the fences.'

'What about an old waistcoat?' suggested Ian after a moment.

Jenny tried to picture it in her mind. 'You know, Ian,' she said. 'I think that just might work.'

An old waistcoat of Fraser's made a terrific harness once they had taken in the back. Jenny cut holes in the bottoms of the pockets.

'There,' she exclaimed. 'The waistcoat goes round Jess's middle and the bottles slide into the pockets. It's perfect. Jess can take milk to the lambs in the fields – one bottle on each side.'

'And you think it'll work?' Ian asked doubtfully.

'It's *got* to work,' Jenny said determinedly.

'Dad just *can't* afford to lose any more lambs.'

At that moment Mrs Grace came back downstairs and stared at Jess. Jenny explained what they were doing.

The housekeeper shook her head. 'Well, well,' she said. 'I've seen a lot of things in my time but I reckon this beats the lot.'

There was a sound in the yard outside and Jenny whirled round. 'That'll be Matt. He said he'd come back for me.'

Mrs Grace took off her apron. 'I'm coming to have a look too,' she decided. 'I wouldn't miss this for the world!'

'What on earth are you doing with Jess out here?' thundered Fraser Miles as Matt stopped the jeep at the edge of the top field. Jenny winced but she was determined.

'Just let her show you her idea, Fraser,' Mrs Grace suggested.

Fraser Miles looked as if he was going to say no, but Mrs Grace was so calm and reasonable that he nodded reluctantly.

'If that dog upsets the ewes you'll be in trouble, Jenny,' he warned.

'He won't, Dad,' she assured him. 'Just give him a chance.' Jenny led Jess to where two lambs lay side by side, their eyes closed.

'I tried to set those two on to another ewe after their mother rejected them,' Matt said. 'It didn't work. The poor things don't stand a chance.'

Jenny knew that 'setting on' was when a sheep farmer covered a lamb with the skin of a stillborn or dead lamb. That way the mother of the dead lamb might be persuaded to think it was her own lamb, and feed it.

'Those were too weak even to bring into the house,' Fraser added.

Jenny looked down at the lambs. They lay side by side, their eyes closed, hardly breathing. 'Come, Jess,' she said softly.

Gently moving the lambs a little she made room for Jess to lie down between them. As the sheepdog pup nestled his body into place, he began to lick the lambs. Jenny held her breath as first one and then the other lamb opened its eyes.

'At least they're still alive,' she breathed.

She manoeuvred the bottles of milk into

place, lifting the lambs' heads towards the teats. For a moment she thought the lambs were too weak to suck, then she noticed one of them squirming closer to Jess's warm body. The little lamb lifted its head and fastened on the teat. Then he began to suck.

Jess lay perfectly still as Jenny repeated the procedure with the other lamb. But this other one was much weaker.

'You're wasting your time, Jenny,' Fraser Miles said to her gently. 'That one will never make it.'

Jenny looked sadly down at the lamb. It lay quite still, its eyes closed. As she watched she saw a tremor run through its body, then it lay motionless again.

She looked up at her father. 'It's dead, isn't it?' she asked.

Fraser nodded. 'I told you that pair were too far gone.'

Jenny felt a lump in her throat. Not only was the little lamb dead, but her father would ask her to take Jess away.

'This one isn't,' said Matt. 'Look at him.'

Matt was right. The other lamb was sucking

gustily at the bottle of milk. Suddenly it lifted its head and bleated, then, exhausted, it lay down. Jess moved, shifting the bottle nearer the lamb's mouth and Fraser Miles laughed.

'That pup is actually trying to feed the lamb,' he said. 'I've never seen anything like it.'

'That's what I wanted to show you,' Jenny said eagerly. 'I can strap two bottles at a time on Jess and he can feed the lambs here in the fields. The kitchen is full and so is the lamb warmer – but Jess can help out here.'

Fraser Miles scratched his head. 'I don't know about that,' he said.

The lamb finished the milk in the bottle and lay back. Matt picked him up and Jess scampered away. Jenny watched the pup. He nosed around the ewes until he found an abandoned lamb, lay down and began the procedure all over again with the unused milk bottle.

Matt held the lamb close to his chest. 'I reckon Jess has just saved one lamb,' he said. 'And look at him – he's doing it again.'

'Well . . .' said Fraser, clearly bemused. 'I've just never come across anything like this.'

Ellen Grace smiled. 'There's a first time for everything, Fraser,' she said. 'And if you take my advice – go with it. After all, if it works, why not?'

Fraser rubbed his forehead. 'I must admit, I'd be glad of any help at the moment,' he said. 'OK, Jenny, that dog has got a job to do. But if he even *looks* like upsetting the ewes he's out. Understand?'

Jenny nodded, her eyes shining. 'I understand,' she said. 'But he won't. He'll be such a help. You'll see.'

'Hmmph!' said her father but Jenny was watching his eyes. Fraser Miles was looking at Jess with a new respect.

6

Jenny was so busy working with Jess she hardly noticed the time passing. Matt had run the jeep down to the farm, taking Mrs Grace back and bringing up a churn of milk to fill the bottles. Mrs Grace had insisted that they return to the house for a bite to eat at lunchtime, and they had taken it in turns to do so: Jenny going first with Matt, and Ian going with Fraser afterwards. Even so, they had all been back in the fields by one o'clock and had been hard at work ever since.

Later that afternoon, Jenny stopped to look at her watch. 'Almost five o'clock, Jess,' she said. 'I'm getting hungry again!'

Jess had been working tirelessly, seeking out lambs in danger. Even her father was impressed. He and Matt were up at the far end of the top field now. Ian was with them, learning about lambing and loving it.

Jenny smiled. Calum McLay might have made sure that her father couldn't afford to outbid him for casual workers but now Fraser had Matt, Ian and Jenny – and Jess – to help him.

'We're going to beat you yet, Mr McLay,' Jenny whispered under her breath. 'Your dirty tricks haven't worked after all.' She looked down at her puppy. 'Isn't it wonderful, Jess? I can work in the fields *and* have you with me.'

Jess barked and wagged his tail and Jenny looked towards the top field. She could make out two figures up there, moving amongst the ewes. She saw Nell flowing like a shadow in and out of the flock, her distinctive white ears clearly visible. But where was Jake?

Jenny cast around her. Jake was an outrunner. Sheepdogs were usually one of two types. Nell was the kind of sheepdog that worked best close in to the sheep, controlling them with her eyes, outstaring them and making them do as she wanted. Jake was the other kind. He could run for miles, rounding up the flock and driving them where the shepherd wanted them to go. An outrunner was absolutely essential on a farm like theirs with its hilly terrain. Like all outrunners, Jake had excellent hearing. He could hear her father whistle from half a mile away.

Jenny screwed up her eyes, searching the top field. Maybe her father had sent the dog out to round up a batch of stray ewes. But, if so, her father would be standing straight, intent on his dog, whistling his instructions to it. But Jenny could see that Fraser Miles was crouched low over the bulk of a ewe. Clearly he was busy with a difficult birth. Ian was with him, also bending down. Matt was even further away, attending to another ewe. And still there was no sign of Jake.

Jenny pursed her mouth and whistled, then she scanned the fields once more but no black and white shape responded to her call. She frowned, trying to remember when she had last seen Jake. It must have been around lunchtime, but she'd been so busy since that she hadn't noticed if he'd passed through the field she was working in.

Jenny turned to Jess. The sheepdog puppy was standing, legs stiff and nose pointing over the hill towards the McLay farm. His ears were pricked, every sense alert. Jenny looked at him thoughtfully. Had he heard something she hadn't?

She whistled again, but this time she watched Jess. He turned briefly towards her, but he knew Jenny would never whistle for him while he was standing so close to her. Jess turned back, his nose still pointing in the same direction, towards the McLay farm, then he gave a short, sharp bark.

Jess had definitely heard something that was beyond human range of hearing. Jenny wondered what to do. Her father, Matt and Ian were all obviously very busy.

Jenny made up her mind. If Jake was in trouble then it was up to her and Jess to find out.

She bent down to the puppy. 'Jake,' she said urgently to the little dog. 'Find Jake, Jess.'

Jess looked up at her, his head on one side.

'*Jake*,' Jenny repeated insistently.

At once Jess dropped his head and began to move across the field. Jenny followed him, her heart hammering. Stumbling over the field, she went after Jess up the hill towards the stile that led to the adjoining field, the one that bordered Calum McLay's land. It seemed much farther than she remembered, she thought, as she crossed the stile and dropped into the next field.

Then, at last, she came in sight of the boundary. Ahead she could see the fence her father had been worried about. One section of it gleamed, shining in the rays of the sun. Jenny frowned. That whole fence had been old and rusty. Part of it shouldn't be shining like that. Then her attention was caught by a dark shape lying beside the fence.

Jess had seen it too and was running towards it. Jenny hurried after him. Maybe it was just a patch of mud, she told herself. But even as she tried to tell herself that, she knew it wasn't true. She recognised that shape. She recognised the white pattern within the black that she could now see as she drew closer. It was the white patch on Jake's chest. It was Jake – and he was lying as still as death.

Jenny raced the last twenty metres towards the dog. Her legs jarred on the uneven ground beneath her feet, and her heart thumped with the effort of putting on one last spurt. Then she was there. She threw herself down beside the sheepdog, struggling for breath.

Jess had already reached Jake. The puppy was licking the older dog's face. As Jenny put her hand out to touch Jake, Jess lifted his head and howled.

Jake opened his eyes at the sound, and tried to move. Then he gave a soft whine and slumped back. Jenny gasped with relief. At least he wasn't dead. She ran her hand along his flank, then cried out when her hand came away covered in blood.

More gently, she parted the dog's thick coat. It was matted with blood and there was an old piece of barbed wire caught in the skin of the dog's side. 'Oh, Jake,' Jenny gasped.

She looked at the new piece of fencing, puzzled. Why had Calum McLay replaced only one small section of the old and dangerous barbed-wire fence? And when had he done it?

But that would have to be dealt with later. Jake was badly injured and there was no time to lose. Jenny looked at Jess. 'Stay!' she commanded.

Jess lay down close to Jake as Jenny got to her feet and sped back the way she had come. Behind her Jess let out another howl but Jenny knew he would stay with the injured dog. She had to get help as quickly as possible.

The breath rasped in her throat as Jenny pounded down the hill. She scrambled on to the stile that connected the two fields and stood on top of it, shouting and waving. Nell looked up and moved towards her. Then Fraser Miles turned and began to run towards her, closely followed by Matt and Ian. Jenny jumped down from the stile and ran on, her legs weak under her, stumbling on the rough ground.

Matt was the first to reach her. 'What's wrong?' he yelled.

Jenny collapsed into his arms. 'It's Jake,' she gasped breathlessly. 'He's hurt . . . The boundary fence in the far field . . . Jess is with him.'

Fraser Miles arrived and looked at her. 'How badly hurt?' he asked.

'Pretty badly, I think,' Jenny answered. 'There's a lot of blood – and barbed wire.'

Fraser Miles's mouth set in a tight line. 'Get the jeep up, Matt,' he said. 'Bring it round by the other gate. We'll take Jake directly to Tom Palmer.' Then he whistled to Nell and started to run across the field towards the stile.

Matt looked at Jenny. 'Are you all right?' he asked.

Jenny nodded. 'Go on,' she gasped out. 'I'll follow when I've got my breath back.'

'I only hope Tom Palmer is there,' Matt said anxiously. Mr Palmer was the local vet.

Ian caught his arm. 'I'll run down to the farm and ring him,' he said. 'I'll get him on his mobile and make sure he's ready for you.'

Matt ran a hand through his hair. 'It's a long way back to the house,' he said.

'I used to do cross-country running at my last school,' Ian reassured him. 'Anyway, Jenny can't run all that way. She's done enough already.'

'She certainly has,' agreed Matt. 'OK, Ian, get going. Jenny, get back to Jake and we'll drop you and Jess off at the road end.'

Jenny nodded as Ian turned and began to run down the hill towards the farmhouse. It *was* a long way but he was covering the ground well.

Jenny sank to the ground and watched Matt, running long-legged down the field towards the jeep. Her heartbeat steadied and she began to get her breath back. She saw her father disappear over the brow of the hill and got to her feet, her legs still a little shaky.

Doggedly, she began to walk back the way she had come. Her steps were heavy. She couldn't get the picture of Jake out of her mind. He had looked so bad and there had been so much blood. She felt tears thick in her throat and took a deep breath. Crying wouldn't help. If Jake died, her father would have enough to worry about without her being upset.

Head up, she began to stride towards the stile. As she clambered over it, the wind caught her hair and lifted it from her face. She looked out over the farm towards the sea. Jake was part of Windy Hill. He *had* to be all right.

'Drink this and you'll feel better,' Mrs Grace said to Jenny.

Jenny looked up at the housekeeper and warmed her hands on the steaming mug of cocoa. She and Ian were sitting at the big kitchen table in the farmhouse. Matt had dropped her off at the end of the road and Ian had managed to get in touch with Tom Palmer. All she and Ian and Mrs Grace could do now was wait.

'They should be home soon,' Ian said as Jenny took a sip of cocoa.

'It might take a little time,' Ellen Grace warned him. 'And, don't forget, those lambs will be needing another feed soon.'

Jenny smiled weakly. 'We won't forget,' she said. She smiled at Ian. 'Thanks for today,' she said.

Ian smiled back. 'Any time,' he replied. 'I really enjoyed working with the sheep. I just wish Jake hadn't been hurt. It was lucky you found him.'

'It was Jess that found him,' Jenny said.

Jess was curled up asleep between two lambs. He had wanted to go with Jake to the vet and had howled as the jeep drove off. Poor Jess. He knew something was wrong.

'Tom Palmer is a good vet, Jenny,' Mrs Grace said comfortingly.

Jenny nodded. 'I know. He looked after Jess's leg. He'll do his very best for Jake. He knows how important Jake is to Dad.'

Ellen Grace gave Jenny a hug. 'And meanwhile,' she said briskly, 'there's one thing to remember about living on a farm – you're never short of a job to take your mind off your worries. There's a lot of lambs around here who would be grateful for a feed!'

Jenny smiled. Mrs Grace was right. Moping wouldn't help but feeding the lambs would! She and Ian finished their cocoa and started making up the bottles.

When the jeep turned into the yard Jenny looked up, surprised. It was later than she had thought. Feeding the lambs really had taken her mind off Jake for a while.

Her father and Matt came into the kitchen together. Jenny swallowed. Jake wasn't with them.

'Is he . . . ?' Jenny couldn't finish the sentence.

Fraser Miles reached out and ruffled her hair. 'He's going to be all right,' he reassured her.

Jenny let out a huge sigh of relief.

'But you haven't brought him home,' Ian said.

'Tom operated on him straight away,' Matt explained. 'The barbed wire was embedded quite deep, and the wound was inflamed. It'll be a while before he recovers.'

Ellen Grace looked worried. 'What about the lambing?' she asked. 'How will you manage without him?'

Fraser Miles sat down heavily at the table. 'We'll have to do the best we can with Nell,' he sighed.

'I can't understand how it happened,' Matt said.

'Jake was probably trying to rescue a stray ewe from McLay land,' Fraser guessed.

Matt frowned. 'But there was no gap in the fencing just there. In fact, a section of fencing had been repaired.'

Fraser looked at his son. 'When I passed by that section of fencing yesterday it was still broken and rusting,' he said, gravely. 'A sheep, still with its thick winter coat, would be protected against the wire as it pushed its way through. But Jake was unlucky. And,' Fraser concluded, 'I'd be willing to bet that the broken section of fence was replaced with a new section *after* Jake got caught in it. Sheep farmers usually keep a spare roll of wire fencing in the back of their truck,' he explained. 'It wouldn't have taken McLay long to replace that small section, so that he couldn't be blamed for having a dangerous fence.'

Jenny gasped. 'But if the fence was fixed *after* Jake was injured that means somebody just left Jake lying there, hurt! Somebody repaired the fence and ignored him!'

'Surely nobody would do a thing like that?' protested Ellen Grace.

'Nobody with any decency,' said Fraser Miles. 'But if Calum McLay wanted to hide the fact that it was his old fence that caused the injury—'

'Of course,' Matt broke in. 'We can't prove a thing. McLay could say he had already repaired the fence – that he'd never seen Jake.'

'Exactly,' said Fraser.

Jenny laid a hand on her father's arm. She was longing to ask him why Calum McLay had such a grudge against him but one look at his grey, exhausted face was enough. Now wasn't the time for questions like that. 'Jess and I will help,' she offered.

'And so will I,' Ian put in.

Fraser Miles smiled. 'Thanks for the offers,' he said. 'You two will be a good help. But you know how I feel about Jess, Jenny. He isn't a sheepdog. He did really well with his bottles of milk, but he can't replace Jake.'

'Maybe not,' said Matt briskly. 'But he's all we've got. We might be glad of him.'

Fraser Miles shook his head. 'I'm tired,' he confessed. 'I suppose you might be right, Matt. Goodness knows we couldn't be any worse off than we are now.'

Jenny's head came up. 'You said we'd hang

on to Windy Hill – no matter what,' she declared. 'You promised.'

Fraser Miles flushed. 'And I meant it, Jenny,' he said. 'You're right. Of course we'll get through this.'

Jess woke up and began to round up a couple of stray lambs that had escaped from their boxes. Jenny saw her father's face relax as he watched the pup.

'And Jess will do his best to help,' she said softly.

'That's all any of us can do, lassie,' Fraser replied.

Jenny didn't say anything more. She just hoped their best was good enough.

7

Jenny was reluctant to go back to school at the end of the Easter break. Normally she liked school – apart from the hassle she got from Fiona McLay – but she wouldn't be able to help her father as much as she had been doing, and neither would Ian. Fraser and Matt would have to cope.

'They'll manage,' Carrie comforted her as they took their places in class and got out their maths workbooks. 'After all, the peak of the lambing is over. It's gone well, hasn't it?'

Jenny smiled. 'They've had a hundred and forty per cent yield so far,' she said.

'What does that mean?' asked Carrie.

'Well, from eight hundred of our ewes, we've got about eleven hundred lambs. But there are still around two hundred ewes waiting to give birth,' Jenny answered.

Carrie's jaw dropped. 'Wow!' she said. 'That's an awful lot of lambs.'

'Dad was hoping to get closer to a hundred and fifty per cent yield by the end of the lambing,' Jenny replied. 'That would mean a yield of fifteen hundred lambs, but I don't think he can do that without Jake. Sheepdogs can help such a lot, picking out ewes in distress and rounding them up for the farmer, so he can help the sheep to deliver their lambs safely.'

'How *is* Jake?' asked Carrie.

Jenny smiled. 'He's recovering,' she told her friend. 'But he's still weak. He lost a lot of blood and he needed quite a few stitches. He can't understand why he can't be out in the fields with Nell. Poor Jake.'

'But Jess is helping,' Carrie went on.

'He's doing his best,' Jenny agreed. 'But he's no substitute for Jake. Dad's right. There's a big difference between a working dog and a house dog.'

Carrie looked at Jenny sympathetically. 'It'll work out all right, you'll see.'

Jenny nodded. Carrie usually managed to cheer her up but this time it didn't seem to be working.

'The selection for the Graston Lass will be on Saturday in the village hall,' Mrs Barker announced from the front of the class.

There were excited murmurs among the girls and Carrie turned to Jenny. 'We'll go together,' she said.

Jenny shook her head. 'I can't,' she explained. 'Dad needs me on the farm. I can't let him down.'

'You wouldn't be chosen anyway,' said a voice behind them and Jenny turned to see Fiona McLay leaning over her desk. She must have been listening to every word they said.

Carrie stuck her chin out. 'Says who?' she demanded, sticking up for her friend.

'I can't come to the selection anyway,' Jenny said. 'It doesn't matter.'

'Poor little good girl,' Fiona mocked. 'She has to help her dad on the farm. Some sheep farmer that needs a girl to help him.'

Carrie leaned across Fiona's desk. 'And I suppose you think you're going to be the Graston Lass?' she said.

Fiona shrugged and tucked her hair back. 'Why not?' she replied confidently. 'Who else do you think they'll choose? Not you anyway. You're an incomer. You only moved here last year.'

Carrie looked as if she was going to explode and Jenny laid a hand on her arm. 'Leave it, Carrie,' she urged.

Carrie looked at Jenny's pale face and her angry expression subsided. 'OK,' she said. 'Fiona isn't worth arguing with anyway.'

This time it was Fiona's turn to flush. 'What do you mean by that?' she almost shouted.

'Quieten down at the back,' Mrs Barker called. 'Where is your maths workbook, Fiona? We're nearly ready to start . . .'

★ ★ ★

Fraser Miles always tried to come into the house for a quick cup of tea when Jenny got back from school. Jenny would have a snack and then spend a couple of hours helping him until it got dark.

That afternoon both he and Matt were there. Jenny took that as a good sign. Things weren't quite as hectic as they had been two weeks ago. Matt was slumped comfortably in an armchair and her father watched Jenny as she sat with Jake in front of the Aga. His side was still heavily bandaged but his temperature had gone down a lot and the infection seemed to be under control. Jess was curled up beside the bigger dog as they both snoozed in front of the stove.

'Jake owes his life to you, lass,' Fraser said to her. 'Tom reckoned that if he'd lost any more blood he wouldn't have been able to save him.'

Jenny looked up from her position beside the dogs. The sheepdog was in the farm kitchen for the duration of his convalescence. Even Fraser had agreed that Jake needed extra warmth and comfort while he recovered. 'It was Jess that led me to him,' she said.

Jess stirred in his sleep and Jenny put her

hand out, smoothing his ears. He snuffled and half woke, licking her hand.

'It seems a pity to disturb him,' Mr Miles said. 'Do you want to have a break this afternoon, Jenny?'

Jenny grinned. 'Are you trying to get rid of us, Dad?' she asked. 'I was only waiting for Ian to arrive. I don't need a break.'

Right at that moment there was the sound of bicycle wheels on the cobbles outside. 'That sounds like him now,' said Fraser.

'Let's go then,' said Jenny, rising to her feet.

Matt laughed. 'You're a slave driver, Jen,' he accused her. 'I was just getting comfortable.'

Jenny grinned. Matt might sound as if he was complaining but he got up quickly enough and made his way to the door.

As they approached it, the door opened and Ian came in. 'Ready?' he said.

'Just waiting for you,' said Jenny. 'Where have you *been*?'

Ian grinned as Jess jumped up and ran to him, wagging his tail. 'You could have gone without me,' he said.

Jenny shook her head. 'We wouldn't,' she said.

'You're far too useful – isn't he, Dad?'

Fraser Miles scratched his head. 'I reckon we could make a sheep farmer of him yet,' he said.

'What about me?' asked Jenny.

'Oh, you,' her father replied as he headed out into the yard. 'You're like Jess. It's in your blood.'

Jenny stopped for a moment on her way to the door. Just like Jess, she thought. Her father couldn't have paid her a bigger compliment.

Though the lambing had quietened a little, the work that afternoon was still hard, and Jess was a great help, running to and fro with his bottles of milk, feeding the lambs. There was only one interruption. A van drove up the rough track to the top field and they all turned, looking at it.

A young man with a camera got out and smiled, his eyes on Jess. 'So it's true,' he declared. 'When I heard about this I thought it was a joke.'

He introduced himself as a reporter from the local newspaper. 'Gary Baker,' he said. 'I was told that this is the puppy who featured in the recent animal welfare advertising campaign. And he's moved on to more amazing things! I'd like to take a picture of him feeding the lambs, and write an article about him, if that's OK?'

Matt laughed. 'Go ahead,' he said. 'If it's all right with you, Jen?'

Gary turned to Jenny. 'He's your dog, is he?' he asked. 'Can you tell me something about him? Does he do any more tricks?'

Jenny told the young man all about Jess.

'Wow!' he said, scribbling furiously in his notebook. 'He's had quite an exciting life for such a young pup, hasn't he? First he escaped death by a hair's breadth and now he's saving lambs! This is going to make a terrific story.'

Gary got Jenny to pose with Jess and two newborn lambs and snapped a few pictures.

'And how old are you, Jenny?' he asked. Jenny told him.

'Ah,' the reporter replied. 'So you'll be in the senior class at Graston School. You'll be going to the Graston Lass selection on Saturday, then?' he asked, conversationally.

Jenny shook her head. 'I won't be entering,'

she replied. 'I'll be too busy for that.'

Gary Baker raised his eyebrows. 'There aren't many girls of your age in Graston that would miss it,' he said cheerfully. 'You *are* an unusual girl.'

'She certainly is,' said Matt, smiling at Jenny.

Matt and Jenny waved as the reporter drove off.

'You didn't mention the Graston Lass selection to Dad and me,' Matt said, looking intently at his sister.

Jenny shrugged. 'It isn't important,' she replied. 'The lambing is much more important.'

Matt smiled at her and ruffled her hair affectionately. 'Jenny Miles,' he said. 'You're a *real* Graston lass, no matter who gets the title.'

8

It was a relief when Jake was fit enough to go back to work two weeks later. Jess had been valuable, but he didn't have Jake's experience, and never would have.

'I'm glad about that really, Jess,' Jenny murmured to the little dog as she stuck another paper flag on to a string of bunting. 'I'd much rather have you as my very own pet.' She yawned as Ellen Grace came into the kitchen.

'That's enough for tonight,' the housekeeper declared. 'You're yawning your head off, Jenny. You've been really marvellous helping me with the decorations for the common riding.'

Jenny smiled and it turned into another yawn. 'I enjoy doing the decorations,' she said. 'I'm really looking forward to the celebrations.'

'Everyone is,' said Ellen Grace. 'It means the hard work of lambing is over. Your father says things are getting much easier now. There are fewer than a hundred ewes left to lamb.'

'Ian has been great,' Jenny said. She frowned. 'Is he still out with Dad?'

Mrs Grace nodded. 'They'll be in soon,' she said. She looked thoughtful. 'I'm glad you and Ian are friends now.'

Jenny rose from the table. 'So am I,' she said. 'It's good having him around the place.'

Mrs Grace looked suddenly worried.

'What's wrong?' asked Jenny.

Mrs Grace smiled ruefully. 'It's just that I don't know if Ian and I are going to be around much longer. Calum McLay won't promise to renew my lease on the cottage and I don't know what we're going to do when it runs out.'

'You mean he's going to make you leave?' Jenny cried, shocked.

Ellen Grace shook her head. 'I don't know yet,' she confessed. 'I think that's the worst thing – the uncertainty. I've written to him to say I want an answer one way or another.'

Jenny was outraged. 'What *is* it about Mr McLay?' she demanded. 'He seems to have it in for everybody – but most of all, Dad.' Her face darkened. 'I wish I knew why.'

Ellen Grace looked at her seriously. 'You remember, Jenny, your father saying a while ago that Calum McLay has wanted to take Windy Hill from him all the while your father's lived here?' she asked.

Jenny nodded.

'Well,' Mrs Grace continued, 'Your father came to live here when he married your mother.'

Jenny looked confused. 'I don't understand,' she said. 'Why did Dad and Mum getting married matter to Calum McLay?'

Mrs Grace smiled at Jenny. 'Because Calum McLay wanted your mother to marry *him*,' she explained. 'Calum had been sweet on Sheena since he was no more than a boy. He'd even persuaded her to accept his proposal. But in the end Sheena couldn't go through with it. She left Calum at the altar and chose your dad instead, even though Fraser was very poor compared to Calum. It was a huge blow to Calum, being jilted like that.'

'I'll bet it was,' said Jenny, wide-eyed. 'Wow! So *that's* why he's got this grudge against Dad!'

'There's a bit more to it than that,' Mrs Grace went on. 'Windy Hill was your mother's family's farm. So when your mum chose to marry your dad, Calum lost a sheep farm as well as a wife. Ever since then, Calum's wanted vengeance. He went on to marry Anna – Fiona and Paul's mum, of course. But even after all these years, Calum's pride must still hurt, as it's clear he wants to take Windy Hill from your father – by fair means or foul.'

'Goodness!' said Jenny. 'I remember Dad saying that he had won a prize over Calum's head. I wonder if he meant the farm.'

Mrs Grace smiled. 'I think he probably meant your mum,' she said gently.

Jenny looked at her for a moment. 'Of course

he did,' she said. 'Oh, I wish Mum hadn't died.'

Mrs Grace put an arm round Jenny. 'Your mum was special,' she said. 'In fact, I've been meaning to tell you, I came across an old photograph the other day of your mum when she was the Graston Lass. I was one of her maids of honour that year.'

'Mum was a Graston Lass?' Jenny squeaked. 'I never knew that.'

'She certainly was,' said Mrs Grace. Jenny hovered impatiently while Mrs Grace dug in her bag and brought out a photograph and handed it to her.

Jenny looked at the old black-and-white photo and gasped. It showed a girl of about eleven, sitting on a brown pony, her long skirts draped over the pony's flank and a crown on her head. The girl was smiling, her eyes alight with laughter, and her honey-brown hair flowing down her back.

'But she looks exactly like . . .' Jenny hesitated. Maybe it was her imagination.

'She looks just like you,' Ellen Grace confirmed. 'She's the same age as you in that picture, of course. If it wasn't in black-and-white anybody would think it *was* you. You could be twins.'

Jenny felt a lump in her throat. She had seen other photographs of her mother, family photographs, but none when her mum had been eleven. 'Oh, Mrs Grace,' she began. Then she stopped, unable to go on.

'I thought you might like to keep that photo,' Mrs Grace said gently.

'Oh, I would,' said Jenny gratefully. 'I'll keep it for ever.'

Jenny heard her father and Ian come in as she went upstairs. Ellen Grace's soft voice joined in the conversation downstairs as Jenny got ready for bed. Jenny put the photograph on her bedside table and gazed at it. The resemblance really was amazing.

She turned over what Mrs Grace had told her in her mind. Now she knew what Calum McLay had against her father. Her eyes opened wide. Was that why her father had been so patient with Calum McLay that time he came to warn Fraser Miles about trespassing? Did her father feel sorry for Mr McLay? She tried to feel sorry for Calum McLay, but then she remembered that he was threatening to evict Mrs Grace, as well as battling to take Windy Hill away from them.

Jenny's eyes closed in sleep. She would think about all these problems tomorrow.

'There's a letter for you, Jenny,' Mrs Grace said the following Saturday as she laid the table for lunch.

Jenny looked up from the lamb she was feeding. There were only three lambs left in the kitchen at Windy Hill. The lambing was nearly over and it had gone better than any of them had hoped. 'A letter! For me?' she exclaimed.

She took the envelope and looked at it curiously.

'It looks official,' Ian said, impressed. 'The address is typed.'

'I wonder what it can be,' Jenny mused.

'There's only one way to find out,' Matt advised her. 'Open it.'

'Don't keep us in suspense, Jenny,' Fraser Miles smiled.

Jenny wiped her hands on her jeans and

carefully opened the envelope, drawing out a single sheet of typed paper. She scanned the letter and looked at the others in turn.

'This can't be right,' she said wonderingly. 'I didn't even enter it.'

'Enter what?' asked Ian.

'The selection,' Jenny told him. 'There must be some mistake. This letter says I'm to be the Graston Lass.'

Ian whooped with delight. 'Won't Fiona be green with envy!' he exclaimed.

'I told you that you were a *real* Graston lass,' Matt said, his face wreathed in smiles. 'Well done, Jen!'

Jenny shook her head. 'It *must* be a mistake,' she insisted.

Mrs Grace came and stood beside her. 'It isn't a mistake,' she said quietly. 'Carrie Turner wrote to the committee telling us you'd decided to help with the lambing rather than go to the selection. The committee decided Matt is right – you *are* a real Graston lass.'

Jenny looked at Mrs Grace in wonder. 'Carrie?' she said. 'And the committee didn't mind? I mean I thought you would have to be

grown-up to do a thing like that.'

'Carrie is a very determined young lady,' Mrs Grace said, smiling, 'And, besides, it was nice to have someone nominated by a person of their own age.'

'Wow!' said Jenny. 'Imagine writing to the committee! Carrie's amazing.' She looked at Ian. 'Did you know she'd done it?'

Ian grinned. 'She might just have mentioned it,' he said. 'I thought it was a great idea. It gave me something to think about too.'

'What?' asked Jenny suspiciously.

Ian just grinned even more. Jenny sighed. If he was up to something she would find out sooner or later.

Jenny looked at her father. Fraser Miles was smiling at her. 'I'm proud of you, Jenny,' he said. 'Your mother was the Graston Lass once. She would be proud of you too.'

Jenny drew in her breath. Her father *never* talked about her mother. 'Mrs Grace gave me a picture of Mum at the common riding,' she told him, shyly.

'Did she?' Fraser asked. 'I'd like to see that sometime,' he said, quietly.

'We'll frame it,' suggested Matt. 'We'll put it in a double frame with one of Jenny at *her* common riding. We'll have to get you up on Mercury soon, Jen. You know the Lass has to ride round the town and you'll need some practice. It's a long time since you've been on a horse.'

'I'll help,' offered Ian. 'The common riding is next weekend – we don't have much time.'

Jenny looked round all the eager faces. Everyone was looking at her expectantly but all she could think of was the bombshell Matt had just dropped in her lap: she would have to ride *Mercury*.

9

'I can't do it!' Jenny burst out, her mouth dry.

'Can't?' asked her father, clearly puzzled.

Jenny gazed at him. He was so proud of her, so pleased she was following in her mother's footsteps. How could she tell him she could never do it?

'I can't be the Graston Lass if it means riding Mercury,' she said at last. 'They'll have to find someone else.'

Fraser Miles leaned across and covered his daughter's hand with his own. 'I know you're nervous of Mercury,' he sympathised. 'But I thought you were beginning to like him at last. Jess likes him.'

Jenny swallowed hard. 'I don't hate him the way I used to, but nothing would make me get up on him.'

'But why not?' her father persisted.

Jenny took a deep breath. There was no way out. 'Because Mercury killed Mum,' she said in a small voice.

She saw the shock on her father's face and heard his indrawn breath but she kept her eyes steadily on him. 'You sold him because you couldn't bear the sight of him. What I don't understand is why you took him back. Mercury killed Mum and you don't seem to mind!'

Fraser Miles took a deep breath and stared down at the table for a long moment. Ellen Grace put her hand on Jenny's shoulder. Jenny was glad of the warmth of her touch. Seeing her father's shocked face was almost too much for her.

At last Fraser looked up. His eyes were

surprisingly gentle. 'Mercury didn't kill your mother,' he said softly. 'It was an accident. There was a storm, and your mother was hurrying towards Darktarn Keep. As she was preparing Mercury to jump the drystone wall below the keep, an old, dead tree nearby was struck by lightning and fell across their path. Your mum tried to turn Mercury to avoid the tree, but the horse had already got into his stride for the jump. He wasn't able to swerve in time, and had to stop dead to avoid the tree. Your mum was thrown. She hit her head on the wall and she died. It wasn't Mercury's fault. Any horse would have been terrified.'

Jenny swallowed hard. She couldn't take it in. 'How do you know all this?' she asked.

Fraser Miles spread his hands. 'I saw it, Jenny,' he said. 'I was out walking and I took shelter in the keep when the storm started. I think your mum was trying to get to the keep to do the same.'

'You saw it happen?' Jenny whispered.

Fraser Miles was silent for a long moment. 'I could see she was going to try and jump the wall. She'd done it before. Your mum was always a bit of a daredevil. I tried to call to her. I didn't think it was safe to jump in those conditions but the storm was loud. She didn't hear me. By the time I got to her she was dead.'

Jenny felt tears burn hot behind her eyes. The picture was clear in her mind – her father, running down the hill from the keep through the storm, bending over her mother's lifeless body. She couldn't bear to think of it.

'Why didn't you tell me?' she said in a low voice. 'Why did you let me think it was Mercury's fault?'

'I didn't *know* you thought that,' her father said. 'Matt and I thought you disliked Mercury because of his association with your mum's accident. We didn't know you *blamed* him. Your mother wouldn't have blamed him – and neither do I.' He rested his head in his hand for a moment. 'I'm sorry, lass. It was wrong of me not to talk to you about what happened but even thinking about it was so painful.'

'You wouldn't let me ride Mercury,' Jenny said. 'But you let Matt ride him.'

Fraser looked up at her. 'So you thought I wouldn't let you ride Mercury because he was dangerous,' he said. 'It wasn't just that, Jenny,' he confessed. 'It's true I sold Mercury right after the accident because he reminded me too much of what had happened to your mother. But the other reason I wouldn't let you ride him, even when he'd settled down, was that I knew if I saw you on Mercury it would be like seeing your mother all over again. I didn't think I could bear that.'

Tears were sliding down Jenny's face. 'But you don't mind now,' she said. 'You want me to ride him as the Graston Lass?'

Her father nodded. 'It's what your mum would have wanted,' he said. 'She would have been so proud of you, Jenny. I can't stand in the way of that. I've been wrong and I've caused you a lot of pain. I'm sorry.'

Jenny dashed the tears from her eyes. Suddenly she realised that she and her father were alone. The others must have left very quietly – probably Mrs Grace had thought of that.

'Oh, Dad,' she said. 'I wish you'd talk to me about Mum. I miss her so much.'

Fraser Miles reached over and drew Jenny

close, hugging her. 'I *will* talk about her from now on,' he promised. 'Perhaps it will help me too.'

'And I'll be the Graston Lass,' Jenny said. 'I'll do it for you – and for Mum.'

10

'There,' said Mrs Grace, setting the crown on top of Jenny's hair. 'You look really beautiful.'

Jenny blushed at the compliment as she looked at herself in the old speckled mirror at the back of Graston village hall. It was the day of the common riding and Mrs Grace had kept the promise she had made ages ago to do something with Jenny's hair.

She had brushed it till it shone and now it rippled down Jenny's back almost to her shoulder blades. Mrs Grace had caught the sides up into a loose knot that fitted under the Graston Lass crown. The crown was made of silver wire intertwined with flowers and Ellen Grace had made Jenny a long blue dress with wide sleeves and a full skirt.

'I tried to copy the one your mum wore as well as I could,' she told Jenny.

Jenny twirled in front of the mirror, the long skirt belling out round her ankles, the sleeves floating. Usually she didn't give two hoots what she wore but this was different. Today was special. 'It's lovely, Mrs Grace,' she said. 'Thank you so much.'

'Aren't you ready yet?' Ian asked, poking his head round the door of the village hall. He stopped and looked at her. 'You look like something out of an advert,' he said.

Jenny grinned. 'You look like a bandit,' she replied. She wasn't going to risk asking him what she looked like an advert for!

Ian looked down at his leather jerkin and breeches and pulled a face. 'I'm supposed to be your groom,' he said. 'Come on. Mercury and Jess are waiting.'

Jenny followed him outside. As she emerged from the village hall the crowd outside cheered good-naturedly and Jenny blushed even more.

'You look great,' enthused Carrie, rushing up to her friend.

'So do you,' Jenny replied. Carrie was dressed up as a Border reiver – complete with sword.

'I'm supposed to be Jess of Beacon Brae,' Carrie grinned. 'Oops! I'd better remember to limp.'

'And, Carrie,' Jenny went on, 'thanks for nominating me. If it hadn't been for you I might never have found out what really happened to my mother. I might have gone on blaming Mercury for ever – and blaming Dad too for keeping him.'

Carrie looked serious for a moment. 'I'm glad it worked out in the end,' she said.

'Get back on your float, Carrie Turner,' yelled an official.

'Good luck!' whispered Carrie as she scuttled back to the decorated lorry and scrambled up into place.

Jenny caught her breath. The float looked great. It had a cardboard keep on it – a copy of Darktarn. Carrie was standing beside a mock bonfire with a papier-mâché torch in her hand. She waved the torch at Jenny and the other reivers around her ducked. Jenny looked closely and recognised some of her classmates. Young Paul McLay was there too, dressed as a shepherd, with a little Blackface lamb in his arms. His mother, Anna McLay, walked alongside the float. Jenny gave them all a wave.

'Playing the princess – waving to your subjects,' sneered a voice behind her.

Jenny turned. It was Fiona McLay, dressed in ordinary clothes. She had refused to take part in the pageant because she hadn't been chosen as the Graston Lass.

'Push off, Fiona,' Ian said shortly. 'Come on, Jenny. It's time to go.'

'I'm a bit nervous,' Jenny whispered to Ian as he gave her a boost into the saddle. 'Look at all these people!'

Mercury shifted slightly, then settled down. Jess was sitting patiently at the big horse's side, waiting for the fun to start.

'Don't be nervous,' said Ian. 'You look great up there on Mercury.'

Jenny smiled. At first she had still been a little nervous of the big black horse, and worried that she might have forgotten how to ride. But once she had been in the saddle for a while she had begun to feel perfectly at home – just the way she used to.

Mercury had needed to get accustomed to yet another new rider, but Ian had been a great help, and so had Jess, of course.

'Ready?' Ian asked, looking up at her.

'Ready!' she replied.

'By the way, did I tell you there might be another surprise in store for you today?' Ian asked her innocently.

Jenny looked down at him. 'What kind of surprise?' she asked.

'Wait and see,' said Ian, maddeningly. 'Walk on, Mercury!'

Jenny was so intrigued by Ian's statement she completely forgot her nervousness. She was halfway down the main street, waving and smiling to the crowds, before she realised.

Oh, well, she thought, it looks as if I'm

managing after all. But what was Ian's surprise?

Round the town and out beyond to the boundaries of Graston the procession went with crowds streaming behind. Mercury performed beautifully and Jess was in his element, trotting along beside the horse.

Jenny began to enjoy herself. The sun shone, the crowds cheered and everyone seemed to be having a great time. When they arrived back in Graston itself she was flushed with triumph and pleasure.

'Well done, lass,' her father said as Matt lifted her down off Mercury's back.

'Mercury was wonderful,' Jenny said, giving the big horse a rub.

Her father's eyes were misty. 'It's like taking a trip back in time, watching you on Mercury,' he said.

Jenny laid a hand on his arm. She knew he was thinking of her mother. 'I'm glad I did it,' she told him.

Jess scampered under Mercury's hoofs and ran round Jenny's legs. Matt laughed. 'I reckon Jess is glad too,' he said. 'I'll just go and give Mercury a rub down. I'll see you later at the sheepdog trials.'

Jenny's face lit up. Jake and Nell were both in the trials. Jake was completely recovered now and working better than ever.

'They're going to announce the Graston Hero Prize now,' Ian informed them. 'Come on, Jenny. As Graston Lass, you've got to pin the rosette on.'

Jenny looked suspiciously at Ian. His face was flushed with excitement, his green eyes sparkling.

'Why are you so interested in the hero prize?' she asked as he dragged her towards the podium in the middle of the square.

'Wait and see,' Ian replied mysteriously. 'Come on, Jess.'

Jess trotted obediently along after them. Jenny had to leave him with Ian while she took her place on the podium. The Graston Hero Prize was one of the highlights of the celebrations. It always went to someone who had done something really special.

Local vet Tom Palmer was the committee chairman. He stood up and cleared his throat, his big red face wreathed in smiles. He talked about past heroes, all of whom had done something for Graston. Then he cleared his throat again.

'This year's prize goes to a somewhat unusual hero,' he said, smiling. 'But I'm sure you'll all agree that this year's hero is very deserving. Will the Graston Hero and the person who nominated him please come up to the podium. Ladies and gentlemen, I give you the Graston Hero – Jess of Windy Hill.'

Jenny gasped in surprise as Ian led Jess up on to the podium. Almost dropping the rosette Mr Palmer handed to her, she turned to Ian.

'You nominated Jess?' she asked disbelievingly.

Ian grinned at her. 'There's nothing in the rules that says the hero can't be a dog.'

Jenny gaped at Ian as Tom Palmer read out the citation. 'For his work in saving so many lambs at Windy Hill . . . newspaper reports . . . Jess has made Graston quite famous . . . As a vet, I think it's terrific to have a doggy hero . . .'

Jenny only took in half of it. When it was time to pin on the rosette she bent down and Jess flew into her arms.

THE CHALLENGE

'Oh, Jess,' she murmured as she attached the ribbon to his collar. 'You're certainly *my* hero!'

'Just hold it there,' said a cheerful voice.

Jenny looked round. It was Gary Baker, the reporter from the local paper, here to cover the parade. He snapped a picture of Jenny and Jess, and grinned. 'I'm getting used to covering your dog's exploits,' he said.

Jess barked and licked Jenny's face as the crowd cheered once more.

Jenny stood back and smiled as Ian took Jess for a victory trot around the podium. She could see Matt at the front of the crowd, waving and cheering with the rest. Right at the back, a little separate from the others, were Fraser Miles and Ellen Grace. Jenny waved and they waved back.

Jenny was flooded with happiness. The lambing had been good and they wouldn't have to sell Windy Hill. Jake was fully recovered in spite of Calum McLay's dirty tricks and she and Ian were friends. She had been chosen as the Graston Lass and Jess was the Graston Hero. What a day for the Miles family!

Ian led Jess back to her and Jenny took the

puppy in her arms. Jenny saw Ian's eyes search the crowd until they found his aunt. Ian looked a little worried. Jenny remembered about the lease on Mrs Grace's cottage and frowned.

'What's wrong?' she asked.

Ian pursed his lips. 'Aunt Ellen has just told me she had a bit of bad news in the post this morning,' he replied.

'Was it a letter from Mr McLay?' Jenny asked anxiously.

Ian looked surprised. 'How did you know?' he said.

'Mrs Grace told me she was worried about her lease,' Jenny replied. 'What did the letter say?'

'Mr McLay isn't going to renew it,' Ian told her gloomily. 'Aunt Ellen is going to have to find somewhere else to live in a couple of months' time.'

'You mean she'll have to leave Graston?' Jenny asked.

Ian shrugged. 'Maybe,' he said.

Jenny turned to look once more towards the back of the crowd. She saw Ellen Grace turn and say something to Mr Miles. Her father replied, smiling down at Mrs Grace. Jenny smiled too. Maybe Mrs Grace wouldn't have to leave Graston after all. Jenny was beginning to get other ideas about that!

She bent her head to Jess and buried her face in his soft fur. 'We'll just have to see what we can do about sorting out *that* problem, won't we, Jess?' she said. 'After all, there's plenty of room at Windy Hill . . .'

THE
RUNAWAY

The Runaway

Special thanks to Helen Magee

Text copyright © 1998 Working Partners Ltd
Series created by Ben M. Baglio, London W6 0QT
Illustrations copyright © 1998 Trevor Parkin

First published as a single volume in Great Britain in 1998
by Hodder Children's Books

1

'Stay, Jess,' Jenny Miles commanded, trying to sound severe.

Jess, her black-and-white Border collie, looked up at her pleadingly, his head to one side. Six months old now, Jess looked just as appealing as he had done when he was a tiny puppy. He had four white socks and a white chest and muzzle. The rest of him was coal black.

'Don't look at me like that,' Jenny said firmly as she shut the farm gate. 'You know you can't come to school with me.'

Jess put his two front paws on the bottom bar of the gate and howled.

'Oh, Jess,' Jenny said, giving his ears a rub. 'I'll miss you too but it's not long till the summer holidays. Then we'll have *weeks* together. And Matt will be home for the summer too.' Matt was Jenny's brother. He was now nineteen and away at agricultural college.

'Don't you worry about Jess, Jenny,' Mrs Grace reassured her. Ellen Grace was the housekeeper at Windy Hill Farm. 'He'll be fine once you're out of sight,' she continued. 'He always is.'

Jenny looked into Ellen Grace's warm blue eyes and smiled gratefully. 'You aren't just saying that are you, Mrs Grace?' she asked anxiously. 'I hate leaving him behind.'

Mrs Grace smiled. 'Jess knows that,' she said reassuringly. 'He just keeps hoping one day you'll take him with you. Once you've gone he settles down.'

Jenny bent once more and stroked Jess's soft

coat. 'Be good,' she whispered. 'I'll be back this afternoon.'

'And Jess will be waiting for you as usual,' Ellen Grace said.

Jenny gave Jess a final pat then jumped on her bicycle and pedalled off, turning at the bend in the farm track to wave once more.

Jess gave a last howl before he was lost to sight. Jenny sighed as she pedalled down the track. She didn't think she would ever get used to leaving Jess behind, but Mrs Grace wouldn't lie to her. Ellen Grace had been housekeeper at Windy Hill for nearly five months now and she loved Jess almost as much as Jenny did.

Windy Hill, she thought, as the breeze blew strands of hair over her face. The Mileses' farm was certainly well named. If she turned her head she could see up towards Darktarn Keep. It stood on a hill above the farm, its rugged outline softened by the sunshine.

Jenny slewed her bike to a stop halfway along the track. Here, the track followed the boundary fence of the farm's top field. Her father, a tall man with dark hair, walked across the field towards her with Nell and Jake, his two Border collies, at his heels. Around him, the flock of Blackface sheep bleated and bumped one another, parting before him. The lambs scrambled after their mothers, their little black faces looking comical against the soft white wool of their coats.

Jenny waved. 'Hi, Dad!' she called. She looked beyond Fraser Miles to where two young men were rounding up sheep. Her father had hired extra help for the sheep dipping.

'Morning, lass,' her father called back. 'How's Jess today?'

Fraser Miles reached the fence and leaned on a post. Beside him, Nell and Jake crouched low, waiting obediently for his next command. Jenny leaned over the fence and gave each of them a pat. Nell and Jake were Jess's parents.

'Just the same,' Jenny said. 'I think he'd rather be out with you and the sheep than having to stay at home.'

Fraser Miles smiled. 'He was a good help with the lambing,' he agreed.

Jess had been wonderful during the lambing earlier in the year. Jenny had strapped bottles of milk to a harness for him and he had managed to feed lots of lambs. The poor little things might have died otherwise.

'But he is a house dog, Jenny,' her father continued.

Jenny nodded. 'I know – and I'd much rather have him as a pet,' she agreed. 'How's the dipping going?'

Fraser Miles looked up at the sky. 'Fine! The weather couldn't be better for it,' he said. 'Sunshine and a south wind.'

Jenny knew that sheep dipping was best carried out in fine weather when the fleeces got a chance to dry off afterwards. 'Will you get them all done in time?' she asked.

'If the weather holds for another few days,' her father replied. 'We start shearing next month.'

'Matt will be home to give you a hand by then,' Jenny said, smiling. She was looking forward to having her brother home for the holidays.

'I'll certainly need his help,' Fraser Miles replied. 'Shearing nearly a thousand sheep is a big job.'

'You'll manage, Dad,' Jenny said encouragingly. 'You always do.'

Mr Miles laughed and ruffled his daughter's hair. 'With that vote of confidence how can I fail?' he said. 'Have a good day at school, lass.'

Jenny pulled a face. 'OK, I'm going. I can take a hint,' she said. 'See you later, Dad.'

Mr Miles turned away and whistled to his dogs. Nell and Jake sprang up, alert to his commands. Jenny watched them racing along the edge of the flock, gathering together the ewes her father had selected for dipping. Mr Miles and his helpers would dip them in batches in the swimbath.

Jenny stood where she was for a few minutes, admiring the sheepdogs as they worked. Blackfaces were a skittish breed and it took a good dog to manage them. But Nell and Jake were doing fine. Jenny watched Jake. He seemed to have made a complete recovery. During lambing he'd become entangled with some barbed wire and very nearly bled to death. But now he was back out in the fields with Nell, as though it had never happened. They really *were* the best working dogs in the Borders.

Reluctantly, she turned away and pushed her bike off. She would much rather have stayed and watched – or, better still, helped!

Jenny pedalled on towards the road that led to the large village of Graston nearby. The wind whipped her honey-brown hair out behind her as she crested the hill that ran down to Graston School. She could see Graston village laid out below her. The village nestled in a valley, surrounded by farmland. The bell-tower of the little church rose above the roofs of the houses. The school was at the edge of the village and its pupils came not only from Graston itself, but also from the surrounding farms and the fishing village of Cliffbay, on the nearby coast. To the east of the village the sea sparkled in the summer sunshine.

Jenny freewheeled the last stretch of hill down to Graston and turned in at the school gates just as a bright orange Mini with a sunflower painted on the roof drew up.

'Hi, Jenny!' Carrie Turner, Jenny's best friend, leaped out of the passenger seat of the car almost before it had stopped.

Jenny waved. 'Hi, Carrie. Hi, Mrs Turner.'

Mrs Turner smiled at Jenny, tooted the car horn in reply and sped off, looking just as cheerful as the sunflower on the car roof. The Turners lived in Cliffbay, in a house right next to the sea. Mr Turner ran boat trips from the harbour there. Mrs Turner often dropped Carrie off at school, but Carrie could easily walk home: it was only a mile or so – and downhill all the way.

'Mum's in a hurry this morning,' Carrie explained. 'She's teaching a painting class in Greybridge and she's late already.'

Mrs Turner was an artist. She had painted a picture of Jess that had been used in a national fundraising campaign in aid of animal welfare. Jenny had a framed copy of the illustration on her bedroom wall.

'So what's new?' Jenny grinned at Carrie. 'Your mum's always running late. It must be the artistic temperament.'

Carrie grinned back. Like her mother, she had red hair and a dusting of freckles across her nose.

'How was Jess this morning?' Carrie asked, slinging her schoolbag carelessly over her shoulder.

'Watch out, Carrie!' said a boy coming in at the gate behind her.

'Oops, sorry, Ian,' Carrie apologised, whirling round, her schoolbag flying again. Jenny ducked and Ian Amery gave her a grin.

'You've been practising avoiding that schoolbag,' he said.

Jenny nodded. Ian was Mrs Grace's nephew. He was staying with his aunt while his parents set up home in Canada.

'Carrie's schoolbag is lethal,' Jenny replied, smiling.

Carrie turned up her nose. 'It's all the heavy books I have to carry,' she explained. 'Anyway, how is Jess?'

'Still howling,' Jenny sighed. 'He's been like this ever since I went back to school after the Easter holidays. He got so used to me being around that he can't understand why I keep going away now.'

'He probably misses working with the sheep too,' Ian said.

Jenny nodded. 'Poor Jess,' she sighed again. 'He looks so miserable when I leave him behind.'

Ian looked sympathetic but Carrie's attention was distracted. 'There's somebody else who looks miserable,' she said, pointing across the playground. 'I wonder what's wrong with Paul.'

Jenny looked over to where Carrie was pointing. A small boy was standing in the far corner by himself, feet scuffing the ground, head down.

'That isn't like Paul,' Carrie said, concerned. 'He's usually running around, playing.'

Paul McLay was seven years old and the son of the farmer who owned Dunraven, the farm next to Windy Hill. Calum McLay and Jenny's dad didn't get on with each other and Paul's older sister, Fiona, was always being spiteful. But Paul was quite different – much nicer than his father and sister.

'Maybe we'd better see if he's all right,' said Carrie.

'You go, Jenny,' Ian suggested. 'Paul likes you and you're really tactful – usually!'

Jenny flushed. She and Ian had had a blazing row the first time they had met. They were still just a little wary of each other.

'Ian's right,' said Carrie. 'You go and talk to Paul.'

Jenny made her way across to the little boy. She made sure that he could see her before she started speaking. Paul had been deaf since he was four when he'd suffered a viral infection which had affected his hearing. But he could now lip-read very well indeed, if you spoke directly to him. 'Hi, Paul! Is anything the matter?' Jenny asked, as she approached him.

Paul's wide grey eyes looked sadly up at her, and he nodded. He really did seem miserable.

'What is it?' Jenny asked.

Paul's lip trembled and he drew a hand across his eyes. 'Mum and Dad want me to go into hospital,' he said, his voice unsteady. 'I'm supposed to have an operation on my ears.'

Jenny frowned. 'What's the operation for?' she asked. Then her face brightened. 'Will it bring your hearing back?'

Paul shrugged. 'It *might*,' he replied. 'But I don't want to go. I'm scared,' he confessed.

'Have you told your mum and dad you're scared?' Jenny asked.

Paul nodded. 'I told Mum,' he replied. 'The

last time I was in hospital, it hurt.'

Jenny looked at him sympathetically. 'Ears *are* painful when they get infected,' she agreed. 'But maybe it won't hurt so much this time.'

Paul stared down at his feet, his hair hanging over his eyes. 'It will,' he murmured.

Jenny touched his arm and he looked at her. She drew in her breath at the sadness in his eyes. It reminded her of Jess when she left him each morning to go to school.

'Jess had to have an operation to fix his leg,' she told Paul. 'It wasn't very easy for him but he can run around much better now. He was really brave about it.' Jess had been born with a twisted leg and had needed to spend weeks in a cast to set it straight.

'I'm not brave,' Paul said, his eyes filling with tears.

Jenny took a deep breath. 'It's all right to be frightened, Paul,' she said. 'I was scared when Jess had his operation. Being frightened doesn't mean you aren't brave.'

Paul still didn't say anything, but Jenny could tell he was thinking hard about what she was saying. She went on speaking. 'Sometimes, when I'm feeling sad or upset, I go to Darktarn Keep. That's my favourite place. My mum used to take me there a lot when I was your age. She told me all sorts of stories about the Border reivers who used to live around Graston.'

'Your mum died, didn't she?' Paul asked.

Jenny felt a sharp pang. A whole year had passed since her mother's death, but it still wasn't easy to talk about it. 'Yes,' she said softly. 'She died in a riding accident last summer.'

'Is that why you get sad and go to the keep?' Paul asked.

Jenny nodded. 'And when I get upset about anything else it really helps to go to my favourite place. Do *you* have a favourite place?'

Paul shook his head. He looked so downcast, Jenny's heart went out to him. She had an idea. 'Would you like to come to Windy Hill and visit Jess?' she suggested. 'Then you could see how well he's done since having his operation.'

Paul's face lit up. 'I'd like that,' he said. Then his face fell. 'But Dad won't let me come to Windy Hill. He doesn't like your dad.'

Jenny sighed. Paul was right. Mr McLay didn't like Fraser Miles. He wouldn't let Paul come to Windy Hill. Many years earlier, before Jenny's parents had married, Jenny's mother, Sheena, was to marry Calum McLay. But at the last moment, Sheena had changed her mind and married Fraser Miles instead. Calum had been furious at losing both Sheena and her farm, Windy Hill, to Fraser. He had wanted revenge on Fraser ever since, by trying to take Windy Hill Farm away from him.

'Maybe we could meet at the keep,' Jenny suggested to Paul. 'You know where it is, don't you? It's near the little lake above our farm.'

Paul nodded. 'Ian took me bird-watching at that lake once,' he said. 'Only he called it a tarn.'

'Lakes like that are called tarns in the Borders,' Jenny smiled. 'Ian was quite right. I could bring Jess there. That would be OK, wouldn't it?'

Paul looked eagerly at her, his face brightening. 'When?' he asked.

'Saturday afternoon,' Jenny said decisively. 'Two o'clock. Will that be all right?'

Paul nodded. 'I'll bring my new binoculars,' he said. 'I can look at the birds on the tarn.'

Paul was a very keen bird-watcher and the lake below the keep was a great place for divers and ducks.

Jenny smiled in relief. Paul's face had lost almost all of its sadness now. 'It's a date, Paul,' she said.

'Saturday,' Paul repeated, smiling up at her. 'And don't forget Jess.'

Jenny smiled. 'I could *never* forget Jess,' she said.

2

Jenny shivered slightly as she and Jess waited for Paul the following Saturday. The weather had been good all week but now it looked as if it had taken a turn for the worse. Dark clouds were beginning to mass out to sea. Jess barked, drawing her attention to Paul as the little boy appeared, walking towards Darktarn Keep. Jenny waved at Paul from her perch on one of the broken walls of the keep.

Paul waved back and Jenny bent to Jess. 'Go and show him the way, Jess,' she whispered in the collie's ear. 'Go and get Paul!'

Jess gave a short bark and raced off down the slope of the hill towards Paul. Jenny watched as her dog wended his way round the fallen rock and long grass at the base of the keep. He scampered towards the drystone wall that bordered the field beyond, scrambled over it and darted under the weathered trunk of a fallen tree, making straight for Paul.

Jenny's eyes rested on the fallen tree for a moment. That was where Sheena Miles, Jenny's mother, had been killed last year. Her father had told her how her mother had been out riding when a sudden storm blew up. Lightning had struck the tree, forcing her mother to pull Mercury up in order to avoid it. Then her mother had been thrown from the horse and had died. Jenny gazed at the tree, feeling a swift pang of grief at the thought of her mother's death.

She lifted her head as a sudden wind blew up, letting it stream through her hair. Her mother had always loved this place. Darktarn

Keep stood on top of a rise above Windy Hill. It was a ruin now, its broken tower jutting upwards, dark against the sky, but the view was magnificent.

From here, Jenny could look out over her father's fields stretching right down to the cliffs that bordered the sea. She could see Puffin Island, a bird sanctuary, gleaming in the sun as the heavy clouds parted for a moment. Gulls wheeled round its low, rocky headland.

Jenny turned as she heard Paul cry out delightedly. Jess had reached the little boy and was running round him, barking a welcome. She smiled. Jess's twisted leg was almost straight now and most people would never guess there had ever been anything wrong with it.

Paul bent to the collie and ruffled the young dog's ears in greeting while Jess leaped up, almost knocking Paul over in his eagerness to welcome him. Jenny heard Paul laugh as the collie ran a few paces forward and looked back. Jess never barked at Paul, seeming to know that Paul couldn't hear him.

'OK, I'm coming,' Paul called to Jess.

Then boy and dog made their way up

through the fallen rocks to the place where Jenny was sitting.

'Wow!' said Paul as they arrived. 'I've never been up here before. This is great.'

'It used to be a stronghold for the Border reivers,' Jenny explained, turning to Paul as he plonked himself down beside her.

'What are reivers?' Paul asked.

'Robbers,' Jenny told him. 'I used to come up here with Mum when I was little. She told me loads of stories about the reivers – how they used to steal each other's sheep in the olden days.'

'That must have been really exciting,' Paul said, his hand on Jess's neck.

Jess lay contentedly between them, his pink tongue hanging out. Jenny nodded. 'Dangerous too, I should think,' she agreed. 'I love it up here. Look, you can see Puffin Island.'

Paul undid the case of his binoculars and raised them to his eyes. 'Wow!' he said. 'I can see kittiwakes nesting on the cliffs out there.'

'Those must be really good binoculars,' Jenny laughed.

'They are,' agreed Paul. 'Mum gave them to

me because I was upset about going into hospital.'

'Are you still worried?' she asked.

Paul sighed heavily. 'I don't want to go,' he replied. He looked away from her, fiddling with the strap on his binoculars. 'The doctor puts you to sleep,' he said.

Jenny touched his arm and he turned back to her. 'That's so that the operation doesn't hurt,' she told him. 'You go to sleep, then when you wake up it's all over.'

Paul swallowed and his lower lip trembled.

'What is it, Paul?' Jenny asked. 'What are you *really* worried about?'

Paul gulped. 'What if I don't wake up?' he asked in a small voice.

Jenny gasped. 'But of course you will,' she said.

'Fiona says sometimes people *don't* wake up,' he said. 'They just sleep and sleep for ever!'

Jenny looked at him, shocked. Fiona was Paul's elder sister. 'Has Fiona been scaring you?' she asked, hardly able to believe it.

Paul hung his head but didn't answer. Jenny felt anger rising in her. How dare Fiona scare her own little brother like this!

Paul stretched out a hand to Jess. The puppy came and laid his head in Paul's lap. Paul buried his fingers in Jess's soft fur.

Jenny looked at Paul with concern. The little boy was clearly struggling against tears. 'I don't think you should listen to Fiona,' she told him. 'Why don't you talk to your mum and dad about it? If you really don't want to go to hospital they wouldn't make you.'

'Dad wants me to go,' Paul confided. He swallowed hard. 'I don't think Dad likes me being deaf,' he said softly.

Jenny sighed. This was very difficult. 'I'm sure he'd rather you were able to hear – for *your* sake,' she said, looking into Paul's troubled eyes. 'But that doesn't mean he or your mum would want you to be unhappy – or that they love you any less for being deaf.'

Just then, Jess raised his head, ears back, eyes alert.

'What is it, Jess?' Jenny said, laying a hand on the dog's neck.'

Jess scrambled to his feet and barked, his tail wagging.

'Ooh!' Paul exclaimed as Jess's plumy tail brushed his cheek. 'That tickles, Jess.'

Jenny smiled. Jess seemed to have taken Paul's mind off his worries – at least for a little while.

Jess strained forward and Jenny looked out across the fields. Down below them, beyond the tarn, was a horse and rider.

Paul raised his binoculars to his eyes. 'It's Ian,' he cried.

'That must be Mercury he's riding,' Jenny explained. 'Ian exercises him for Matt while he's at college.' Matt was home for the weekend but Fraser Miles had needed him to help on the farm.

'What a wonderful horse,' Paul breathed, as they watched the gleaming black creature canter across the fields towards them.

Jenny smiled. 'Ian and Matt have done wonders with him,' she said.

Mercury had belonged to Sheena Miles. Fraser Miles had sold the horse immediately after the accident that had killed his wife. But Matt had found Mercury a few months later at the livestock market in Greybridge, a local town. The horse had been in a very sorry state.

He had been ill-treated and was extremely nervous.

At first Jenny had feared and hated Mercury, blaming the horse for her mother's death. But later, her father had explained that the accident had not been the horse's fault, and gradually Jenny had come to love Mercury.

Jess barked again and looked pleadingly at Jenny.

'All right,' Jenny said to him. 'Go on! Go and say hello to Mercury.'

Quick as the wind, Jess was off, streaking downhill towards the horse and rider.

'Jess and Mercury are great friends,' Jenny explained to Paul. 'When Mercury first came back to Windy Hill he was very nervous but Jess really helped to calm him down.'

Paul's eyes turned back to the Border collie as he scampered down the hill past fallen rocks, skirting the tarn and scaring ducks into the air.

'Wow! A diver!' Paul cried, training his binoculars on the flight of birds Jess had alarmed.

Jenny looked at Paul. He seemed much

happier now. Maybe he would forget his fears, she thought, as she raised her head to watch the birds wheeling against the sky. She frowned as she felt a large drop of rain on her upturned face. More followed, quickly spattering her cheeks and hair.

Well-prepared, she and Paul pulled on their hoods and zipped up their waterproof jackets. The clouds were huge now, low and threatening. As Jenny wiped the rain from her cheeks, a flash of lightning lit up the sky and she heard the first rumble of thunder. It sounded very near. Another flash followed and the thunder rolled even nearer. The heavens opened and the rain began to fall more heavily.

Jenny was about to beckon Paul up to shelter in the keep, when he grabbed her arm.

'Look!' he cried.

She turned at the alarm in the little boy's voice. 'What is it?' she asked, anxiously. Then she saw where he was pointing. As yet another streak of lightning flashed across the sky, Mercury reared up on his two hind legs in terror. Thunder rolled, seeming to rebound off the walls of the keep. Jenny's heart thundered

too for this had happened once before.

Mercury's forelegs came crashing down again and he began to gallop furiously. Jenny could see Ian hanging on grimly, straining at the reins, trying to hold the big horse. She caught her breath in horror as she watched Mercury race, out of control, across the turf below them. It seemed that Mercury, too, was remembering that terrible storm of the previous year.

'He's bolted!' Paul cried. 'Mercury is running away!'

Jenny grabbed the binoculars and focused them on Ian, trying desperately to see through the pouring rain. Ian's face was set and white; his hands gripped the reins.

The lightning flashed and flashed again. Jenny could feel the force of the thunder when it came. Mercury tossed his head and reared again in blind panic.

Then Jenny was running down the hill. Behind her, Paul called out in alarm.

'We've got to stop them,' Jenny called back, for once forgetting to face Paul as she spoke to him. 'The storm has frightened Mercury. He's running blind. Ian is going to be killed if we can't do something!'

Jenny ran on, her heart thumping, the breath ragged in her throat, the rain washing over her. Down the hill she pounded, leaping over fallen rocks, heedless of rabbit-holes that might trip her up. At the bottom she plunged forward, racing round the tarn, praying she could do something, *anything*, to stop Mercury before Ian was pitched off his back. For this was how Jenny's mother had been killed.

3

The breath rasped in Jenny's throat as she raced towards the horse and rider. Jess was already scrabbling over the rough drystone wall below the keep. Jenny saw Ian try again to rein in the big horse, twisting his body, gripping desperately with his legs to find control over the animal. Mercury reared and Jenny's breath stopped altogether as she saw Ian clinging to the reins and saddle. Then Jess reached the top of the wall and leaped for the ground beyond.

'No, Jess!' Jenny cried. But the little dog was over and running for the horse. Jenny reached the wall herself and clung to the rough stones, panting, as Paul came up behind her.

The little boy threw himself at the wall, heaving himself up on to it.

Jenny reached out an arm and grabbed him, turning him towards her. 'If you go running over there you'll frighten Mercury even more,' she said, breathlessly. 'That isn't the way to save Jess – or Ian.'

Paul looked at her. 'But what are we going to do?' he asked.

Jenny shook the rain from her eyes. 'I'm going to go over – very quietly. Stay here, Paul – please.'

Paul nodded again. 'Be careful,' he whispered.

Jenny laid a hand on the wall and pulled herself up, slipping on the wet stones. Jess had almost reached Mercury now. She kept her eyes on him as she dropped carefully over the wall and began to walk towards the terrified horse.

Ian had somehow managed to bring Mercury out of his headlong gallop but the horse's eyes were rolling and he reared again as another streak of lightning split the sky.

Ian turned and caught sight of her. Then all his attention was on the reins again as he brought Mercury down, leaning well into the saddle. Jenny could see his lips moving. He was talking to the horse, trying to calm him.

Jenny saw Jess stop within a metre of Mercury. The young dog laid back his ears and crouched low to the ground, crawling forward until he was almost under Mercury's dancing hoofs. Jenny forced herself not to call out but she couldn't help increasing her pace a little.

Then she stopped in her tracks as she realised what Jess was doing. The Border collie was working true to his instinct. Moving slowly, close to the ground, he made his way towards Mercury.

Mercury whinnied and for a moment his hoofs stopped dancing, then he threw his head up and neighed. Jess barked once, then crawled forward, lying right in front of the horse's forefeet. Jenny held her breath. If Mercury reared now he would come down on top of the collie. Jess wouldn't stand a chance.

She glanced quickly at Ian. His hair was

plastered to his head with the rain but his green eyes were intent. focused on Jess. He leaned forward, daring to take one hand off the reins, and laid a hand on Mercury's neck.

The big horse bent his head towards the little dog and Jess reached up, nuzzling Mercury's nose. Jenny watched, hardly breathing, as the two animals seemed to communicate with each other. Then Mercury took a step back and gradually his body seemed to relax.

Lightning tore through the sky again, but more distant now. Mercury flinched, but didn't rear up. Thunder rolled, but Mercury remained calm. Then the rain eased, and stopped as suddenly as it had begun.

Jenny looked at Ian and saw him relax too. He slid gently from Mercury's back on to the ground and staggered a little.

Jenny went to him as he leaned against Mercury's flank, resting his hand on the horse's neck. Mercury blew gently through his lips and shook his head slowly from side to side.

'Are you all right?' Jenny asked Ian anxiously.

Ian nodded. He was still pale and shaken. 'My legs feel like jelly,' he confessed. 'Can you hold

Mercury's head while I sit down for a minute?'

Jenny took the reins and stroked Mercury's neck, murmuring to him, but the horse was calm now – thanks to Jess.

Ian flopped down on the wet grass and lay there, looking up at her. 'Phew!' he said. 'What happened?'

Jenny didn't answer his question. She frowned. 'Have you ridden Mercury up here before?' she asked.

Ian nodded. 'Any number of times,' he replied. 'He's never bolted before. I can't understand it.'

'It must have been the storm,' Jenny explained. She bit her lip, her eyes shadowed. 'Do you remember Dad explaining how my mother got killed here last summer?' she asked Ian. 'Mum was riding Mercury towards the keep to take shelter from a sudden storm. They were just about to jump the wall below the keep when a bolt of lightning brought a tree down right in front of them. Mercury must have been terrified when the storm blew up today. I was scared it was all going to happen again.'

Ian's mouth dropped open. 'Oh, Jenny, you must feel awful,' he said. 'I'm sorry I gave you such a fright but I just couldn't control him.'

'It wasn't your fault,' Jenny assured him. 'But I think we should get Mercury home and talk to Dad and Matt about this.'

Ian looked at her seriously. 'You always said Mercury was dangerous,' he said.

Jenny nodded. 'I know,' she confessed. 'I blamed him for killing Mum. But it wasn't his fault. Not last time and not this time either. It must have been awful for him when the lightning began.'

'But if he's going to bolt every time there's a storm then he *is* dangerous,' Ian said, his face troubled.

'Jess managed to calm him,' Jenny replied thoughtfully. 'Maybe he just needs time to forget how frightened he was last time.'

'What's your dad going to say?' Ian asked, shoving his hair out of his eyes. 'Do you think he'll give Mercury more time? Or do you think he'll get rid of him?'

Jenny looked at Jess and Mercury. 'I don't know,' she replied. 'But Jess would miss Mercury so much – and so would Matt. And I'd miss him too, now.'

There had been a time, only weeks ago, when Jenny would gladly have got rid of Mercury. Now she felt quite differently about the big horse. She had seen for herself how gentle and affectionate he could be when she had ridden him in the Graston Parade at the end of the lambing season.

'Can I come over now?' called a small voice.

Jenny turned. 'Oh, Paul,' she answered apologetically. 'I'm sorry. Of course you can. Everything is all right now.'

Paul scrambled over the wall and came to stand beside them. 'Jess was really brave, wasn't he?' he said, bending down and giving Jess a pat.

Jenny nodded. Then a thought struck her. 'So were you, Paul,' she said.

The little boy looked up, surprised. 'Me?' he said.

'Yes, you!' replied Jenny. 'You were all set to climb over the wall to save Jess. I'll tell you something, Paul: whatever anybody says, you're a very brave boy.'

Paul looked up at her, his face breaking into a smile. 'Brave,' he repeated. 'Just like Jess.'

4

Jenny and Ian found Mr Miles in the farmyard, unloading supplies of insecticide from the jeep for the sheep dipping. The sheep Nell and Jake had gathered were already waiting in the holding pen before being dipped in the swimbath.

Fraser Miles turned to wave to them. 'I was getting a little worried about you, being out in that storm—' He stopped as he saw the expressions on their faces. 'What's happened?' he asked, as Jenny and Ian led Mercury into the farmyard.

Jess scampered over to Jake and Nell, wagging his tail. The two dogs lay still, allowing the puppy to nuzzle them.

'Mercury bolted,' Ian explained, unsaddling the horse. 'I was riding him up towards Darktarn Keep as the storm blew up, and he panicked.'

'Are you hurt?' Fraser asked urgently.

Jess looked up and barked at the sharp tone of Mr Miles's voice. Jenny laid a hand on his neck. 'It's all right, Jess,' she whispered.

'We're OK, Mr Miles,' Ian said quickly.

Jenny looked at her father. Fraser Miles's blue eyes looked worried.

'Nobody got hurt, Dad,' she reassured him. 'Little Paul McLay was up there too but we sent him home. We didn't think it would be a good idea to bring him back to Windy Hill.'

'His father certainly wouldn't like that,' Fraser agreed. 'Now, tell me exactly what happened.'

Jenny took a deep breath and began to explain. 'It was the storm that scared Mercury, I'm sure of that,' she finished, as Ian rubbed the big horse down. 'And if it hadn't been for Jess I don't know if we'd have got him calmed down.'

Fraser smiled. 'Jess has always been able to calm Mercury,' he said. 'You often find that with nervous horses. Being around a smaller animal seems to reassure them. Sometimes it's a cat or even a goat.' Then Fraser Miles looked serious. 'But if Mercury is going to bolt like that then we'll have to think again about keeping him. I'm not prepared to keep a dangerous animal,' he told Jenny firmly. 'I'll talk to Matt about it.'

'But it was the storm,' Jenny protested weakly. 'It came so suddenly – Mercury was frightened.' But she knew her father was right. She had been terrified herself that Ian would be thrown, as her mother had been.

Her father's eyes darkened. 'And what if there's another sudden storm when Ian or Matt is out on Mercury? They might get thrown next time – and we know what can happen then, don't we?' He put a hand on Jenny's shoulder. 'Look lass, we know Mercury didn't mean to harm your mother. And he didn't mean any harm to Ian today. But this panicking in storms – you must see I can't run any more risks like that.'

Jenny looked at her father in dismay. Poor Matt. He would be devastated. And poor Mercury.

'But if he really *is* dangerous, you couldn't sell him, could you?' asked Ian.

Jenny's heart lurched. She hadn't thought of that. If they couldn't sell Mercury, then he might have to be put down! She couldn't bear to think about it.

'Someone might be willing to take him and try to school the fear out of him,' Fraser replied. 'If not, then we'll have to send him to an animal sanctuary on the understanding that nobody can ride him.'

Jenny breathed a sigh of relief. At least the very worst wasn't going to happen.

Mr Miles whistled to his two dogs. Nell and Jake came to heel at once and followed Fraser out of the farm gate.

'I've got to get these sheep dipped,' Mr Miles said as he closed the gate. 'Don't take Mercury out again unless you have my permission, Ian. Matt's inside. Tell him he isn't to take him out

either. I've got to think this through.'

Jenny and Ian looked at each other in dismay.

'Oh dear! What's Matt going to say?' Jenny asked. 'He loves Mercury.'

'We'd better go and tell him,' Ian said glumly. 'It's all my fault. If I'd been a better rider this would never have happened.'

'No, Ian,' Jenny replied. 'It was the storm, not your riding that caused Mercury to panic. You did well to stay on him while he was bolting.' She sighed. 'I'm afraid Dad is right. Mercury's fear of storms does make him dangerous to have around.'

'Come on,' Ian said. 'Let's get Mercury stabled and find Matt.'

Matt was in the kitchen with Ellen Grace. There was a delicious smell coming from the oven as Mrs Grace bent to take out a baking tray.

'That smells great!' said Matt.

'Ah, I might have known you two would appear just as these were ready,' Mrs Grace said, smiling, as she saw Jenny and Ian. Then her face changed. 'You look as if you've lost a pound and found a penny. What's wrong?'

Jenny and Ian told their story again.

Matt listened intently, his blue eyes concerned. 'I've never had Mercury out in a storm.
It must have reminded him so much of what
happened last time. Horses can be amazing
sometimes, the way they remember things.'

'The place wouldn't seem the same without
Mercury, now,' Mrs Grace said sympathetically,
as she placed a pot of tea and a plate of hot
scones on the kitchen table.

'A lot of things look like changing, Ellen,'
Matt replied, taking a scone. 'What are we
going to do if *you* leave us?'

Jenny drew in her breath. In her concern
about Mercury, she had forgotten her worry
about Mrs Grace. The lease on the cottage she
rented was nearly at an end, and her landlord,
Calum McLay, had refused to renew it. It
seemed this was because Ellen Grace now
worked for Fraser Miles, whom Calum disliked.
'How long have you got now, Mrs Grace?' she
asked.

'There's another month before my lease runs
out,' the housekeeper told her, sighing. 'I've
been looking around but there isn't another

cottage to let in the area. It looks as if I'm going to have to move quite far away.'

Ian's mouth set stubbornly. 'There must be something we can do about Calum McLay,' he said. 'He's nothing but a troublemaker. He shouldn't be able to force you out of your home.'

'He *can* force me out because he owns the cottage,' Ellen Grace said quietly. 'There isn't a thing we can do.'

Jenny opened her mouth to make a suggestion. She'd had an idea growing in her mind for some time now. Why couldn't Mrs Grace move into Windy Hill? There was plenty of room for her and Ian. But Jenny knew she needed to speak to her father about it first. She would ask him just as soon as she could.

'I reckon Fiona takes after her dad rather than her mum,' she said instead. 'She's being really rotten to Paul. She's scaring him stiff with horror stories about going into hospital.'

'That's awful,' Ellen Grace said. 'Can't you speak to her – tell her to stop?'

Jenny shrugged. 'I can try,' she said. 'But Fiona never listens to anybody – especially me.'

'If she's anything like her father there's no point in *anyone* talking to her,' Matt said, getting up from the table. 'I'm just going to have a look at Mercury, then I've got to get back to college. I've got loads of reading to do for Monday and if I stay here, I know I won't get it done,' he said, smiling.

Jenny watched him go. He didn't look like his usual self at all. His feet dragged as he made his way to the door. 'Dad says he wants to talk to you before he does anything about Mercury,' she offered as he opened the door.

Matt turned and smiled slightly. 'At least that means Mercury will still be here when I come home next weekend,' he said. 'That's something, I suppose.'

Jenny sighed. Matt had put so much work into restoring Mercury to health. He must feel it was all for nothing.

She looked around the table. Ian was staring into his cup, the scone on his plate untouched. Mrs Grace was looking out of the window. She looked so sad. Jenny thought of Paul and his worries about going into hospital. She sighed again. Mercury, Mrs Grace's lease – and Paul.

Right now the world seemed full of problems.

She sat up. She could almost *hear* Carrie's voice saying, '*That's no way to think!* Do *something!*'

Well, she *would* do something. She would speak to her father about Mrs Grace coming to live at Windy Hill and she would try and talk to Fiona. But what about Mercury? There didn't seem any hope of a solution to *that* problem.

5

Jenny tried to speak to Fiona about Paul at school on Monday but Fiona wasn't in the mood to listen – not that she ever *was* in the mood to listen to Jenny.

'Why don't you mind your own business?' Fiona sneered.

'But Paul is only seven,' protested Jenny. 'You're scaring him with all your stories.' She shoved her hair out of her eyes. Jenny's hair always reflected her moods. Right now it was nearly standing on end, she was so angry.

'Little Miss Busybody,' Fiona said nastily. 'And just look at your hair. Haven't you ever *heard* of a hairbrush?' Fiona flicked her sleek short hair into place and flounced off, leaving Jenny fuming. Fiona was always making rude comments about Jenny's appearance – saying she couldn't afford new trainers or decent clothes.

'Don't take any notice of her,' Carrie advised, coming to stand beside Jenny.

'I don't care what she says about me,' Jenny replied. 'But why is she being so cruel to Paul? He's her brother. It's just so frustrating!'

'If you ask me, I reckon she's jealous of Paul,' Carrie replied thoughtfully.

Jenny looked at her friend in astonishment. Carrie's usually cheerful face was serious for once. 'But why?' she asked.

'Maybe Fiona thinks Paul gets too much attention at home,' Carrie went on. 'I heard her telling him he was a mummy's boy just the other day.'

'But that's ridiculous,' Jenny retorted. 'He's only little and he isn't spoiled. How can she be jealous of him? He's the one that's deaf. I just don't understand her.'

Carrie shook her head. 'Of course you don't understand her,' she agreed. 'I can't imagine you being jealous of anybody. But you've got to look at it from Fiona's point of view. Maybe she feels left out at home. Perhaps it seems that Paul is getting all the attention because of his deafness.'

Jenny opened her mouth to protest but closed it again. Maybe Carrie had a point. 'You might be right, Carrie,' she admitted. 'But I don't think I'll ever understand Fiona.'

'Well, thank goodness for that,' Carrie replied, grinning. 'I reckon you're far to nice to understand a creep like Fiona.'

Jenny couldn't help smiling. But a doubt nagged at the back of her mind. If what Carrie said was true then maybe Fiona wasn't such a creep after all; maybe she was just insecure. But that still didn't justify what she was doing to Paul.

'I'd like to ask Paul over to Windy Hill to play with Jess,' she confided to Carrie. 'He really likes Jess and it cheers him up such a lot, but his father would never let him visit us.'

Carrie looked thoughtful. 'It doesn't have to be Windy Hill,' she said at last. 'I could ask Paul to Cliff House – after all, you often come to see me, and you know how much Jess likes his runs on Cliffbay beach. If Paul just happened to be there at the same time . . .'

'Carrie, you're brilliant!' Jenny exclaimed.

'Oh, I know *that*,' Carrie agreed. 'But how about talented, beautiful, charming – let's see, what else?'

Jenny grinned. 'Anything you like,' she said. 'Let's go and find Paul.'

On Friday afternoon, Mrs Turner pulled up outside school in her orange Mini to pick up Carrie, Jenny and Paul. She had Jess with her. She'd collected him from Windy Hill on her way. Jenny grinned as she saw her pet's black-and-white face gazing out of the car window. The young collie gave them a joyful welcome as they climbed into the car.

'Ow!' Jenny protested as Jess hurled himself at her. 'You're getting heavy, Jess.' But Jess took no notice, licking her face ecstatically.

'I think he's gorgeous!' Paul announced, and Jess promptly launched himself at the little boy.

By the time they got to Cliffbay, Jess had calmed down and was lying comfortably across Jenny's lap, his head on Paul's knees. Jenny glanced at Paul and smiled. The little boy was stroking Jess's ears contentedly. What a pity he didn't have a pet of his own.

'Mum says she'll send Fiona to collect me later,' Paul said as Mrs Turner pulled up in front of Cliff House.

'I rang your mum,' Mrs Turner told him. 'She said that Fiona will come in time to take you home for tea – but that doesn't mean you can't have a quick snack. How would you like that?'

'I'd love it,' Paul said, as Jess scrambled out of the car, his tail wagging. 'And I'm going to love playing with Jess too.'

Jenny looked out to sea as they made their way down to the beach from Cliff House after tucking into apple juice and raisin biscuits. It was calm now but Jenny knew how quickly that could change. The storm at the keep had been the first of several. Luckily Mr Miles had managed to get the flock dipped between storms. Now his major worry was the effect of the weather on the lambs. They were still only a couple of months old and very dependent on their mothers for food and warmth. Mr Miles had had to take quite a few of the ewes and their lambs into the shearing shed for protection during the bad spell.

Jenny had enjoyed having the little black-faced lambs around the farm, but she knew they were better off out on the hills where they could learn to graze by watching their mothers. They would be weaned in another two months' time and they needed to learn to survive on their own.

'Dad put the lambs back out in the fields this morning now that the weather has improved,' she said to Carrie, as they watched Paul throwing a stick for Jess.

Carrie plonked herself down on the sand and looked up at her friend. 'Thank goodness those storms are over,' she said. 'My dad hasn't been able to take the boat out all week, it's been so bad. A lot of the fishing boats have been tied up at Cliffbay too.'

Jenny looked up at the sky. It was swept clean by rain and wind and the sun was shining. She sat down beside Carrie, enjoying the sunshine.

'Fetch, Jess!' Paul yelled, throwing the stick into the sea.

Jess bounded off, plunging into the water, swimming strongly. In no time at all he was back, ready to fetch again. Paul bent and fussed over him then he threw the stick once more.

'He'll never let you stop, Paul,' Jenny called when the little boy turned to grin at them.

Paul's grin widened. 'I could do this all day,' he replied. 'I'd never get tired of it.'

Jess ran up the beach, the stick in his mouth, and shook himself all over Paul but the little boy only laughed and made even more fuss of the young collie.

Jenny and Carrie lolled on the shore, watching Paul and Jess scamper around. Jenny was happy just to watch. Paul and Jess were having a marvellous time and, as she told Carrie, she could play with Jess any time she wanted. For Paul, this was really special.

Paul was soon wet through but the sun would dry him off. Jess came racing up the beach, stopped and shook himself, spraying Paul all over again.

'Good boy,' Paul said, bending down to pat the collie. Jess's tail wagged harder than ever as Paul held the stick up.

Jenny waved to catch the little boy's attention. 'Throw it further out, Paul,' she said, miming the action. 'Jess likes to swim.'

Paul nodded and threw the stick as far as he could.

Carrie screwed her eyes up against the sun, watching Paul and Jess.

'Those two get on really well,' she said.

Jenny nodded. 'Jess is wonderful with Paul,' she replied. 'It's amazing to watch. He never barks to get Paul's attention. He always puts himself where Paul can see him. It's as if he knows that Paul can't hear him.'

Carrie watched as Jess came scampering back up the beach. Paul had turned away to look at a fishing boat just setting out from the harbour at Cliffbay but, instead of barking, Jess ran across the beach until he was in Paul's direct line of vision.

'I see what you mean,' Carrie said admiringly.

'That's clever of Jess.'

'They're working out a kind of communication between them,' Jenny told her. 'It's quite different from the way Jess behaves with me.'

'Wow!' said Carrie. 'It's impressive.'

'I was wondering if it would be good for Paul to have a pet of his own,' Jenny said thoughtfully.

Carrie considered for a moment. 'I think that's a great idea,' she agreed. 'Do you think he would be allowed to have a puppy?'

Jenny shrugged. 'I don't know,' she replied. 'I don't want to suggest it to him in case he ends up disappointed. I wondered about mentioning it to Fiona, but she wouldn't listen to me.'

'Can you imagine suggesting *anything* to Fiona? Or Mr McLay, for that matter?' Carrie asked gloomily. 'They're both impossible.'

'That's what I thought,' Jenny replied. 'But what about *Mrs* McLay? I've only met her a couple of times but she seems really nice.'

'Yes, my mum seems to like her, too,' Carrie agreed. 'Have you got a puppy in mind?'

Jenny shook her head. 'I thought I would ask Mr Palmer,' she replied. 'If there just happened to be a puppy looking for a home, maybe Mrs McLay would agree.' Tom Palmer was the vet in Graston. He had treated Jess's bad leg and, since then, Jenny and the vet had become good friends.

Carrie smiled at Jenny. 'Good idea, Jen. It can't do any harm – so long as you don't get Paul's hopes up before we know whether or not he'd be allowed a puppy.'

'Maybe if he had a puppy to look forward to he'd be happier about going into hospital,' Jenny mused. 'He'd be a marvellous pet owner.'

There was a sound behind them and Jenny looked up. Fiona McLay stood over her, block-ing the sun. Jenny scrambled to a half-sitting position. 'Hi, Fiona,' she said pleasantly.

'I've come to collect Paul,' the other girl said shortly. 'Were you talking about him just now?'

'You mean about the puppy?' Jenny said. 'It was just an idea. He and Jess get on so well together.'

'I've told you before, Jenny Miles,' Fiona snapped. 'Mind your own business. Paul can't have a puppy. He can't even hear.'

'What difference does that make?' Carrie

protested. 'Deaf people have hearing dogs. The dogs help them – just like guide dogs for the blind.'

'Keep out of it, Carrie,' Fiona retorted. She turned once again to Jenny. 'If Dad knew Paul was down here with you he'd be furious,' she said. 'He wouldn't want any of your daft ideas about dogs either.'

'A puppy,' said a small voice. 'For me?'

Jenny looked round, horrified. Paul had come up behind her. He had obviously read his sister's lips. 'It was only an idea, Paul,' she said.

Paul's eyes were shining. 'I'd *love* a puppy like Jess,' he said.

'Well you can't have one,' Fiona snapped. 'Mum's got enough to do looking after you without a puppy as well.'

Paul's face fell and Jenny's heart went out to him as she saw his disappointment.

Fiona didn't seem to notice. She put her hands on her hips and looked sternly down at Paul. 'It's time to go home,' she said. 'If Dad hears you've been playing with Jenny Miles you'll be in trouble.'

'It isn't Paul's fault,' Jenny protested, scrambling to her feet. 'It was my idea.'

Fiona turned to her. 'You've got too many ideas, Jenny Miles,' she sneered. 'Just keep them to yourself in future. Don't you *dare* mention anything about a puppy to my parents.'

With that, she grabbed Paul's hand and marched him up the beach towards the cliff path.

Jenny watched them go, fuming. Paul turned back once and gave them a wave, then they were lost to sight round the headland. 'What is *wrong* with her?' she said.

'Do you have to ask?' Carrie replied.

Jenny sighed. 'I suppose she'd be even more jealous of Paul if he got a puppy,' she said. 'Maybe I'd better give up the idea. The last thing I want to do is make Fiona resent Paul even more.'

Carrie shook her head. 'Just look at Jess,' she said. The Border collie was standing with the stick in his mouth, looking hopefully after Paul. 'It's a pity Paul might not be able to have a dog of his own – just because we don't want to upset horrible Fiona.'

Jenny threw herself down on the sand and looked up at the sky. It was blue from hills to horizon – not a cloud to be seen. She wished life was like that. Just at the moment she seemed to have quite a few problems.

'There is *one* thing I can do,' she said, sitting up determinedly.

'What's that?' asked Carrie.

'I can talk to Dad about Mrs Grace coming to live with us,' Jenny said firmly. 'At least I can solve *one* problem – maybe!'

6

'Come on,' said Carrie. 'Time for tea. You're coming to us, remember?'

Jenny rose and walked slowly along the beach with Carrie, calling to Jess. The puppy scampered up, wagging his tail and licking Jenny's hand. Jenny kneeled down and gave him a cuddle. 'Did you hear what Paul said, Jess?' she asked. 'He said he'd *love* a puppy like you.'

Jess's tail wagged even harder and he sat down

abruptly on the sand. Jenny laughed and felt better. Jess could always make her feel better.

Carrie's parents made her feel better too. They were both in the kitchen when the girls arrived. Mr Turner was ladling spaghetti into a big white bowl. Mrs Turner gave the bolognese sauce a final stir and tipped it over the pasta. She had obviously spent the day painting. There was a smear of bright blue paint on her cheek.

She rubbed at it absently when Carrie pointed it out. 'I've just had Tom Palmer on the phone,' she announced. 'He's got an abandoned puppy he wants to find a home for and he wants me to put a notice on the harbour notice-board.' She chuckled. 'He suggested I do a little illustration. It's a Border terrier. I think a little sketch would look sweet.'

'What!' screeched Carrie. 'But we were just talking about asking Mr Palmer to find a puppy for little Paul McLay. This is amazing! It's like we made it happen!'

'Does Paul want a puppy?' Mr Turner asked Jenny, as he sat down at the kitchen table.

'*He* would love one,' said Jenny. 'But we haven't actually mentioned it to his parents.'

'I see,' said Mr Turner, his blue eyes twinkling. 'Do I smell a plot?'

'Just a tiny one,' Carrie grinned. 'But don't you see? This is a *sign*! Paul wants a puppy. We were talking about getting him a puppy! And now Mr Palmer has a puppy that needs a home! It's fate!'

'Mmm,' said Mrs Turner, setting plates out in front of them all. 'I don't know about fate but it would certainly be convenient.'

'Fate,' repeated Carrie firmly. 'This puppy was *sent* for Paul. Just you wait and see.'

Mr Turner looked at Jenny and winked. 'Oh well,' he said. 'In that case there's no problem.' Then he turned to his wife. 'Don't bother about the notice, Pam. That puppy is home and dry!'

Home and dry, Jenny thought as she reached the top of the cliff path on her way home after tea. She turned and looked out to sea. Puffin Island was still bathed in sunlight but now Jenny could see a mass of clouds beginning to gather on the horizon. She shivered. Maybe there were more storms to come after all.

'Come on, Jess,' she called to her pet. 'Time to go home!'

As Jenny and Jess raced into the farmyard, Jenny let out a whoop of delight. 'Matt's home!' she cried delightedly. 'There's his motorbike, Jess!' For a moment her pleasure was tinged with concern as she remembered that this weekend her father would decide Mercury's fate. He had been waiting until Matt returned.

Jess barked madly and wagged his tail, streaking towards the kitchen door. Jenny followed at a run.

'Where's Matt, Mrs Grace?' Jenny called, as she and Jess burst into the kitchen. Ian was sitting at the kitchen table, his homework spread out before him.

Mrs Grace smiled. 'And hello to you too,' she said.

Jenny looked apologetic. 'Oops, sorry. Hello, Mrs Grace. Hi, Ian! – where's Matt? Has Dad said anything about Mercury?'

Mrs Grace laughed. 'One question at a time. Matt is out helping your father to move all the sheep into the top field. They're driving the flock up the track now. Your dad reckons there's another storm on the way and the bottom field is already waterlogged. I don't think they've had time to talk about Mercury yet.'

'Maybe I should go and help them,' Jenny suggested, a frown creasing her brow. Her father had so much work to do looking after the sheep all on his own. Matt had managed to be at Windy Hill for the lambing, but for the rest of the college term he was only able to be home to help at weekends.

'He'd be better pleased if you got on with your homework – like Ian,' Mrs Grace replied, smiling.

'I offered to help,' Ian said, looking disappointed.

'I think your father and Matt can manage, Jenny,' Mrs Grace said firmly. 'They've probably finished by now, anyway.'

Jenny made a face. 'Lucky Matt. Helping on the farm is much more interesting than homework,' she said. 'Isn't it, Jess?'

Jess gave a short bark and wagged his tail. He obviously agreed with Jenny.

At that moment the phone rang and Mrs Grace answered it. Jenny watched the housekeeper's face change from friendly interest to concern.

'When did this happen?' she asked sharply.

At once Jenny was all attention. Something was wrong.

Mrs Grace listened for a few moments more then spoke again. 'I'll let them know straight away,' she said. 'They'll come over to you immediately. I'm sure of that.'

'What is it, Aunt Ellen?' Ian asked as Ellen Grace put the phone down.

The housekeeper's face looked very serious. 'That was Anna McLay from Dunraven,' she answered. 'Paul's mother. She's in a dreadful state. Paul's gone missing.'

'Missing?' repeated Jenny. 'But I saw him this afternoon just before tea.'

Ellen Grace looked intently at her. 'Where?' she asked sharply.

'Down on the beach,' Jenny answered. 'He came with Carrie and me to Cliffbay, after school.'

'Did you leave him there on his own?' Mrs Grace asked.

Jenny felt herself flushing. 'No, of course not,'

she replied. 'Fiona came to take him home.
They both went off together. The last time I
saw them they were heading for the cliff path.'

Mrs Grace nodded. 'That fits,' she said. 'Anna
McLay says Paul ran away from Fiona when
she was bringing him home. He's been missing
for two hours now.'

Jenny frowned. 'That's not like Paul,' she said.
Then she flushed. 'He was a bit upset.'

Mrs Grace fired questions at her and Jenny
answered as best she could, telling the housekeeper about her idea for a puppy for Paul.

'But Fiona said he couldn't have a puppy, it
would be too much trouble,' Jenny finished.
'Do you think that's what made him run away?'

Mrs Grace shook her head. 'Who knows?'
she said. 'The important thing is to find him.
Anna McLay is out of her mind with worry. If
he's up on the cliffs he could be in danger, and
if he's wandered into the hills it might be even
worse. The tarns up there are deep and the river
is swollen from all the recent storms. Anna
wants a search party organised straight away.'

'Have they told the police?' Ian asked.

Ellen Grace nodded. 'The police say two

hours isn't very long but they sent a patrol car out. The trouble is, a patrol car can't get into the hills. If they don't find him soon they'll call up Greybridge for police dog handlers and send out a search party on foot. Run and tell your father and Matt, Jenny. Tell them they're needed urgently. We've got to go and help find Paul.'

Jenny leaped to her feet. 'Come on, Jess,' she called. 'Let's go!'

Jenny ran so hard her heart was hammering by the time she got to the track. Ahead of her the road was crammed with sheep, all trying to get through the field gate at the same time. Jake and Nell were weaving amongst them, rounding up the stragglers, driving the last of the sheep forward and into the field. Her father was following behind his dogs.

Jenny ran forward, waving her arms. 'Dad! You've got to come quickly. Matt too!'

Fraser Miles turned. The sheep bleated and began to jostle one another. Mr Miles strode towards Jenny and bent down, scooping Jess up. 'Now, Jenny. You know I don't want Jess out with the sheep. He's a house dog.'

'I'm sorry, Dad,' Jenny apologised, taking Jess

from him. 'But this is an emergency.'

Matt whistled to Nell and Jake and shepherded the last of the sheep through the gate, shutting it behind them. He turned and walked back towards Jenny and her father. 'What's the matter, Jen?' he asked.

'It's Paul McLay,' Jenny blurted out, putting Jess back down on the track. 'He's gone missing and the McLays are organising a search party. They need all the help they can get.'

'Where did they last see him?' Fraser Miles asked.

'Fiona lost him somewhere between the cliff path and Dunraven,' she said breathlessly, as her father began to stride down the hill towards the farmhouse. Nell and Jake came to heel at once.

'How long has he been missing?' Matt put in.

'About two hours,' Jenny replied. 'The police have sent out a patrol car but Mrs McLay is afraid Paul is lost in the hills.'

'If he is we could have a devil of a job finding him,' Mr Miles said. 'I'll take the jeep up there.'

'I'll get Mercury saddled up,' Matt said. 'A

horse can go places even a jeep can't.'

Fraser Miles hesitated. Jenny knew what he was thinking. Mercury hadn't been ridden since he'd bolted with Ian. But this was an emergency! Paul's life could be in danger. 'It was only the storm that spooked Mercury,' she said. 'He's OK otherwise.'

'All right, Matt,' Mr Miles said after a moment. 'But be careful.'

'I will,' Matt promised, beginning to run.

Jenny watched him vault over the wall that bordered the track, taking the shortest route back to the farm. 'What about me?' she asked.

'You?' her father said.

'I want to help look for Paul,' Jenny pleaded. 'Jess can help too. Jess knows Paul's scent.'

'You're far too young,' Fraser Miles told her. 'The last thing we want is another youngster lost on the hills.'

Jenny put a hand on her father's arm. She didn't dare put her real fear into words. She couldn't help thinking that maybe it was her fault Paul had run away. If she hadn't half promised him a puppy he wouldn't have been so disappointed when Fiona said he couldn't have one. Was that why he had run off?

'Please, Dad,' she pleaded. 'How would you feel if I got lost? You'd want everybody to help, wouldn't you?'

Fraser Miles stopped for a moment and looked down at her. 'I reckon I would,' he said. 'OK, but when I tell you it's time to go home, you go home. Right?'

'Right,' said Jenny. 'I promise.'

Jenny and Ian saw Carrie as soon as they arrived at Dunraven. She came running towards them. 'Mum and I came straight here. Mrs McLay called to tell us what had happened,' she said, her expression worried. 'I've tried to think but I don't remember Paul saying anything that might give us a clue.'

'Neither do I,' Jenny sympathised. 'But at least we can help search for him.'

The crowd of searchers gathered in the farmyard and stood listening attentively to Sergeant Scott from Graston police station.

'We've covered most of the roads round about,' he explained. 'That isn't to say the little boy couldn't be hiding in a ditch. But we've done the best we could. I'm afraid we can't ask for a search and rescue helicopter just yet. Paul hasn't been missing long enough to merit a full-scale operation.'

'How long does he have to be missing before you people take it seriously?' snapped Calum McLay. The big man's face was white with strain and he looked belligerently at Sergeant Scott.

'I know how you must be feeling, Mr McLay,' Sergeant Scott replied. 'But we're doing the best we can. Children that age often run off for a few hours, then they turn up as right as rain, wondering what all the fuss was about. We've already requested a couple of police dogs. They should be here any time now.'

'But Paul isn't the type to run off,' Mrs McLay protested. Paul's mother was usually a picture of neatness but now her fair hair was ruffled and her waxed jacket was dragged on just anyhow.

'Let's just get on with it,' Calum McLay ordered.

Sergeant Scott sighed. At the best of times, Calum McLay wasn't the easiest person to deal with. When he was as worried as he was now he was just impossible.

The sergeant handed out Ordnance Survey maps. 'I want a note of which route everyone is taking,' he explained. 'That way we can cover the most ground and keep a check on which parts have been searched. Matt Miles is going to patrol the search parties on his horse. We haven't got a rough terrain vehicle for the hills around here so we'll search there on foot while we still have daylight on our side.'

'That won't be long,' Ian whispered to Jenny. 'Look at those clouds.'

Jenny hadn't noticed the weather. Ian was right. The clouds did look threatening. There was a frightening yellowish tinge to the underside of them. She shivered. 'Let's just hope the weather holds for a while.'

'And let's hope Mr McLay's temper holds as well,' said Matt, behind them. 'He isn't doing anybody any good behaving like this.'

'Mrs McLay is really upset,' Ian commented.

Anna McLay was standing huddled in her jacket, wringing her hands. Jenny smiled tentatively at her.

Mrs McLay came across to them. 'I can't tell you all how grateful I am,' she said, her voice shaking with emotion. 'All these people turning out to look for Paul. It's so kind of you.'

'We all really like Paul a lot,' Ian said to her.

Mrs McLay smiled. 'I can see that,' she said. 'I didn't realise so many people knew him.'

'We'll find him, Mrs McLay,' Matt said.

Anna McLay nodded. 'I wish I could help in the search,' she said. 'The police think it would be better if I stayed here – just in case he comes back home.'

'I hope he does, Mrs McLay,' Carrie said. 'I hope he comes running in and you give him a good scolding for worrying everybody.'

A tear slid down Anna McLay's face. 'I'd be glad to,' she said. 'If only he *would* come running in the door I wouldn't mind what he'd done.'

Jenny watched sympathetically as Mrs McLay walked away. 'It must be so hard just having to wait,' she said.

Carrie nodded. 'At least when you're search-ing you feel as if you're doing something. Poor Mrs McLay. I like her a lot.'

'Fiona is upset too,' Jenny said. 'Look at her.

I'll go and have a word with her.'

Fiona McLay stood apart from the others. Her face was chalk white and streaked with tears. 'I know what you're going to say,' she burst out as Jenny came up to her. 'It's my fault, isn't it? That's what Dad thinks.'

'What happened exactly?' Jenny asked.

Fiona ran a hand through her short dark hair, making it stand on end. For once, she didn't seem to be bothered how she looked. 'Paul was in a bad mood all the way home,' she said distractedly. 'All he could talk about was that puppy. I told him he couldn't have one. How could he look after a puppy? He's deaf. And he's got to go into hospital. I certainly wasn't going to look after a puppy for him while he was in hospital, and Mum shouldn't have to either.'

'I shouldn't have said anything about a puppy,' Jenny said miserably.

'No, you shouldn't have,' Fiona retorted. Then she looked away and brushed a hand across her eyes. 'He ran away from me,' she went on. 'I thought he was just sulking. I thought if I walked on he would come to his senses and follow me.'

'But he didn't,' Jenny said.

Fiona shook her head. 'When I went back to look for him I was furious. Then I began to get scared. Where *is* he?' she wailed. She couldn't hold back a sob.

Jenny laid a sympathetic hand on Fiona's arm. 'We'll find him,' she said comfortingly.

Fiona swallowed. 'What if we don't?' she asked. 'What if he's out there, lying hurt? What if he's fallen into one of the tarns and drowned? What if he's fallen over the cliff and broken his leg? Or what – what if he's dead?' Fiona's voice was becoming hysterical.

Jenny took a deep breath, trying to keep her own voice calm. 'He's probably just lost,' she said. 'There are going to be loads of us searching, Fiona. We're bound to find him.'

Fiona turned on her. 'It's all right for you,' she said snappishly. 'You weren't the one who lost him. Nobody is blaming *you*!' She turned on her heel and walked away.

'Don't let her upset you,' Ian said, coming up behind Jenny.

Jenny sighed. 'Fiona's right though,' Jenny said. 'Nobody *does* blame me. But it might be my fault after all. If I hadn't mentioned a puppy maybe none of this would have happened.'

'So, there's only one thing to do,' said Ian.

'What's that?' Jenny asked.

Ian's green eyes were steady. 'Find him,' he said.

Dear Dad

~~~~~
~~~~
~~~~
~~~~

Jenny

7

Ian, Carrie and Jenny joined the search party led by Fraser Miles. They drove up into the hills as far as the jeep would take them, then Fraser handed out whistles.

'Remember, it's no good shouting,' he reminded them. 'Paul won't be able to hear you. We'll have to search every metre of ground. Spread out, and whatever you do, don't lose touch. If you come across any sign of Paul give three blasts on your whistle.'

Matt rode up on Mercury just in time to hear his father's last words. 'I'm going to be keeping all the search parties in contact,' he said. 'If you want to talk to me use the whistle. Mercury will hear it, even if I don't.'

'Why can't we use mobile phones?' Mrs Turner asked.

'We can – if they work,' said Fraser Miles. 'But up here in the hills the signals are pretty unreliable.'

Mrs Turner put her mobile back in her pocket. 'So much for modern technology,' she remarked. 'Let's get going.'

'Isn't your dad here?' Ian asked Carrie.

Carrie looked sideways at him. 'He's out in his boat,' she said.

Ian looked disapproving for a moment then his face changed. 'Oh, I see,' he said. 'Sorry I asked.'

'Why?' said Jenny, puzzled.

Carrie swallowed hard. 'Dad's doing a patrol of the sea beneath the cliffs with the other boats from Cliffbay,' she explained. 'It was high tide a couple of hours ago. The coastguard has sent a boat out too.'

Jenny felt herself go suddenly cold. 'Do the police think Paul might have fallen over the cliff?' she asked.

'They reckoned it was best to have a look,' Carrie said. 'They're searching between here and Puffin Island.'

Jenny looked out to sea. The water looked grey and cold beneath the cloudy sky and the waves were choppy.

'Come on, Jenny,' Ian urged her. 'We're ready to go.'

Jenny looked down at Jess. 'Find Paul,' she said urgently. 'The police dogs aren't here yet but you know his scent so well. Please, Jess, find Paul!'

Two hours passed. It was getting dark, and Jenny was footsore and weary. The police dogs had arrived more than an hour earlier, but there hadn't been any sign of the missing boy. It was hard work. They had to search every fold in the hill, every ditch, behind every rock. Paul could be lying unconscious, or hiding in fear, anywhere.

At last Fraser Miles called a break as Matt came riding up.

'No luck?' asked Matt.

Fraser shook his head.

'It's the same with the others,' Matt said. 'If we don't find him soon we're going to have an even harder job. The light is getting really bad now.' Matt was right. The dark storm clouds were quickly taking away the little that was left of the daylight. The rain couldn't hold off much longer.

'What's happening?' asked Mrs Turner. 'Are the police sending for reinforcements yet?'

Matt nodded. 'They're trying to get a helicopter now in order to search places we can't reach on foot, but it might take some time,' he said. 'The police dogs haven't been able to find any trace of Paul and the darker it gets the more difficult it is for the dog handlers. I'm going to take Mercury home and join up with the climbing party on the cliffs.'

Fraser Miles looked at Jenny's tired face. 'Take Jenny home too, will you, Matt?' he said. 'She looks dead-beat.'

Jenny looked up, appalled. 'But you can't send

me home, Dad,' she protested. 'We haven't found Paul yet.'

'Remember your promise,' Fraser said.

Jenny bent her head. She *had* promised to go home when her father told her to.

'I'm taking Carrie home too,' Mrs Turner said. 'What about you, Ian? Do you want a lift?'

'I'd better get in touch with Aunt Ellen,' Ian replied. 'Have you seen her, Matt?'

'She stayed at Dunraven to keep Paul's mum company,' Matt replied.

'I'll drop you off there as we pass,' Mrs Turner offered.

Ian nodded. 'I'll follow on to Windy Hill after I've seen Aunt Ellen,' he told Jenny. 'That way we can wait together for news.'

Matt reached out a hand to Jenny. 'Come on, Jen,' he said. 'Hop aboard. Mercury won't mind carrying the two of us home.'

Jenny put her foot in Matt's stirrup and he hauled her up, settling her in front of him. Mercury stood steady as a rock while she grasped his bridle. She turned and called Jess. The collie pup ran obediently over and fell into line beside the horse.

'Where are the police searching next?' Fraser called after his son as Matt turned Mercury's head.

'The far side of the bay and the hills above,' Matt called back. 'Somebody from Greybridge was driving to Cliffbay and saw someone up there an hour or so ago.'

'Was it Paul?' Jenny asked eagerly.

Matt shook his head. 'They don't think so,' he replied. 'The description didn't fit very well. The driver was a long way off. It could have been a hillwalker but it's the only lead they've got.'

They made their way back to Windy Hill, Jess running alongside. The hills beyond Cliff-bay were the wildest in the area. Jenny hoped against hope that Paul wasn't lost up there. But then again, if he was, the police would be on his trail.

'Can you rub Mercury down for me?' Matt asked Jenny as he helped her down off the big horse's back. 'I want to get back up there as quickly as possible.'

Jenny nodded. 'Of course. Good luck, Matt!'

she said as her brother turned to go.

Matt smiled. 'We'll do the best we can,' he said. 'You know that.'

Jenny watched Matt set off. 'Oh, Jess,' she said, bending to give the young collie a hug. 'I hope they find him soon.'

Mercury whickered and Jenny looked up. 'It's OK, Mercury,' she said. 'I'm coming. Let's get you rubbed down.'

Jenny led Mercury into the stable and un-saddled him. She couldn't get her mind off Paul. Where *was* he? Wherever he was he must be feeling really bad. She wiped Mercury's flanks automatically, feeling the horse relax under her hands. She wished *she* could relax but she was too worried for that.

'If it wasn't so late I'd go up to Darktarn Keep, Jess,' she said.

Jenny's hands stopped moving and Mercury shifted uneasily, looking round at her. Jenny was remembering her conversation with Paul. She had told him the keep was where she always went when she got worried. He had liked the keep too. What if he had gone there? The searchers would never find him. They were looking in completely the wrong direction.

Jenny made a move towards the stable door. She should phone Mrs McLay. Then she stopped. She couldn't do that. What if she was wrong? She couldn't bear to think of getting Mrs McLay's hopes up all for nothing.

Jenny bit her lip. 'What am I going to do, Jess?' she asked.

Jess looked up at her, his head on one side.

In an instant Jenny made up her mind. She reached for Mercury's saddle. 'Sorry about this, boy,' she said to the horse. 'I know you were all ready to be tucked up in your stable but I've just got to check this out. If Paul is at the keep we've got to find him. It's dangerous up there – especially when it gets dark.'

Jenny threw the saddle over Mercury's broad back. 'You've got to help me, Mercury,' she whispered. 'You and Jess. If Paul is up there we have to find him. If he's hurt you'll have to carry him home, Mercury. Don't let me down, boy. Please don't let me down.'

Jenny gave Jess a drink, found a torch and scribbled a quick note for her father. She left the note on the kitchen table. Writing it took up precious time but the last thing she wanted was to have her father thinking she had gone missing too.

She led Mercury through the farm gate then climbed on to the fence. She had to stand on the fence to mount him.

'Steady, boy,' she murmured to him. 'I know you're tired but do this for me – and for Paul.'

She needed the big horse. Paul might be hurt. Parts of the keep were unstable. Jenny knew which areas to stay away from but Paul didn't. Anyway, Mercury could get to the keep far quicker than Jenny could on foot.

'Come on, Jess,' she called.

Jess pricked up his ears and trotted after Mercury, keeping close to the big horse's hoofs. Jenny smiled down at her pet. Jess was such a comfort.

As she rode up the track and out into the open ground above the top field she heard the rumble of thunder in the distance. She turned briefly and looked out to sea. The water was steel grey now, the waves rolling in topped by white caps which gleamed in the fading light. Above her, thick clouds held the promise of rain, and as she reached open country the first drops began to fall.

Jenny shivered as another roll of thunder sounded far in the distance. She only hoped it wasn't moving this way. If it did, would Mercury bolt again? Jenny pushed the thought away. She was halfway to the keep now. It would be as bad to turn back as to go on. She dug her heels into Mercury's flanks, urging him on.

'Come on, boy,' she whispered as another roll of thunder sounded in the distance. 'There's nothing to be afraid of.'

Jess ran along beside Mercury, keeping close to the big horse's hoofs. A sudden gust of wind whipped Jenny's hair over her face and she clawed it back. The rain was getting heavier now, stinging her face as it was blown on the wind.

Jenny peered into the gloom. Far above her was the keep. She could see its jagged outline, dark against the sky.

'That's where we're going, Mercury,' she whispered, bending low over the horse's ears. 'Darktarn Keep.'

Up ahead was the drystone wall and, beyond that, the tarn, glimmering in the failing light. At that moment Jenny heard a rumbling noise coming from the other side of the hill. The thunder *was* moving – and it was coming closer.

Mercury's head came up and he whinnied. Jenny clenched her hands on the reins then, very deliberately, relaxed them. She mustn't risk transmitting any of her nervousness to him.

'Jess!' she called softly.

Jess barked once and moved closer to the big horse, pacing him. Jenny felt Mercury's muscles bunch under her and Jess, seeming to sense his agitation, moved under the big horse. Immediately Mercury relaxed, his tense muscles softening.

'Good boy,' Jenny whispered, leaning close to his ear.

She rubbed her hand gently over his neck, murmuring to him, soothing him. Mercury's ears pricked and he turned his head a little, as if listening. Jenny went on talking in a low voice, hardly knowing what she was saying. After a moment she realised that it wasn't her words that were calming the big horse, it was the tone of her voice. As she felt him respond to her murmurs she grew in confidence, gripping less tightly with her knees, loosening the reins, showing Mercury that she had faith in him. And Mercury, his ears up, snuffled gently, his hoofs stepping firmly over the rough ground. Jenny sat up in the saddle, trying to see how far they were from the keep.

At that moment, another rumble of thunder sounded, much closer now. There was no doubt about it – a storm was building up. Jess wove his way in and out of Mercury's hoofs. 'We'll be all right, Jess,' Jenny called softly.

If only she could get to the shelter of the keep before the storm broke. Mercury whinnied nervously, and Jenny bent over his neck once more, whispering to him. To her relief, Mercury tensed, but did not shy at the next roll of thunder. His fear was under control – so far.

Jess barked and Jenny looked up. There was the keep, closer than she had thought.

'Come on, boy,' she murmured to Mercury. 'You can do it.'

Jenny steered Mercury away to the left to a break in the drystone wall, leaving the horse to pick his way through. Then they were passing the tarn, approaching the rise on which Darktarn Keep stood.

At the top of the rise, Jenny slid from the saddle and dropped to the ground. Her legs felt a little weak. A furry bundle launched itself at her and licked her hand. 'Oh, Jess, what would I do without you?' she said gratefully.

Then the thunder rolled louder. Jenny shivered, laying her hand on Mercury's neck. Mercury whickered and Jenny felt his warm breath on her cheek. She took hold of the reins, leading the horse towards the keep. 'There's no time to waste, Jess,' she said. 'Find Paul!'

Jess scampered over a low ruined wall and into the keep as Jenny led the big horse between the fallen stones of the wall of the building. Carefully, picking his way through the ruins, Mercury followed her until they came out into what had once been the courtyard of the keep.

Jess was standing in the middle of the courtyard, barking frantically. Jenny looked beyond

Jess, into the shadows of the far wall of the keep. Paul was sitting on the wall, his back to them. He hadn't noticed their approach.

Jenny's breath caught in her throat. The boy was sitting right on the edge of the wall, under the shelter of an overhanging archway. She knew exactly what was on the other side. That part of the wall dropped sheer into the river below. And Jenny knew the wall was unsafe.

Her first instinct was to run to Paul, and snatch him back from danger. But what if she startled him? What if he slipped and toppled over?

At that moment, before Jenny could do anything, a massive bolt of lightning flashed directly overhead.

Paul looked up, his terrified face illuminated for a moment in the searing light. He stood up, balancing precariously on the top of the narrow wall. As he turned he caught sight of Jenny.

She tried to smile reassuringly as she took a step towards him. She had to get him down from that wall. He didn't realise how dangerous it was.

Behind Jenny, Mercury shifted. Jenny turned

back to the big horse as the thunder followed the flash. She laid a hand on his flank. The last thing she wanted was Mercury to bolt now.

Mercury whickered and settled under her touch.

'Good boy,' Jenny muttered, relieved that the horse had stayed calm. She beckoned Jess over. 'Stay with Mercury, Jess,' she said to the puppy. Then she moved forward again towards Paul.

Another flash of lightning ripped through the sky immediately above. Jenny saw Paul's face turn upwards again and his look of shock was plain to see in the brief flash of the light. He moved as if to scramble down from the wall but his foot slipped and he teetered for a moment, rocking on his narrow perch.

'Paul!' Jenny cried, racing forward.

Overhead, the thunder rolled almost immediately, bouncing off the walls of the old ruined keep.

Jenny saw Paul's face, pale in the garish light, then he gave a cry as he shifted his position, trying to keep his balance. He stepped back, his left foot slipping on the wet surface of the stones. He spread his arms out to steady himself

but, as he did so, a shower of small stones fell from the archway above him, shaken loose by the force of the thunder. Paul put his hands up to protect himself as the stones rattled and bounced down on the wall beside him.

He took another step, his hands covering his head, but slipped again. He swayed on top of the wall, desperately trying to regain his balance.

Jenny rushed forward, but it was too late. Paul tipped backwards out of her reach, and fell from view.

8

'Oh, no! Paul!' Jenny cried. Lightning flashed and thunder rolled again. Jenny heard Mercury whinny behind her. She turned, alarmed at the sound, but Mercury was standing where she had left him, Jess at his heels, keeping him calm.

Jenny turned back to the wall, clinging to the stones. 'Paul!' she yelled into the darkness below.

The rain fell more heavily now, stinging her

eyes, washing down the wall under her hands in great sheets. She shook the hair out of her face and peered down. Below, she could hear the river roaring down the hill, surging and crashing against its banks.

It was no good. She couldn't see where the little boy had fallen. She clung to the wall, powerless to help. Then, as the next bolt of lightning lit up the area again, Jenny spotted him.

He had tumbled down to the bottom of the slope and into the river, but had managed to stop himself from being swept away by grabbing hold of a bush at the river's bank.

Her heart in her mouth, Jenny watched the little boy, half submerged in the roaring river, struggling to keep his head out of the foaming water as it rushed past him. She drew a hand across her eyes, clearing the rain from them. 'I'm coming, Paul!' Jenny yelled. 'Just hang on!'

The water tore at Paul's clothes. The bush was the only thing stopping him from being carried away by the river. How long would his grip hold?

'Jenny!' shouted a voice behind her.

Jenny turned, one foot already on the wall. 'Ian!' she cried. 'Thank goodness you're here!'

Ian was standing on the far side of the courtyard, his hand on Mercury's neck. He ran towards her. His hair was plastered close to his head as the rain beat down. 'I went back to Windy Hill and saw your note,' he gasped, taking a crumpled piece of paper from his pocket. 'I ran all the way. Did you ride Mercury in that storm?'

'He was all right,' Jenny said. 'He didn't bolt. He's safe. But, Ian, Paul isn't! He's in danger.'

'Is Paul *here*?' Ian asked.

Jenny looked at the dripping figure before her. 'You've got to help,' she urged. 'Paul was hiding in the keep. He's fallen into the river. Come on! We've got to save him.'

Then she was off, slipping and sliding down the wet grass. Jess, seeing Jenny race off, followed her.

'Be careful!' Ian yelled as he plunged after her.

Jenny could think of nothing else but getting to Paul in time. Then she called out in alarm as her foot slipped. She went down, her foot twisting under her painfully as she skidded several metres on her back, the river coming ever closer.

A second later Jess reached her and grabbed hold of her coat in his teeth, helping to slow her fall. Ian caught up with them and helped Jenny up. 'It won't do any good if we all end up in the river,' he said.

She nodded briefly and they edged their way cautiously down the rest of the slope until they reached level ground, Jess ahead of them. The roar of the water and the crash of thunder was so loud they could barely hear each other.

Jenny peered through the gloom. 'There!' she yelled, pointing.

Paul was floundering near the edge of the river, the water pouring around and over his terrified, white face, making him cough and splutter. Jenny could see now he was clinging to the root of a young tree that was sticking out of the riverbank. The recent storms had washed away the earth from the banking, exposing it.

'Quick, then,' said Ian. 'We should be able to reach him.'

But as he spoke, Jenny gasped in horror. 'Look! The tree root is coming away from the bank!'

With a tearing sound, the root Paul was clinging to broke free. Paul cried out in fright as the force of the water whirled him further out into the torrent. Luckily the root didn't break off entirely and Paul managed to hang on as the current dragged at it.

Jenny moved forward but Ian grabbed her. 'No,' he said. 'The river is flowing far too fast and he's too far out now. It's too dangerous.'

'But we have to do something!' Jenny cried, distraught. Paul's eyes were fixed on her. She couldn't think of leaving him even to get help. Then her face lit up. 'Mercury can help! Get Mercury, Ian. Hurry!'

Ian nodded and scrambled off up the slope.

'Ian!' Jenny called. 'You can ride him. It's quicker – but take Jess with you.'

Ian nodded again and beckoned Jess to him.

'Go on, Jess,' Jenny said. 'Go with Ian to Mercury. He might need you.'

The puppy bounded up the hill after Ian.

'I'll be as quick as I can!' Ian promised.

The wind was stronger than ever and lightning split the sky at intervals, followed by the crash of thunder. Jenny hoped that Mercury would stay calm. Ian would have to ride the horse down the far side of the hill and round the base of it.

She kept her eyes on Paul, willing the little boy to hang on, hoping against hope that his fingers would not slip on the wet tree root.

It seemed like years before Ian was back, riding Mercury towards the river, with Jess at the big horse's side.

Jenny made a grab for Mercury's bridle. 'If we can get the reins out to Paul we can pull him in,' she said.

Ian nodded, helping her with the buckles. The leather straps were slippery with rain but at last they managed to get the reins loosened and coupled together again into a long strap.

Jenny took hold of the length of leather and tried to cast it out into the water. Paul's hand came up as he saw what they were doing but the wind beat back upon them, defying their efforts. The reins were not heavy enough to withstand the wind.

'Don't let go, Paul,' Jenny mouthed. 'Don't let go of the tree root.'

'We'll never do it,' said Ian, defeated. His face was running with water, his hair tangled and wet. 'Can't we find something heavy to attach to the reins?'

Jenny shook her head. 'What if we hit Paul? We can't risk throwing anything heavy.'

Jenny scraped a soaking strand of hair away from her own face. She felt frustration rise in her as Jess stood on the riverbank, barking. She looked at the Border collie. Jess was straining towards Paul, every sense alert. He looked up at Jenny and barked again. Jenny gasped. Of course. Jess could help.

'*We* can't do it, but Jess can,' Jenny declared. 'He can swim out with the reins. He's a strong swimmer.'

Ian was silent for a moment. 'But he's only a pup,' he said.

Jenny swallowed. 'We've got to try, Ian,' she said. 'Jess is our only hope.'

She bent and put the reins in Jess's mouth.

'Hold on to Mercury, Ian,' she said, then she turned to Jess. 'Take it to Paul,' she commanded. 'To Paul, Jess!'

Jess didn't hesitate. The little dog plunged into the river and struck out for Paul.

Ian held Mercury's head firmly as Jenny watched Jess trying to swim against the current. Time and again the strength of the water pushed him further downstream, away from Paul. Three times the little collie was washed towards the bank and three times he plunged in again. The last time he scrambled up and began to run towards them.

Tears were streaming down Jenny's face as she realised the little dog had no chance against the force of the river. 'It's all right, Jess,' she said, as the collie came running up to them. 'You did your best.'

Jess barely looked up as he raced past her, the reins still in his mouth. Further upstream he plunged once more into the water.

Jenny gasped as she saw what he was doing. 'Look!' she said to Ian. 'He's letting the current carry him down towards Paul.'

'Clever Jess,' said Ian. 'He's going to do it!'

Jenny watched, as Jess swam towards Paul, paddling desperately to keep his course. He was nearly there.

'*Now*, Ian!' Jenny said, stepping into the water.

'Hang on to Mercury,' Ian warned as he followed her.

Together they waded into the river as far as they dared. Jess had reached Paul. Jenny's heart seemed to stop as Paul's free hand came up and grabbed at the reins.

'Now the other hand, Paul,' she whispered under her breath. 'You'll need both hands.'

Ian and Jenny looked on, the water swirling round their legs, as Paul let go of the tree root. For a moment the water caught him, spinning him round as his other hand tightened still further on the reins. Then both hands were grasping the lifeline.

'Back, Mercury,' Ian urged. 'Steady now, boy.'

The big horse backed obediently towards the bank. Paul hung on but Jenny was watching Jess. The collie was trying desperately to swim beside Paul but he was already exhausted after his fight against the current. As Jenny watched, she saw the puppy beginning to lose the battle

against the force of the water.

'Jess!' she yelled, lunging forward.

Paul saw the panic on her face and let go of the reins with one hand. Jenny breathed a sigh of relief as he grabbed Jess's collar. But now Paul was in danger again. With only one hand on the reins and Jess's weight pulling him back, he wouldn't be able to hold on much longer.

'Hurry, Mercury,' Ian urged, his face set.

The horse took another step backwards and his hoof slipped on the stones beneath the water. Paul had to let go of Jess's collar to grasp the reins again with both hands and Jess spun round in the current. The young collie struggled furiously against the raging torrent, his head disappearing beneath the water as the force of it overcame him. He was being swept away!

'No!' cried Jenny, leaning as far as she dared towards the little dog, her hands desperately searching. Water filled her mouth and her eyes as she scrabbled blindly for Jess's body. 'Jess!' she called, her breath coming in great gasps.

She felt the force of the current dragging at her, but then her searching hands found a bundle of wet fur. Jess! With a sob of relief she somehow managed to grab Jess's collar, and his familiar black and white head emerged. A hand reached out and grabbed her.

'Hang on!' said Ian's voice. 'Nearly there.'

The next few moments were a confusion of noise and water and cold. Then Mercury was stepping back on to the bank, Paul still just managing to hang on to his reins.

Jenny lurched as Ian gave her a sharp pull on to the bank, after lifting Paul clear. She lay there for a moment, the water singing in her ears. Though more distant now, lightning still flashed and thunder rolled overhead.

Jenny felt a warm tongue licking her ear. 'Oh, Jess,' she gasped, cradling the little dog to her. 'You're safe.'

'We've got to get Paul back quickly, Jen,' Ian said.

Jenny looked up at the urgency in his voice. 'Of course,' she said, getting to her feet. 'He must be in shock after his experience.'

Ian nodded. 'He is,' he agreed. 'But there's more than that.'

Jenny's mouth went dry. She looked beyond

Ian to where Paul was lying on the grass. He was doubled up and clutching the lower part of his left leg. 'What is it?' she asked.

'I think he might have broken his ankle,' Ian replied. 'Can you give me a hand to lift him up on to Mercury? The sooner we get help, the better.'

9

They made their way slowly back to Windy Hill. Ian led Mercury, while Jenny rode with Paul, holding the injured little boy fast in the saddle. A tired Jess stayed at the big horse's side.

Jenny was shining her torch a little ahead of Ian, but it wasn't really necessary. Mercury knew the way back to the farm and his stable very well.

Paul was white with pain and exhaustion but

the little boy hadn't complained once, not even when they had lifted him up on to Mercury's back. Jenny had made a pad out of her jumper and placed it between Paul's foot and Mercury's flank, like a cushion, but even so, it wasn't an easy journey for him.

'I'm sorry I ran away, Jenny,' Paul whispered in Jenny's ear as they approached the farm-house.

Jenny drew the torch back a little so that its glow illuminated her face and Paul could read her lips.

'Why *did* you run away?' she asked as he looked up at her.

Paul snuggled closer to her. 'I didn't want to go to hospital,' he burst out.

Jenny turned his face so that he was looking at her again. 'I'm sure your parents wouldn't force you to go if they knew how you felt,' she said. 'Have you told them?'

Paul nodded. 'They don't take any notice,' he replied. 'They just say nobody ever wants to go into hospital.'

'Have you told them *why* you're so worried?' Jenny persisted.

Paul bit his lip. 'Fiona says there's no point,' he told her. 'She says they'll just think I'm a scaredy-cat. She says the nurses and doctors won't like me. They'll think I'm making a fuss.'

Jenny's heart went out to the little boy. 'Lots of people like you, Paul,' she said gently. 'Think of all the people out looking for you. Your dad is really upset and your mum is worried sick. Fiona was crying because you were missing.'

Paul stared at her, surprise written on his face. 'Fiona?' he said wonderingly.

Jenny nodded. 'Then there's my dad and Matt, and Carrie and Ian, and loads of other people. And they all like you. And they're all worried about you.'

'They don't really like me,' said Paul. 'They just feel sorry for me.'

Jenny took a deep breath. 'Did Fiona tell you that?'

Paul nodded.

Jenny tried to control her anger. 'That just isn't true, Paul,' she said firmly. 'Jess likes you just for yourself – and so do I.'

'Do you?' asked Paul. 'Don't you feel sorry for me?'

Jenny thought for a moment. It was important to get this right – to tell Paul exactly how she felt. 'I feel sorry that you can't hear,' she said carefully. 'But I don't feel sorry for *you*. Why should I? You're bright and good fun, and popular – and very brave! You're a friend.'

'A friend,' said Paul slowly. He looked up and smiled at her.

Jenny smiled back. She felt Paul relax a little as he took in everything she had said. Far in the distance the thunder still rumbled but the storm was moving away, out to sea.

'Look,' said Jenny. 'There's Windy Hill. Everybody there likes you.'

Light spilled out from the door of the farmhouse as they clattered into the yard and Mrs Grace came rushing out.

'You've found him!' she cried, her eyes on Paul. 'I've just got back from Dunraven. I was beginning to worry about you two. Where did you go?' The rain had eased off now but Mrs Grace took in their dirty, bedraggled appearance. 'Explanations later,' she went on. 'Let's get you inside. Hot showers all round while I phone your mother, Paul.'

'Paul has hurt his ankle, Aunt Ellen,' Ian said. 'It might be broken.'

Mrs Grace helped Ian and Jenny lift Paul gently down from Mercury's back. Paul winced as he slid from the saddle but he managed a smile. 'It was Jess who saved me,' he told Mrs Grace.

Mrs Grace smiled at him as she carried him into the farmhouse. 'You can tell me all about it later,' she said. 'Let's make you comfortable first and let your family know that you're safe.'

By the time Jenny came back from her shower, Paul was tucked up on the sofa in a pair of her pyjamas, under a mound of blankets. Mrs Grace had made a temporary splint to support Paul's ankle until they could get him to hospital. Jess, having been rubbed dry, was now curled up at Paul's side

'Mrs McLay is on her way,' said the house-keeper. 'She'll take Paul to Greybridge Hospital to get his ankle seen to. Mr McLay is still out looking for him but Mrs McLay says she'll try to get him on his mobile phone. Now, who wants a hot drink?'

Ian and Jenny had told Mrs Grace the whole story, but Jenny noticed that the housekeeper hadn't asked Paul any questions. The little boy was still rather pale.

At the sound of a vehicle pulling up in the yard, she looked at Paul, saying, 'That'll be your parents, Paul.'

Paul's eyes widened. 'Will they be angry with me?' he asked.

Jenny heard the sound of car doors slamming, then feet running across the farmyard. The door burst open and Mrs McLay stood there, her eyes going at once to Paul. 'Paul!' she cried, rushing to him.

Paul took one look at her then opened his arms and burst into tears. Anna McLay scooped her son into her arms, hugging him as if she would never let him go, burying her face in his hair.

Paul struggled and laughed a little. 'You're squashing me,' he said, looking up at his mother.

Jenny felt a smile spread over her face. Mrs McLay loosened her grip a little, but Paul still snuggled close to her.

Jenny looked at the door. Mr McLay and

Fiona were standing there. Mr McLay looked white and strained. His hair was standing on end and his legs were covered in mud to the knees. Fiona's face was pale with shock and she looked as if she had been crying again.

Jenny got up from the table and went to her. 'It's all right now, Fiona,' she said. 'Paul's safe.'

'It was my fault he ran away, wasn't it?' Fiona asked miserably.

Jenny looked at her. Until tonight, she had never seen the other girl so unsure of herself. Usually Fiona went around telling everybody what to do and bullying them. 'It's all over now,' she said. 'You didn't know this was going to happen.'

'But it's still my fault that he ran away and got hurt,' Fiona said brokenly, a tear sliding down her cheek. 'Paul will hate me now.'

Jenny looked at the little boy. 'I don't think he will,' she said. 'If you take back all the stories you told him.'

Fiona flushed a deep red. 'I will,' she said. 'I've told Mum and Dad it was my fault Paul was so scared of going into hospital. I've told them all about it.'

Jenny put a hand on Fiona's arm. 'That's a start then, isn't it?' she said. 'Paul won't hold it against you, not once he understands that you felt left out.'

For a moment the old anger flared in Fiona's eyes. Then she went even redder. 'You're right,' she said. 'I was jealous of all the attention Mum and Dad were giving to Paul. But I didn't want this to happen.'

'You weren't the only one to blame, lass,' Calum McLay said gruffly. 'I've been a bit hard on Paul too.'

Jenny looked up at him. He looked completely washed out, not at all his usual confident self.

Mrs Grace coughed. 'I'm sure the McLays would like to have a few minutes alone together,' she said. 'I think I hear the jeep.'

Jenny and Ian took the hint and went with Mrs Grace to meet Mr Miles and Matt. Jess trotted alongside.

'I hear you two found him,' Fraser Miles said, getting out of the jeep as Matt parked it in the yard.

Jenny and Ian launched into their story once more.

But then Fraser Miles's smile began to turn into a frown. 'You mean you took Mercury out in that storm?' he said. 'After I had expressly forbidden it? You did well to find Paul, Jenny, but that was foolhardy after what happened the other day.'

Jenny flushed. 'I was just so anxious to find out if Paul was there,' she explained. 'And, besides, the storm hadn't started when I left.'

'Was Mercury all right?' her father asked.

'Oh, Dad, he was wonderful,' Jenny said, smiling. 'He got a bit of a scare when he first heard the thunder but I talked to him – and Jess ran beside him. It was amazing. Mercury seemed to be listening to me. I just kept on talking to him and he settled down. Even when the storm was really close, even when the lightning was flashing all round the keep, he was all right. I think he's got over his fear. And we couldn't have saved Paul without him.'

Her father looked doubtful. 'He didn't bolt?' he asked.

Jenny shook her head. 'Truly, Dad, he was fine. He faced up to the storm and conquered his fear.'

'I rode him down to the river in the storm,' Ian put in. 'He was completely under control. And he was marvellous when we needed him to pull Paul out of the water. Really, Mr Miles, I think Jenny is right.'

'He's cured, Dad,' Jenny said. 'I know he is.'

Fraser Miles looked at his son. 'What do you think, Matt?' he asked.

'It certainly sounds like we should give Mercury another chance,' agreed Matt. Jenny heard the eagerness in her brother's voice.

'Well, I'm willing to,' said his father. 'It sounds as if Jenny and Jess might have done the trick.' Jess barked and he looked down at the little dog. 'So you're the hero of the hour again, Jess, are you?' he said, bending down to give the collie's ears a rub. 'Good boy!'

Jenny looked on as her father petted Jess. Jess's tail wagged so hard he nearly overbalanced!

The kitchen door opened then, and Calum McLay came out carrying his son tightly, followed by Anna McLay and Fiona. He nodded to them as he passed on his way to his vehicle.

Anna McLay came over. 'We can't thank you

all enough,' she said, her eyes filling again, with tears of relief. 'We're taking Paul to Casualty in Greybridge now.'

Jenny bit her lip. 'I know he has to go to hospital to have his ankle treated,' she said. 'But it was the thought of going to hospital that frightened him into running away. Do you think he'll be all right?'

Anna McLay smiled. 'I've explained to him that we're all going with him,' she said. 'And that I'll stay there with him if the hospital decide to keep him overnight.'

'What did he say?' asked Ian.

Mrs McLay laughed. 'He said he wanted to see the pictures of his insides.'

'Oh yes! They'll X-ray his ankle, won't they?' Jenny exclaimed.

Anna McLay nodded. 'He seems really interested in that. Who knows, maybe he'll change his mind about not liking hospitals.' She looked over at the Land Rover, where Calum McLay was hovering anxiously, making sure his son was comfortable on the back seat.

'It nearly took a tragedy to knock some sense into Calum,' Mrs McLay went on. 'But I think the message has got through. He realises what is really important now. And, if ever he looks like forgetting it, I'll be there to remind him. I'm not going to turn a blind eye to his bullying any longer. It's high time I stood up to my husband.'

'Good for you,' Fraser Miles said approvingly.

'And don't you worry any more about his plans to hound you out of Windy Hill, either, Fraser,' Anna McLay declared. 'After all, if it hadn't been for the people here, we might have lost Paul. There'll be no more dirty tricks if I've got anything to do with it. I'll see that Calum behaves himself.'

Matt laughed. 'I almost feel sorry for Calum,' he said.

'Don't be,' said Anna firmly. 'It's time he had a taste of his own medicine.'

'See you at school, Fiona,' Jenny said, walking with Mrs McLay over to the Land Rover.

Fiona looked at her. 'I suppose you'll tell everybody what I did,' she said.

Jenny shook her head. 'No, I won't,' she replied. 'I don't think you'll do anything like that again. That's all that matters.'

★

'Well,' said Mrs Grace as they watched the McLays drive off. 'It's good to see Anna McLay standing up to Calum at last. They'll both be better for it.'

'I agree, Ellen,' Fraser Miles said. 'He's got away with too much for too long.'

'Mr McLay and Fiona seemed much nicer tonight,' Jenny remarked, as they went back into the house. 'You know, I liked Mrs McLay before but I like her even more now. She must be brave to stand up to Mr McLay.'

'You can show courage, too, when something really important is at stake, Jenny,' Mrs Grace said. 'Look at the way you fought to save Jess when he was a pup.'

'Why don't you get Jenny on to Mr McLay over this lease business, Aunt Ellen?' Ian suggested.

Jenny sat up and Jess stirred and looked at her accusingly. 'I nearly forgot,' she said. 'I meant to talk to you about it, Dad, but then we heard that Paul was missing and it went right out of my mind.'

'What did?' asked Fraser.

'My idea,' said Jenny. She stopped, suddenly shy.

'Come on then, what is it?' encouraged Matt.

'Well,' said Jenny, 'I was wondering if Mrs Grace could come and live with us here at Windy Hill – and Ian too, of course,' she added.

Fraser Miles and Ellen Grace looked at each other.

'It's funny you should suggest that,' said her father. 'Ellen and I were thinking the same thing but we weren't sure if you would like it.'

'Like it?' shrieked Jenny. Jess jumped and shook himself. 'I'd love it!'

'Well then, that's settled,' said Mr Miles, smiling.

Jenny drew Jess towards her and gave him a cuddle. 'One big happy family,' she said, smiling at Ian.

Ian grinned. 'Except when Jenny and I fall out,' he added.

Jenny tossed her head. 'We won't fall out any more,' she declared. 'We're *friends*.'

Children's ward

10

Next morning Jenny answered a phone call from Anna McLay. Paul's ankle had been set and he was doing nicely.

'Did he like the pictures of his foot?' Jenny asked.

Anna McLay chuckled. 'The doctor gave him one of them to keep,' she told Jenny. 'He wants to pin it up on his bedroom wall.'

'That was nice of the doctor,' Jenny remarked.

Mrs McLay agreed. 'They're *all* nice,' she said. 'Paul is having a lovely time; meeting the other children and getting to know the nurses. In fact, when I told his doctor what had happened, and how worried Paul had become about not waking up again after his ear operation, he arranged for the doctor who will be in charge to come and visit Paul, to put his mind at rest. Keep your fingers crossed that it works, Jenny.'

'Oh, I will,' Jenny breathed. 'Mrs McLay, would it be all right if Ian and I came to visit Paul?'

'I was going to ask if you would,' Mrs McLay replied. 'Paul has been asking for you and for Jess.'

'Will we be allowed to bring Jess?' Jenny asked.

'The hospital has a pets policy,' Mrs McLay told her. 'They've discovered that the patients do much better if they're allowed to see their pets – especially the children.'

'Then we'll certainly bring Jess,' Jenny promised. 'Jess would *love* to see Paul!'

Mrs McLay told Jenny which ward to go to. 'There's a door at the end of the building that leads into the children's ward,' she said. 'It's lovely – and it has its own little garden outside. Paul will be so happy when he hears that Jess is coming to see him.'

Jenny rushed to tell Mrs Grace and Ian her news.

'I'll drive you over there tomorrow after-noon,' Ellen Grace promised. 'Anna and I can have a coffee and a chat and let the three of you have some time together.'

'Four,' Ian corrected her, smiling. 'Don't forget Jess.'

'As if I could,' said Mrs Grace as Jess scam-pered up to them at the sound of his name.

'You're going to see Paul tomorrow, Jess,' Jenny said, kneeling down and ruffling Jess's ears. 'Won't that be nice?'

Late that afternoon, the phone rang again and Ellen Grace picked it up. After a few minutes she called over to Jenny. 'Mr Palmer would like to speak with you,' she said, smiling.

Jenny was always delighted to speak to the vet who had helped Jess and Mercury get well. She dislodged Jess from her lap and went to the phone.

'It seems you've found a home for my abandoned puppy,' the vet said.

'Have I?' Jenny asked, confused.

'I've just had a phone call from Calum McLay,' Mr Palmer explained. 'Seems Pam Turner had told him about the pup, and that you'd said he might be perfect for Paul.'

Jenny's heart beat a little faster. 'So what did Mr McLay say?' she asked.

'He says if Paul wants the pup then he can have him,' the vet told her.

Jenny felt a wide smile spreading across her face. 'Oh, that's wonderful,' she breathed. 'Does Paul know, yet?'

'Not yet,' Mr Palmer replied. 'In fact, Mr and Mrs McLay thought you might like to tell him.'

'Oh, yes!' Jenny replied. 'Ian and I are going to see Paul tomorrow. He'll be so excited when he finds out.'

'Well,' Mr Palmer chuckled. 'I think we can do a little better than just telling Paul. We can *show* him! I've just had a word with Mrs Grace,' he explained. 'She's agreed to come and collect the pup on the way to the hospital tomorrow afternoon.'

'Wow!' Jenny said, excitedly. 'That would be fantastic!' Jenny put the phone down and turned to grin at Mrs Grace.

'I take it there will be *five* of you now,' the housekeeper said, smiling.

Jenny nodded happily. 'Ian,' she said. 'Guess what Mr Palmer's just told me!'

The following day, Mrs Grace turned the car into the hospital grounds and Jenny looked out of the side window eagerly. Beside her, Jess lifted his head and peered out of the window too. Ian was in the front seat with the puppy.

'Oh, no you don't,' Ian exclaimed, as the small brown bundle in his lap tried to wriggle out of his grasp. He held the puppy up so that he too could look out of the window.

Jenny smiled. The puppy was adorable, a honey-brown Border terrier with a scattering of darker brown on his back. 'Isn't he gorgeous?' she said.

'And full of life,' Mrs Grace laughed. 'Hold on to him, Ian.'

Mrs Grace parked the car and they made their way to the entrance at the end of the building. Both dogs were on leads. Mr Palmer had provided the puppy's collar and lead. 'A present for Paul,' he had said, smiling. 'Tell him to get well soon.'

A nurse in a white uniform came out of the entrance and looked at Jess. 'I'm Sister Joyce,' she said. 'I'll bet you've come to visit Paul. He's been talking all morning about it.' She looked at the Border terrier. 'I thought there was only one dog,' she said.

'This one is a surprise for Paul,' Ian told her, picking the puppy up. 'I hope you don't mind.'

Sister Joyce laughed. 'I don't mind,' she assured them. 'But it will take you a little while to get through the ward once the children see these two. Paul is out in the garden with his mum but you have to go through the ward to get there,' she said. 'Come on, I'll show you the way.'

They followed the nurse through the door and into the ward. Jenny looked around. The ward *was* lovely. There were bright posters on the walls and a play-area down at the end just in front of the French windows that opened on to the garden.

'Oh, look!' said one little girl, sitting up in bed. 'Puppies!'

Mrs Grace smiled. 'I think Sister Joyce is right,' she said. 'I'll just go and have a word with Anna and tell her you'll be along as soon as you can.'

Jenny looked around as children began to crowd round them. She couldn't just rush through the ward.

'What's that one's name?' asked a little boy in a wheelchair.

'Jess,' said Jenny, leading Jess across to him.

She looked at Ian. He was surrounded by children, all wanting to stroke the puppy. He grinned back. 'What a welcome!' he said.

'We find our pets policy works wonders with the children,' Sister Joyce said.

Jenny smiled. 'It certainly seems to,' she agreed. But there was one face she was looking forward to seeing more than any other – Paul's!

It was a full ten minutes before Jenny and Ian could drag themselves away from the young patients. Jenny put Jess down at the garden door and looked out over the lawn. Paul was sitting in a wheelchair with his mother and Mrs Grace on either side of him on garden chairs. He was chattering away, his face turned up to his mother's.

Jenny unclipped Jess's lead. 'Go and say hello to Paul,' she whispered in the young collie's ear.

Jess looked up at her, then he was off, racing down the garden. Paul turned as Jess came into view and opened his arms wide, his eyes shining, his whole face lighting up.

'Jess!' he cried.

Jess scampered up to him, his tail wagging furiously, and Paul bent to give him a cuddle. Jenny and Ian gave him a moment to welcome Jess.

'Now?' said Ian.

'Now,' Jenny agreed, and together they led the Border terrier pup down the garden.

Paul looked up as they approached. 'A puppy!' he cried. 'Oh, Ian, he's lovely. Is he yours?'

Ian grinned. 'No, he isn't mine, Paul,' he said.

Paul looked at Jenny, puzzled.

'He isn't mine either, Paul,' Jenny told him.

'He's yours – if you'd like him.'

Jenny watched as Paul's face changed from puzzlement to disbelief to joy.

'Mine?' he said. 'My puppy?' He looked at his mother.

'It's true,' she said. 'Dad told me all about it yesterday, but I didn't want to spoil Jenny and Ian's surprise by telling you. Do you like him?'

Paul bent down and stroked the puppy's head. The little dog looked up at him with deep brown, melting eyes. 'Oh, he's gorgeous,' Paul breathed. 'And he's mine! I'll take such good care of him.'

Jenny watched as Ian lifted the puppy to sit on Paul's lap. She was very sure that Paul *would* take good care of his pet.

'Can he come and visit me when I come into hospital next time?' Paul asked.

Jenny's breath caught in her throat. Paul had said 'when', not 'if'.

'So you're going to have the operation for your ears?' she asked him.

Paul nodded. 'I met Dr Tony, who will look after me while I am asleep during the operation. He's nice. He made me laugh. And

Dr Mike said I was very brave when I had my ankle set.'

'And so you were!' said his mother, smiling.

'Shall we go and have some coffee, Anna?' Mrs Grace suggested. 'We'll leave these five to enjoy themselves.'

Jenny watched as Ellen Grace and Anna McLay made their way back into the building. A young nurse passed the French windows and waved to Paul.

'That's Nurse Chrissie,' Paul said. 'She says I can have crutches soon – and Pippa is going to teach me how to use them.'

'Who's Pippa?' Ian asked.

'She's my friend,' Paul said. 'She's got a broken leg but she can get around really fast on her crutches. So can Jack. He's my friend too.'

'You seem to have made a lot of friends,' Jenny said, smiling.

Jess barked and the Border terrier leaped off Paul's lap and began to chase the young collie round the garden. Jess turned and waited for the smaller dog to catch up. The terrier butted Jess playfully on the nose and Jess crouched down and growled softly, batting a paw at the terrier. In a moment the pups were rolling over, playing with each other.

'Do you know what Carrie said about this puppy?' Jenny asked Paul.

Paul shook his head.

'Carrie said he was *meant* for you,' Jenny told him. 'And I think she was right.'

Paul giggled as he watched Jess and the Border terrier chase each other. 'They're going to be friends,' he said delightedly.

Jenny nodded vigorously. 'Just like us,' she said.

Paul beamed.

'What are you going to call him?' Ian asked.

Paul looked at the brown bundle of energy. The puppy broke away from Jess and came running up to Paul. The little boy bent and scooped him up in his arms. 'Toby,' he said. 'I'm going to call him Toby.' He bent his head to bury his nose in the puppy's soft fur.

Jenny and Ian looked at each other over the little boy's head.

'I think the puppy is a success,' Ian said, his eyes twinkling.

'You *could* say that,' Jenny agreed, as Mrs

Grace and Anna McLay appeared.

Jess barked and Jenny looked down at him. 'You've got a playmate. Jess,' she said. She looked at Mrs McLay. 'Can Paul bring Toby to visit Jess?' she asked.

'Toby?' said Mrs McLay, looking at the puppy. 'He certainly can. I'll make sure of it. I can't think of a nicer playmate for Toby than Jess.'

Jenny smiled. 'I can't think of a nicer play-mate for *anybody* than Jess,' she declared.

Perfect Ponies
1: KEEPING FAITH

Lucy Daniels

Josie Grace has grown up with three perfect ponies – Faith, Hope and Charity. They belong to her mother's riding school, and Josie can't imagine life without them. So when her parents are forced to close the stables. Josie is devastated. But she's determined to find each of the ponies a perfect new home . . . whatever it takes . . .

Faith has been at the Grace's stables for as long as Josie can remember. Faith was the first pony Josie ever rode and has a special place in her heart. But Faith is an elderly mare now she needs rest and a gentle owner. Will Josie find dear old Faith the peace and quiet she deserves?

Perfect Ponies
2: LAST HOPE

Lucy Daniels

Josie Grace has grown up with three perfect ponies – Faith, Hope and Charity. They belong to her mother's riding school, and Josie can't imagine life without them. So when her parents are forced to close the stables. Josie is devastated. But she's determined to find each of the ponies a perfect new home . . . whatever it takes . . .

Sweet-natured Hope is gentle and reliable – she's always been a favourite at the riding school. But Josie is worried that Hope's plain looks will stop her being placed in a loving home. Will Josie find the perfect owners for this special pony?

TABBY IN THE TUB
Animal Ark 41

Lucy Daniels

Mandy Hope loves animals more than anything else. She knows quite a lot about them too: both her parents are vets and Mandy helps out in their surgery, Animal Ark.

A feral tabby cat has turned up in Welford and Mandy is worried. The poor thing is about to have kittens and she has no one to look after her. Bill Ward, the postman, comes to the rescue, allowing the tabby to make herself at home in his garden shed. And, before long, the tabby is able to return the favour in a very special way . . .

Another Hodder Children's book

PUPPY IN A PUDDLE
Animal Ark 43

Lucy Daniels

Mandy Hope loves animals more than anything else. She knows quite a lot about them too: both her parents are vets and Mandy helps out in their surgery, Animal Ark.

Mandy's dad diagnoses an undersize Old English Sheepdog puppy as deaf. Mandy feels sorry for it. But it isn't until she finds another Sheepdog pup abandoned and in a bad way, that she and James get suspicious. Could a local breeder be to blame for the condition of these puppies?